◇ Celebrate ▽

60 YEARS OF CRIME

with . . .

'NEMESIS' by ANTHEA FRASER

The author of seven highly successful crime novels begins this haunting tale in a genteel public library where a mousy young woman named Smith meets a handsome young man named Martin . . . and gets spooked by a murderer named Harry.

'TWINS' by ERIC WRIGHT

Canada's foremost crime writer introduces us to a detective writer who plans the perfect crime . . . only to find the execution may not work out exactly like his cleverly devised script.

'CUSTODY' by ELIZABETH FERRARS

This esteemed Silver Dagger award–winner adds a double twist to a cunning tale of a messy divorce . . . the bitter aftermath of love . . . and the killing consequences of an ex-husband's schemes.

'A STICKY BUSINESS' by CHARLOTTE MacLEOD

This lone American among the Brits produces another sterling member of the Kelling clan, the aging Mrs Hypatia Kelling, who is being robbed blind . . . but is savvy to what really moves the human heart.

AND MORE GEMS OF DETECTIVE FICTION FROM THE CRIME CLUB DIAMOND JUBILEE COMMEMORATIVE VOLUME

A
Suit
of
Diamonds

A commemorative volume
of
specially commissioned short stories,
published to celebrate
The Crime Club's Diamond Jubilee

A DELL BOOK

Published by
Dell Publishing
a division of
Bantam Doubleday Dell Publishing Group, Inc.
666 Fifth Avenue
New York, New York 10103

ISBN: 0-440-20840-8

Reprinted by arrangement with William Collins Sons & Co., Ltd., London, England

Interior design by Jeremiah B. Lighter

Printed in the United States of America

Published simultaneously in Canada

November 1991

10 9 8 7 6 5 4 3 2 1

RAD

Contents

Robert Barnard

THE
DANGLING
MAN

'COME IN QUICK. There's something good on *Day-time Live.*'

Jan's mother scurried back down the murky hallway and into the living-room. We were visiting for lunch on my day off, as we do every three or four months—God only knows why, because it is one of those visits we do not want to pay and they do not want to receive. Jan insists that we go, because she says they 'don't have anybody', which is as undeniable as it is understandable.

We took off our coats in the hall, took Helen out of her carrycot and went through. Jan's mother and father were seated as always in front of the television set, a bag of crisps between them.

'That's Rita from *Coronation Street,*' announced Daniel, as we stood awkwardly in the doorway confronted by the screen. Helen just gurgled at the sight of a familiar face. Her reaction, come to think of it, was pretty much that of Jan's mum and dad.

'Ever so interesting, this,' said Mum, crunching noisily. 'Dinner's ready in the microwave. There's only news at one, so I'll put it on then.'

My mother-in-law mentioned her microwave with the same sort of complacent pride that some writers show in talking of their word-processors, though the microwave is to the art of cooking what the word-processor is to the art of writing. Mind you, the culinary arts have never meant a great deal to Jan's mum, even though she did spend her working life in the kitchens of hospitals and old people's homes, where she was known unaffectionately as Salmonella Sal. She and Dad were both retired (Dad had played a part in the long run-down of British Rail), and now spent their lives in front of the television, watching game shows and chat shows, soaps and sit coms, relieved only by bouts of spying out of their windows on their neighbours in the concrete inner-city blocks of high-rise flats they inhabit on an estate just north of the Barbican Centre.

'She's wonderful. Ever so brave. Do you remember when Alan Bradley tried to murder her?' Mum asked, her eyes still glued to the screen, and confusing the actress with the part she played in the manner of all soap addicts. As the interview ended she did not switch off, but scrambled off to the kitchen to perform her culinary mysteries. We had given up waiting to be asked to sit down, and had perched on the upright chairs around the table.

'How's young Daniel, then?' asked Dad.

'All right,' said Daniel.

They had this conversation every time we came, and that's where it petered out every time we came.

When Mum came in with our microwoven meal of pork chops, carrots, instant mashed potatoes and packet gravy, we sat down to it round three sides of the dining table, the fourth side being left empty to allow an unimpeded view out of the window. Mum and Dad, indeed, contrived to get the seats that allowed them both to see out of the window and also to get a good view of the television, though since the principal news item that day was the Prime Minister visiting disaster victims in Lancashire (after a breakneck chase up the M1 to get there before any of the Royals), it was the window that won every time.

'We've got Pakis opposite,' said Dad, gesturing to the seventh-floor flat in the neighbouring block most immediately in view. 'Wouldn't credit it, would you?'

'They look more like Iranians to me,' I said neutrally.

'I wouldn't be surprised,' said Mum, her beady eyes

watching the every move of the couple in the flat opposite. 'There's other darkies come there, and they plot. That's what they do, they sit round that table and they plot. It's probably a bomb factory over there. You mark my words, they're all planning to kill that Solomon Grundy, the writer.'

'Mind you,' said Dad judiciously, 'I blame him. It was all a publicity stunt, wasn't it? To sell his bloody book. Just got a bit out of hand and he got more than he bargained for.'

I didn't bother to correct them about Mr. Rushdie's name, or defend his motives. There was no point with Jan's parents. A brickbat from them was better than a pat on the back from anyone else. It wasn't just other races that were inferior and up to no good, it was other people. Everyone. Everyone in the wide world was sex-mad, money-mad, crooked, having it off with someone's wife, publicity-seeking, hypocrites—they had the most fantastic vocabulary of denigration I've ever known, and hardly any other vocabulary at all. It can't be said that their minds were formed by the *Grub* newspaper, because they'd obviously been miserable sods since before the *Grub* hit our streets, but it was certainly true that their minds were beautifully in key with every attitude and tone of voice of that august journal of opinion.

'Look, she's serving him his dinner,' said Mum, watching avidly still. 'Some horrible foreign mess—sheep's eyes, I shouldn't wonder. Now he's waving his knife at her. He'll take it to her one of these days, and then where will we be?'

'In the window watching, I expect,' I murmured, but no one was listening to me. Embarrassed by their naked interest in the doings of their neighbours, I let my eyes stray, and the moment I let them move upwards I was up from the table, out of the living-room, away from the chops and the instant mashed with the congealing gravy, out of the flat, down the steps and on my way to the next block. Because of their obsessive interest in the Iranian couple on the seventh floor they had missed the fact that in the lighted but curtained window of the flat above them there could be seen the shadow of a pair of legs, dangling in mid-air. Typical of them to be tuned to the wrong channel.

The lift was out of order and I sped up the stairs, thanking my stars I was keeping in reasonable trim these days. On the eighth floor there was a woman coming back from the garbage chute and I stopped her and flashed my ID card at her: Superintendent Perry Trethowan, CID. I looked around distractedly to guess which was the flat I wanted.

'The person in the flat *there*. Do you know him?'

''Course I do. He's my next-door neighbour.'

I rang the doorbell and waited. Silence.

'I got the key,' said the woman. 'He's on his own and a bit of a loner. Worries about his cat. I hope he's all right. You a policeman?'

'Yes.'

'Thought so. Interested in him, aren't you? Want to get in?'

The neighbour unhooked the key from just inside her door, and she stood and watched as I let myself in, with some pale shadow of the interest my in-laws felt in the do-ings of their neighbours. I walked into the next-door living-room, and when I saw what was there I turned.

'Don't come in here. It's not a nice sight. You on the phone? Right—ring for the police.'

When she was well gone I went back in and got a better look. Swinging on a rope from a large hook in the ceiling was a man. He seemed to be in his forties, short, besuited. His neck was in the noose, his hands were tied behind his back with thick string, and his ankles were tied together. All the chairs in the room were neatly placed against table or walls. Who says we've abolished hanging in this country?

I shut the door and went out into the corridor. The next-door neighbour came to her door and stood at it. I had perhaps done her an injustice comparing her to my in-laws, because she seemed genuinely upset.

'They're coming. But he's dead, isn't he?'

'Yes, he is.'

'I *am* sorry. Such a nice man.'

'But you don't seem surprised.'

'I'm not, altogether. He was a worrier, like I said, and he was so depressed most of the time. His marriage had broken up last year—that's why he was here, he'd let his wife have the house. He did love her, poor chap, and he gave the impression that life wasn't worth living any longer.'

'You're assuming he committed suicide, aren't you?'

'Well, yes. He was healthy enough. Didn't he?'

'Not,' I said grimly, 'so far as I can see.'

As we waited for the duty police to arrive she told me what she knew about him. His name was Richard Powell, and he was something in Barclays Bank—'not on the counter, you know, but one of the high-ups: accountant or something, doing accounts for the nobs and some of the local businessmen.' He had moved into the council block when his marriage broke down, and was supposed to be looking for something of his own, though Mrs Smithson, the neighbour, said mostly he didn't seem to have the energy, didn't seem to *want* to start a new life. His cat was the only thing he cherished—she fed him during the day, and as often as not took him in with her.

'He's in there now, Mr Moggins. I suppose I'll keep him. Poor Mr Powell—just never seemed to have a grip on life somehow.'

I was saved from repeating that he had not committed suicide by the sound of several heavy feet in the stairwell: the local bobbies doing their *Pirates of Penzance* imitation. I showed them the flat, told them who I was, and was just about to go when a thought struck me. I turned to Mrs Smithson who was still standing in her door, having shut the cat in the bedroom 'so it shouldn't go in next door and see, poor mite.'

'You said when I told you I was a policeman that we were "interested in" your neighbour. What did you mean?'

'Well—' she looked embarrassed—'wasn't that a policeman came to see him earlier?'

'Could well have been. How do you know?'

'You see . . . you get nervous living on your own—and sometimes if you hear anyone outside here in the corridor . . .'

'Oh, I see: you looked through the spyhole.'

'Yes. I think it was a policeman who came and knocked at Mr Powell's door.'

'When was this?'

'Oh, half an hour ago, maybe a bit more.'

'And was he let in?'

'I couldn't rightly see—not with its being the door next to mine. If it'd been one of the flats opposite I could've, but not Mr Powell's.'

Of course by now this was rightly none of my business, and I could have returned to the local supermarket's own-brand treacle sponge, or whatever delicacy my mother-in-law was serving up for afters. By this time the Australian soaps would have begun on the telly—*The Young Doctors, Country Practice,* or whatever. I decided to stay put.

I knocked on the door to the right of Powell's flat, but got no response. On an impulse I went down a floor, and with some trouble located the flat immediately under the dead man's. The name on the door was Iqbal, and the swarthy man who opened it was polite but unforthcoming.

'Yes?'

'I'm sorry to bother you, Mr Iqbal, but did you know the man in the flat immediately above you on the eighth floor?'

'Mr Powell? Yes, I know him a little . . . But you said "did"?'

'I'm afraid he's dead.'

Immediately the impenetrableness was replaced by a look of concern and grief. He turned back into his living-room and talked at length in a foreign language to his wife, who became equally upset. I stood in the living-room doorway and waited. Finally Mr Iqbal turned back to me.

'Did he commit suicide?'

'We don't think so.'

'You are police? It was murder?'

'It's possible. How did you come to know him?'

'We talked in the lift. Once I went up to apologize to him. I am chairman of the Overseas Students Association of London University. Sometimes we have committee meetings here.' My in-laws' bomb-making conspiracies, no doubt. 'These are difficult times, with the government refusing political asylum to everybody, and our meetings can get very heated. Even quarrels. One was so bad, so much shouting, I apologized for the noise next day to those on either side, and Mr Powell above. After that we talked often. Poor man. Very unhappy.'

'He talked about himself, then?'

'A little. He had been very happy—good job, lovely wife, nice home. Then the wife—well, you see, she is very independent—'

'Independent for British woman, even,' put in his wife.

'Yes, exactly. She had good job, managerial job, with a security firm. So one day she says to him: "I have a new boyfriend—marriage over." He not stop loving her, but he lost his marriage, his home—even lose interest in his job.'

'Ah yes, the job. Did he tell you anything about that?'

'Not really. Once he helped a friend of ours with income tax. I remember he said then that his bank was in the East End—lots of tough characters—gangs, that sort of thing. He said that if he was doing tax return for someone he thought was a little—you know—suspect, he have to be very careful *he* not get involved in anything criminal. He said once it was a sort of challenge, a game, but it had lost all interest. He was very unhappy man. He play very sad music—you know, big orchestra, slow, sad stuff.'

'He played this morning,' said Mrs Iqbal. 'That was not

usual. He play usually at night. But of course today he was not at work.'

'No,' I said. 'Today he stayed home.'

Up on the eighth floor there were police buzzing everywhere. I stopped one young sergeant I knew quite well and asked him what was going on.

'The doc has been. He thinks he'd been dead about an hour when he saw him. That puts the death about a quarter to one. Thanks to you, we got here soon after, so he could be more definite than usual. Apparently he rang the bank this morning and said he wouldn't be coming in. Off-colour. His wife's been contacted, and she's on her way.'

He darted back into the flat, and I took advantage of the corridor being empty to knock again on his other neighbour's door. This time I heard footsteps approaching.

'Police,' I said when the door opened. He nodded and stood aside for me to go through. The living-room was warm and untidy, an old man's room.

'I see there was a lot of coppers around,' the man said. 'Something 'appened next door, 'as it?'

'Something has,' I said.

He was a heavy, lugubrious man who said his name was Ernie Stokes, recently retired from the employ of Fishguard and Patterson, funeral directors, and still employed by them on great occasions. I could see that he might add depths of dole to any burial. There was something about him that was—I almost said shifty, but that wasn't quite it. It seemed as if ordinarily he might have been a straight enough individual, but that at present—for whatever reason—he was uneasy, uncertain, maybe even had suffered some kind of shock. He had also at some time of the morning been drinking, and drinking spirits.

'How well did you know your neighbour?' I asked.

'Dickie Powell? Not to say well, because 'e'd only been 'ere the best part of a year, but well enough . . . 'E's gorn, isn't 'e?'

'Yes, he is. You don't seem terribly surprised.'

'Oh, I don't know about that.'

'Did you expect him to commit suicide?'

'Suicide? Oh no, nothing like that. What's a divorce these days? Hadn't even got a divorce yet. Just a trial separation.'

'What, then? Why weren't you surprised?'

He shifted in his seat, unable to hide his unease.

'Some o' the things 'e used to tell me—about these geezers whose financial affairs 'e 'ad to do wiv. Well, I've lived in the East End all me life. I've known some of these gang bosses—'elped bury some of 'em, come to that. Remember that bloke Calvi they found 'anging under a bridge? That's the sort of thing 'appens to people who get too involved wiv the big gangland men.'

'He was an Italian banker. And if it was murder there was probably Mafia involvement.'

'Well? Are you telling me there's no Mafia in the East End?'

'No. But I'd be surprised if they used the accountancy services of Barclays Bank.'

'Oh well, I'm not saying Mafia necessarily. Most of the gangland people have a legit business, as a front. That was the sort of accounting Dickie used to do now and again. He sometimes had to come down pretty hard on them, so he said. They could turn quite nasty.'

'Did you hear anything from next door this morning?'

'I was out most of the morning—till ha' past twelve.'

'He was probably still alive at half past twelve.'

'There was music playing when I come in. Could 'a bin a cover.'

'Could have.'

I was just about to take this further when I heard a noise from the corridor—crying, a woman's voice. I went to the door, closely followed by Ernie Stokes, and saw a woman leaning against the doorpost of Powell's flat, retching and sobbing.

'It was horrible . . . You shouldn't have shown me
. . . Yes, it was him.'

She took out a handkerchief and wiped her face. They
were real tears, blotching a carefully made-up face. She was
about thirty-five, beautiful in a classic way, yet somehow
hard, and with a mouth too thin and small to match the rest
of the face.

'You'd spoken to your husband earlier, hadn't you?'
asked the inspector on the case, shutting the flat door.

'Yes. He rang. We kept in touch. There were no hard
feelings.'

'He rang you at work?'

'Yes. I told you, we kept in touch.'

'Did he have any particular news?'

'No. Said he was working at home today. Said he was
on to some particularly clever tax fiddle and wanted peace
and quiet to go over the papers. Some local wide-boy who
thought he could put it over Dickie, that's what I gathered
. . . Look, could I get away from here? It upsets me . . .'

'Of course, of course. I'll get one of my men to take
you down to a police car. You can go to the Station, and I'll
be along in ten minutes or so to take a statement from you.'

This was all watched from most of the doors along the
corridor—doors open a mere crack to doors unashamedly
open with their occupants standing watching. As she was
led away most of them closed unobtrusively. I caught Mrs
Smithson, the neighbour on the other side, just as she was
retreating in.

'You've got Mr Powell's cat there, haven't you?'

'I have. Poor little Mr Moggins.'

'Why have you got him, if Mr Powell was off sick from
work?'

'Well, I was just off to the shops about ten when he
came out to fetch his milk in. I was surprised to see him at
home, and asked if there was anything he wanted at the
shops. He said he wasn't feeling too well, but there was
nothing he wanted. Then he asked if I would take Mr Mog-

gins into mine. I thought he was going to go along to the
doctor's, or maybe wanted a quiet lie-down. Mr Moggins is
very lively, and likes to jump all over you if you try and have
a nap. So on my way back from the shops I rang the doorbell. They were playing a game with string on the floor.
That went on for a minute or two, then he picked him up,
stroked him till he purred, and handed him over to me.
That was the last time I saw him.'

She went inside, upset. I stood in the corridor for a few
moments, thinking. The young sergeant I knew well came
out of Powell's flat, on his way back to the Station.

'Looks like this thing is opening up. There seems to be
some sort of gangland connection.'

'A red-herring,' I said.

'Eh?'

'A red herring. Started by the dead man himself—quite
innocently in the first place, I imagine. If you had a dull job
like accountancy with a bank you'd probably play up any
dubious characters you had anything to do with. Recently I
suspect he'd been plugging it a bit.'

'If that's the false trail, what's the real one? Have we
missed something?'

'Maybe. I suggest you ask Ernie Stokes what he was
expecting to have to do, but found someone else had done
for him.'

'Eh?'

'And ask the wife what her new boyfriend does for a
living.'

'Her boyfriend? He hasn't come into it.'

'And if she says he's a security guard—which she will—
ask him what he was doing here about a quarter to one
today.'

'But . . . why should he kill the husband, or her
come to that? Apparently it was all quite amicable.'

'He didn't, and neither did she. Powell killed himself.
He took a sickie from work, said goodbye to the cat, put on
the sort of music that went with his current mood, and

prepared to commit suicide. He'd already arranged with his neighbour Ernie Stokes that when he was dead he would come in and make it look like murder. The man used to work for an undertaker, so he'd have a strong stomach. Even so, he had to go out and get a few whiskies into him during the morning.'

'Why? Insurance?'

'Of course. Powell wanted his wife to benefit from his insurance. He loved her still, that's quite clear—not wisely but too well, judging by her hard little mouth. He also had a sound accountant's instinct: don't waste a good insurance policy you've paid in for.'

'And is that what happened?'

'No, it isn't. He rang his wife, to speak to her for the last time. He must have said something that had her worried, made her think he might be contemplating suicide. Whether she was worried for him or for their insurance policy you'll maybe find out. She works for a security firm, and so, I'm pretty sure, does her boyfriend. She sent him round, and he got here just after Powell'd done it. Mrs Smithson here saw him through the spyhole in her door, and thought he was a policeman—the dark blue uniform, of course. When he didn't get any reply he got into the flat— no problem for a security guard: half of them are recruited from ex-criminals anyway. The body hanging there was the end of any dreams they might have had of cashing in on the policy. Unless something was done.'

'I get you—he faked it.'

'That's right. The thick ball of string was there on the table, waiting for Ernie. Powell and the cat—gruesome touch!—had been playing with it earlier. He tied the hands and feet, put the chair against the wall, and made off smart-ish. Which made for a very bewildered Ernie Stokes, when he went in a few minutes later.'

'Couldn't work out what had happened?'

'That's right. I knocked at his door soon after I arrived, but he wasn't answering. Too bewildered, still trying to figure things out. Finally he decided to stick to the line he'd agreed on with Dickie Powell—that corny gangster stuff, and the idea that he wasn't greatly bothered by the separation from his wife, which was something that was contradicted by everything else I was told.'

'But if the boyfriend hadn't come along—?'

'Everything might have gone as Powell had planned. If ever anyone queered their own pitch . . .'

I left him to put the idea to his boss. When I got back to Cell Block H, Mum and Dad were watching *Neighbours*. Jane had found her long-lost father, or Harold had found his long-lost son—I forget what it was, but I could see a car accident at the end of the episode and a life-support system for weeks to come.

'She's gone,' Mum announced. She always calls Jan 'she', as if she can't quite recall her name. 'She left the car for you and took the Tube. Says you're to bring the things.'

I went around collecting up children's things, and as I did so Mum tore herself briefly away from the doings in Ramsay Street.

'There was someone come to that Paki flat opposite. He stood in the door so we could only see his legs—big, thuggish chap he looked. You ought to be on to them, your lot at the Yard. They're international terrorists, you mark my words.'

'Actually he runs the London University Overseas Students Club,' I said.

'There! What did I tell you?' said Mum triumphantly. 'There's going to be horrible doings in that block before very long.'

On the screen the episode ended and the theme music came up. 'Neighbours, everybody needs good neighbours, with a little understanding . . .'

Gwendoline Butler

LADIES WHO LUNCH

GWENDOLINE BUTLER, *a past winner of the coveted Crime Writers Association Silver Dagger, is a South Londoner by birth.*

She is the widow of Dr Lionel Butler, former Principal of Royal Holloway College, University of London, and now lives in Surrey. She has one daughter, and when not writing her immensely successful crime novels which trace the career of that long-serving policeman who is by now Chief Commander John Coffin in the Second City of London, she spends her time looking at pictures, furniture and buildings.

IN THE MID 1980s there was a small rooftop restaurant in Central London where you could, on a summer's day, lunch in the sun amid potted plants. It's gone now, but it was a great favourite with ladies like me. I was selective about whom I took there, because it had a special place in my life.

I walked down the road which led to the restaurant one May morning with Sally Benson. It was a strange road for that part of London, old, wide and empty. Rather like one of those streets in Bruges, or the east coast of Fife, with little top-heavy houses that look as if they were left over from a film set of *Nicholas Nickleby*. The street is still there. A preservation order on it, I expect. Certainly it is not without historical interest.

The house is still there, too.

Clapped up against one side of a bigger house was the smallest, brownest old house imaginable. Very narrow, with one window beside the front door and above it a hanging bay, and above that, one small oriel window.

'That's the house,' I said to Sally.

'Is it?' She stopped to stare.

'Yes, she did it there.'

'It doesn't seem possible,' said Sally, who could be very naïve. 'Not all those people, all dead there.'

'Only two.'

'And the dog.' Dogs were people to Sally. She had a small dachshund herself, long-haired, placid and greedy. I don't think people get like their dogs, but they choose dogs that echo what they see in the mirror. Sally was a bit like a long-haired dachshund.

'She'll be living there again soon. Next month, I think.'

'Next month? She's coming back there?'

'Yes, you don't stay in for ever these days, you know. Not even for murder.'

'But going back there. To the house where she did it!'

'I don't suppose she has anywhere else to go.' And it was a valuable property in a good if strange street. Places have a lot to answer for, I think.

'It was a terrible thing she did, though,' said Sally with a shudder.

'You might think so, I might think so: she didn't. Fully justified, she said. And the jury almost half believed her.'

I mean that literally since the jury was nearly equally divided between the sexes, seven women and five men. Had the jury been all men I am sure that they would have acquitted Melva since no man could believe that a plain little housewife, neat and respectable, could possibly have committed that terrible murder. The women knew better.

'She nearly got away with it, you know. No blood on her. No knife.'

'I thought that was found.'

'Yes, later. In the Park. But no evidence she'd ever been there in the Park. And some that she had stayed in the house.'

'Yes, I remember,' said Sally. 'But I remember thinking: She's as guilty as hell.'

Sally was refreshingly unguilty herself, always. Do I really mean refreshing? Because sometimes I found this side of her infuriating. Guiltlessness ought to be earned, not come as a blessing.

'They never found any bloodstained clothes, either, did they?' she went on, as we went up in the lift to the restaurant. 'She must have done the deed naked. I've heard people say Lizzie Borden did that. And that man Wallace that killed his wife.' Wallace had been found Not Guilty, but a trifle of misinformation would not worry Sally.

A few minutes later I watched Sally sipping her wine delicately but greedily. She usually ate and drank like a careful-mannered little vulture.

I said: 'I met her, you know? Before, of course. We met in the steam room of the Health Club. I couldn't see her face properly because of the steam. Her body, yes. She had rather large, flat brown nipples which I thought strange on such a slender woman. Her face, no. But I never forgot her voice.'

'It was an unusual voice.' Sally had heard her speak on television. Just the one interview. Before the arrest.

I remembered listening to it myself.

I said: 'She told me what she was going to do. I didn't believe it, of course, we all told tales there. I told mine. Told her what I was going to do. Probably she didn't believe me either.'

We had passed the house now. I gave it a backward glance. It was hard to believe that three souls had died in it so badly. Knifed to death. Two people and a dog. Dogs do have souls, I think, although theologically that is unsound.

Melva Peel, murderess. She had knifed to death her husband, his mistress and their dog. One by one, as far as was known, since Melva never explained and only forensic evidence could be reckoned on.

We ordered our meal. I encouraged Sally to choose lavishly. I felt I owed her a good meal. I usually felt like that about the guests I brought here because so often afterwards a stroke of bad luck seemed to fall upon them. I don't think you could say that the restaurant was unlucky (although, of course, it has since disappeared), so it must have been me.

'We met a few times later on. I brought her to lunch here once or twice.'

'Really?' Sally was forking up smoked salmon. She was a

bit greedy, was Sal. What she fancied she could not deny herself.

Sally and I had been friends since schooldays, we sat next to each other in class, tried to do ballet and joined the school dramatic society together. Sally was prettier but I was a good mimic. I did a splendid parson.

At the moment she had a temporary job promoting a new scent. She was rather a temporary person, was Sally. Transient. She had attachments, destructive while they lasted.

'You do smell, Sal.'

She offered me a sniff at her wrist. 'The new scent. Naturally the firm like me to smell of it. Gives confidence to the customers that it will smell good on them too.' And make them look like me, she might have added, because that was the bottom line. She was beautiful, our Sally. I wasn't bad myself, but Sally had held on to her youthful good looks remarkably. Of all the women I had brought there to lunch, a mixed bunch, she was the best-looking. 'I'll give you a bottle. I get a reduced rate.'

'No, thank you. I don't think it's a smell I'd want to go to bed with.'

Sally looked surprised, as if it was something she hadn't expected me to say. Who was I to dwell on bed, her face said.

'I'm going to visit her when she comes out,' I said over the ice-cream.

'Really? Where?'

'The house, I suppose. She'll go there, I think. She must.'

'I wouldn't,' said Sally with feeling.

'I've visited her in prison, you know.'

'Have you? Really?'

'Don't say Really again, love. Yes, I have.'

'But how did you?'

'I got permission. She seemed quite glad to have me visit her. I don't think she got many visitors.'

'I shouldn't suppose so.' Sally gave a little shudder. 'I think it was brave of you.'

'I took little gifts. Chocolates, cigarettes, although I don't think she smokes, but I suppose they came in useful. I gave her a little money too. From time to time. I don't know what she did with it but she took it.'

I had a sudden picture of that little hand, long, thin, with grubby fingers, snaking out across the table.

'Is it allowed?'

'No, I don't suppose so. But I did it. We were never caught.'

'I believe you are really quite wicked, Grace,' said Sally admiringly. She had replaced her lipstick and was getting ready to go back to her scents. 'See you later, darling. We must have lunch again. On me this time, all girls together.'

'Right,' I said.

'Not just yet, though. I'm going off for a little holiday. Bermuda. I've got friends there.'

'Lovely. I've always wanted to visit it.' I felt quite jealous. I sat waiting to pay the bill (they were always slow in that restaurant) and watching Sally preen herself, and thinking back.

On one of those visits to the open prison where she worked in the library, I reminded Melva of what I had said to her in the steam room.

'Do you remember what I said?'

She had looked vague.

'Do you ever think about what I said to you in the steam room?'

'Yes, I do think about it, as a matter of fact. Quite often.'

'I said that if you wanted to kill your husband and his woman, the safest way to do so was to get someone to help you, to do it for you if you could.'

'It was what you said you'd do if your husband left you. Did you do it?'

'I didn't have to, as it happens. He left me. But he

came back.' The woman he'd been seeing then had had a terrible accident. Something had gone wrong with the brakes of her car. She didn't die, but she was never the same woman.

It was then Melva told me that she believed she would be coming out soon. On a kind of trial run, reporting to her probation officer, but free. 'I've been ill, you see. And I'm no threat to anyone.' She smiled. After all, she'd done what she wanted. 'At least, I hope so.'

She had survived her sojourn there remarkably well, but of course, it had taken a toll of her health. Over the years I had noticed a quiet deterioration. Perhaps every visit a little less firm of outline, as if she was slowly melting away. Or turning into someone else? A kind of pseudo-Melva?

Or, of course, she might just be iller than she knew. If they were going to let her out, then she probably was.

I wondered if she'd asked for a prognosis and decided that she hadn't. She was singularly unquestioning and incurious, was Melva. For instance, she never asked me why I came visiting her. But then I am not sure if I could have found an easy answer, except that I knew we had to keep in touch.

I do like her so much, she has suffered for all women.

Sally had finished repairing her face; I had paid the bill. I stood up.

'I must get back to work,' I said to Sally.

'You don't have a job.'

'Yes, I do. A perfectly beautiful job: looking after my husband.' It took some doing, I can tell you.

'Oh yes, I'd forgotten that. I suppose that counts.'

'You bet it counts.'

Sally accepted this silently. Thinking it over, I decided.

'You sound quite possessive,' she said eventually, as if surprised. 'I never thought it of you.'

After lunch, leaving Sally to go back to her scents and lotions (if that was what she did go back to, I had the gravest doubts), I took myself to stand in front of the house in Oakrey Street. People did stare at it, even now. One or two a year, perhaps, real addicts of crime. Of course, at the time of the murder there had been hundreds.

No, that was an exaggeration, I never saw more than twenty or so, and they never stayed long. In the first place, the police did not encourage you to, and secondly there was something about the house itself that turned you away. Not welcoming. Rather the reverse. I wonder the Peels hadn't noticed this themselves when they moved in. Perhaps Melva had and this was what she wanted. A thoroughly hostile house.

From all this you will gather that I was often one of the watching crowd myself. Not every day, naturally; one has a life to live. Nor did I wish to be obvious.

But I got to know one of the young police constables on duty there, a fair-haired woman with bright blue eyes and a pink skin. I told her I was writing a human-history piece about domestic murder.

I suppose you could say I was. In a way, I am still writing it.

The girl told me how the three bodies, man, woman and a dog, had been found in different rooms, but there had been blood everywhere. She thought the woman had run round the house while bleeding and then collapsed behind the front door.

'It's strange,' the girl had said, 'but all three bodies were found behind doors. The man was leaning against it, half upright.'

'Did you see it yourself?'

'No, ma'am.' The girl shook her head. 'And am I glad! No, but I go out with the chap that went in first. Went all over the house, he did, he didn't know how many dead bodies he was going to find.'

Ten years or more those two had been going out; they were either dead, married or parted by now. Time had passed.

'He found three,' I had said.

'Yes, the dog counts. That really turned him up. The dog had bled all around too. That house was spotted with blood.'

As she had spoken I could see the house, a kind of flat picture, more a diagram than a picture, but blotched with red.

I think we moved apart then, me with that picture of the house inside my head. I didn't go back to Oakrey Street again at that time. The trial came on, which I wished to attend, and did so successfully for the most important days. It was hard to get a seat, but I knew one of the lawyers defending her and he wangled me in.

So I saw her in the dock, heard her give evidence and be cross-examined.

I was surprised how well she stood up to it. Never confessing anything, never giving ground even when pressed hard. All she ever admitted to was being in the house. But upstairs asleep. Sedated because she was so upset about her husband leaving her. Another casualty of Valium, you might say.

Of course, it went in her favour that they had never found the weapon and that there had been no trace of blood on her. No, not a drop, and it's hard stuff to get rid of.

I truly believe she thought she would be found Not Guilty. As with Lizzie Borden.

Just on the grounds that Melva was such a ladylike, quiet person, and looked it, with her neat black dress and no lipstick. Of course they hadn't seen her in the steam room as I had and seen those curious used-looking breasts. There was more to her than you could tell. I knew that. More of life, more of usage from life, more of sensuousness, more of desire.

If there had been an English verdict of Not Proven, I think that that's what she would have got. Like Madelaine Smith.

But there was something about Melva that the jury could not quite stomach. Something that made them uneasy. I saw that as they came back in. They came back in twice to ask advice of the Judge. In the end, he said he would take a majority verdict.

That verdict was Guilty.

I happened, by what you might call planned chance, to follow one of the jury home and heard her say on the bus that she thought that Melva had done the deed while in a drugged state. I would like to have had a word with that woman, but she got off the bus before I could manage it.

There was an appeal, of course. Turned down, as might have been predicted. I was abroad at the time with my husband so I missed any of the details that there might have been, but I expect the newspapers had lost interest.

I did not visit her in prison at first. Not for several years indeed. I wasted those years, I suppose. But she wasted them more.

By the time I started to visit her, she was in an Open Prison where she worked in the library, having been and done whatever makes you a model prisoner. No further violence or wickedness was expected from her.

The prison was in a green field near Worcester. It was made up of a number of bungalow-type buildings with one big central block. I suppose it had been built about twenty years ago and was beginning to show its age. I thought it could do with a repaint. Pleasant enough from the outside, not so good inside. It was impossible to imagine anyone being positively happy there.

As a matter of fact, I thought that some of the prisoners looked in a jollier state than the staff. You see, they were going to get out, away into the normal world. Those others were there for ever.

On the first occasion I went there I was inspected by a prison psychiatrist. At least, it was called an interview but I felt sure that I was being looked over.

Who is this person who comes visiting a convicted

murderess? That was the unspoken question. Why is the visit being made and what is the relationship with the prisoner?

'Just a friend,' I said. I hardly knew Melva really, except in one part, the murderous part of her life, but I didn't say that. 'I think she'll want to see me.'

'She's never wanted to see anyone else.'

'I promised I'd come. I've written once or twice.' She hadn't answered, of course, but I had never expected a reply. My letters were simply a reminder that I was here still.

No doubt the woman had read my letters, I had no idea how private communications were in this place, I suppose I thought of it as being rather like an army at war, but my letters had been extremely ordinary. Not really saying anything very much.

It turned out that this was what worried the psychiatrist.

'Melva showed me your letters. But at first she said she did not know you. Or why you were writing.' I had only used initials, of course.

'That wasn't kind of her.'

'She is not kind.'

Well, I knew that was true. The death of the dog showed that, but then I don't believe I am kind myself. 'She knows me all right,' I said.

'Later, she said she did remember.'

I didn't think for one moment she had forgotten.

'I wanted to see you to warn you,' the woman went on.

'Warn me?'

'She's in a very disturbed state.'

'She's not going to attack me, is she?'

'There will be no opportunity.'

Good, I thought.

I must say when I saw Melva she didn't look in a disturbed state. A bit dried-up and brown, like a leaf left out in the sun, but composed. Possibly to the psychiatrist, who herself had a nervous twitch about the eyes, that quietness was itself a bad sign.

'I didn't come before,' I said, 'because I didn't think you'd want to see me earlier.'

She shrugged. 'I expected nothing.'

'Sorry things didn't work out.'

'I did what I wanted,' she said.

On that visit we did not talk very much, but I went back several times later, taking presents.

It was on that last visit there that she said, after a bit of general conversation (although I will tell you that general conversation in a prison, even an open one, is hard to come by): 'I have been told I may expect to be released quite soon. Sort of ticket of leave.'

I said I was pleased, as I was, very pleased, and we talked a little bit about her coming out. Clothes and that sort of thing. She'd got so much thinner, dwindled somehow.

'I have a heart condition,' she said. 'I don't think they want me to die in prison.' She smiled. 'There was always the feeling that I might not, after all, have been guilty.'

'You did do it though, didn't you.' It wasn't quite a question and didn't get quite an answer.

She just shrugged.

'Do you regret it?'

'Oh no. About it I am good inside. Of course, it changed me. The act changed me.'

Weak of her, I thought then.

For the first time, I wondered about her husband. What sort of man he had really been. Why he had turned to Jacinth or whatever her name was. I had never seen him alive, of course. Pictures in the papers afterwards, but they gave no real impression.

Funny to think that if he had lived he would be an old man now, he was twenty years older than Melva. Married a young wife on purpose, she told me, so that he would have someone to look after him in his old age. Just shows you can never tell what fate has in store for you.

For instance, I married for love and loyalty, all of which I gave, and comfort and support. I'm not at all sure I got that from poor Robert, although he might see things differently. I felt a lack, I must say.

Two months later, I knocked on the door of the house in Oakrey Street. I knew it was inhabited because the curtains had changed. Or been washed. No one came, so I tried the bell.

The bell did not ring. I could understand that. I too would not like to hear a bell ring in a house where murder had been done. Especially if I had done the killing. Still, it would have to be repaired, and if she would not see to it, then I would.

But although the bell did not ring, and no one seemed to have heard my knocking, presently the door opened a crack and Melva peered round it.

'Knew you were there,' I said.

'I guessed you'd call. But I thought you might telephone first.'

'I was afraid you'd run away,' I said playfully.

'I don't run much these days.'

The heart condition, I supposed. She looked fragile, but you can never tell. For instance, one of my lunch guests had bones like a bird, but when she slipped and fell down her area steps on some grease that had got there, she didn't break her neck. Not even an ankle. But she went abroad shortly afterwards for a rest so she must have felt more shaken up than she admitted.

The house was awful. It smelt dead. Worse, as if something was rotting there. The old blood, perhaps. I swear not a duster had been laid on it all the time she was inside. I'd have come round myself if she'd asked me.

You could tell that time had stopped in the house. Everything in it went back to a decade ago, to the day of the killing. Life had stopped in this house on that day. On a table in the hall was a yellowing copy of *The Times,* friable and old. A pile of letters and circulars lay on the floor next to a dead pot plant.

It was like a museum.

She took me through the hall into the kitchen where she appeared to be living. I knew a bit about the geography of this strange little brown house. It stretched further back than you might think from the front. There were two rooms on the ground floor as well as the kitchen, then three rooms on the floor above, with attics above that, lit by tiny windows in the roof. There was a small back garden.

The kitchen was where the rotting smell seemed to be coming from. I thought it came from the refrigerator, and wondered what she had there quietly going putrid. Not that it worried her, she ignored it.

'I expect you're glad to be . . . out,' I said.

'The last place wasn't so bad,' she said in an unemotional voice. 'But the first prison was frightful.' A slight peevishness crept into her tone. 'They put me in a cell with a murderess.'

I blinked.

'My case was quite different. She'd broken into a house to rob it and killed an old man. She was a criminal.'

I suppose we are never criminals to ourselves, I thought.

We had a small talk, not saying much. 'I'll come and see you again soon. I'll bring you some food. How are things going on that side? Have you got an appetite? What are you eating?'

'I don't think I am eating,' said Melva vaguely.

That couldn't be quite true.

'Well, I'm eating something.'

Herself, I thought, by the look of her. Had been for years. Quietly consuming herself ounce by ounce, fat, flesh and bone.

'Let me know if there's anything I can do.'

'I don't think there's anything I want. I'm not lonely.'

You are never alone with a great pain. I knew that myself.

I said: 'You might be able to do something for me. It's my turn.'

After seeing Melva that day, I went back to our flat in Ebury Street. It's a nice flat, sunny and comfortable. Well within walking distance of Oakrey Street. I had prepared a good evening meal of cold chicken salad and strawberry shortbread, an old-fashioned pudding, not much done these days.

Over dinner Robert said: 'You look preoccupied.'

'I've been seeing an old friend. I'm quite worried about her.'

'You're too good to everyone,' Robert said seriously.

'Oh, do you think so? I do try to do what I can.'

Robert poured out some wine. 'Let's go out to dinner next week. Say the Ritz. The Savoy if you prefer.'

'The Ritz will do.'

'A little dinner before I go away.'

Robert is a comfortably built, tall man, always well dressed. You can tell he is a successful business man. He would look down on poor old Charles Peel who had got himself murdered. People didn't do that sort of thing.

'Where is it this time?' I was making the coffee.

'Bermuda. The Hong Kong of the future, you know. We're setting up a branch.'

'I'd love to go there. Always wanted to.'

'I know. Take you next time.'

Next day I went to see Melva, and I said: 'Will you lend me your house?'

'Let?'

'No, just lend. For the day. Possibly just the afternoon. Yes, the afternoon would be enough.'

'Where will I go?'

'I don't know. Just walk around. No one will know you, if that's what is worrying you.'

'I don't want to.'

'I still have a key, you know. I could just walk in. You owe me. I helped you that day as I said I would in the steam room. I didn't do the murder for you, you wanted to do it all yourself, but I came in and took away the knife and the gown you wore. Your butcher's gown.'

'But they found the knife.'

'I couldn't help that. I did the best I could in the time I had. And they never found the gown. It all helped you, you know.'

Still she hesitated.

'And I'll give you something in return.'

'Something solid?'

'It'll be solid to you, I think.' I guessed she wanted an entrance into the world again, to visit people, to be asked around. As if she was normal. 'I'll see you meet my friends. Theatre, dinners, a lunch at my favourite restaurant, that sort of thing.'

I had guessed at her weakness. She had done what she wanted, killed where she could, now she wanted to be admitted to society again, but she had lost the entrance ticket.

'All right, you can have it. Just for the afternoon, mind.'

We settled a date in the coming week, and I went back to make my arrangements. Early on I checked my bank account. As I half expected, Robert had deposited a substantial sum in it. In his way, he is a generous and caring husband.

I spoke to Robert at dinner that night. 'I wish you'd come and see a house I'm interested in.'

'In buying?' Robert always thinks commercially. The word percentage is a love-term to him. 'Yes, it's probably a good time to buy with the market being down. What sort of house?'

'I suppose it's a kind of museum piece,' I said thoughtfully.

'Not been touched for years? Oh, those are usually very promising.'

'I think you'll find this is. Will you come?'

Then I got hold of Sally.

'What, lunch again?'

'Not this time. I want to show you a house.'

'Me, love?' She sounded astonished. 'Are you going to move?'

'No, I don't think so. Well, as a matter of fact, I'll let you into the secret. It's the house in Oakrey Street. I think you ought to see it, just as a curiosity. Well worth it, I assure you.'

'Will she be there?' asked Sally doubtfully.

'I don't think so. I might arrange a meeting for you two later.' In fact it was bound to take place.

'All right. I'll be a devil and come.' It was the sort of way Sally spoke. I supposed it matched her bright pink fingernails and blonde tints. 'Can I bring the dog?'

'Welcome. I was going to suggest you bring him.'

'Really? Are there rats, then?'

There probably were in the basement. It was infested with something, that house.

'Keep him on the leash, though, won't you? I wouldn't want him wandering.'

'Oh no, that would be fatal.'

Quite right, I thought; well spoken.

'Be on time,' I said.

She was indignant. 'Naturally I'll be punctual, I always am.'

She was late, of course, which I had counted upon. Robert had arrived half an hour earlier and was now lying behind the kitchen door, where she would soon see him.

He had come through the front door, murmuring that he seemed to remember the address somehow. Had we come to parties here in the old days? And why was I wearing that get-up?

'No, you've never been here before as far as I know. Have a look round. I'll join you.'

I left him wandering about, looking puzzled. Behind the kitchen door I put on the white robe in which Melva had killed her pair of lovers. A shapeless garment, perhaps she had made it herself. Or bought it at Mowbray's. A kind of surplice. It had been washed.

Then I sprang out at Robert and stuck the knife in his throat.

'Don't,' he said, staggering back against the wall. 'Are you mad?' He tried to grip my wrist but the white linen gown got in his way. It seemed to have a life of its own, that garment. 'I've put a large sum in your bank account.' Trust Robert to speak of money at a time like that.

'I expect there is more than three times that amount in your account in Bermuda,' I said.

I wonder if we really said these things, because it seems to me now that Robert sank to the ground, speechless, covered in blood as I stabbed him again. Perhaps we invent bits of dialogue in times of crisis. Or our memory does it for us afterwards.

When Sally banged on the door, the bell still did not work although I had had it repaired. I was waiting for her.

She screamed when she saw me standing before her, robed in white and stained with blood. It was a slightly phoney scream because she hadn't grasped what was happening to her.

She knew me for what I was, though; she was clever enough for that, whereas Robert had just looked dumfoozled. Never thought the little woman had it in her, you could see him thinking.

'Grace, why are you togged up like that? And what's happened? Have you had an accident?'

She really was stupid. But the dog wasn't. It started to howl straight away.

'Yes, something terrible has happened. Come into the kitchen. It's Robert.'

'Robert!' This time the scream was genuine.

I struck her as she bent over him, so she fell across him. I had managed better than Melva, who had had to chase her second victim round the room.

On the other hand, I got a dog bite in my wrist, which I think Melva did not. Never heard it mentioned, anyway. I regretted killing the dog, but I did it anyway.

Then I tossed the knife, an old one from the kitchen, stolen by me on an earlier visit and sharpened up, into the kitchen sink and let the tap run over it. Not because I wanted to wash it, but because if there were no fingerprints to be found on it, not Melva's where they might have been expected (I had worn gloves), it would be assumed they had been washed away.

I let the robe drop to the floor. It had been laundered but I had no doubt that forensic evidence would reveal the old, original bloodstains underneath. Blood is so terribly difficult to wash out, as any housewife knows. They would have to work out for themselves where Melva had hidden the robe. I couldn't do everything for them.

Then I sat in the public garden across the road, nursing my bitten wrist, till Melva came back. I reckoned I had a fair chance of getting away with it. It would look so very much as if Melva had simply repeated her crime, killing two perfectly innocent people. I couldn't see any protests of Melva's carrying much weight. And I hadn't used my own name at the prison, nor kept, quite, to my own appearance. I always used the same get-up when I visited her. In my own life I am tall and thin, still quite young, with pretty fair hair.

She would have blood on her hands, I had left plenty on all the door handles for her to pick up. A little bit on the telephone too, just to make sure.

I sat there in the sun, waiting till I saw her go in. I hung on until a police car and first one ambulance and then another turned up. Then a third. Since they would not be using an ambulance for the doggy, one of the ambulances must be for Melva. She had finally gone over the top.

As I walked home to await the inevitable telephone call, telling me the sad news about Robert, I did regret missing my meal at the Ritz, but you couldn't have everything.

I would go on my own. Or perhaps the Savoy. I have always liked the Savoy. And then, all being well, I might take a look at Bermuda where all that money would now be mine.

But to my surprise I was finding that Melva was right after all: one is changed by the act of killing.

Two of us will go to Bermuda. My other self, the dressed-up one that did the killing, is hanging on and will come with me for ever. I shall never be alone now.

A nurse and two doctors, one a psychiatrist, stood by Melva's bed, where she lay, eyes open but apparently not seeing anyone.

The psychiatrist said: 'The last year in prison she was showing signs of disturbance, but I thought we had it under control.'

'What form did it take?' asked the physician.

'She had this dream. It seemed to have been a dream within a dream. She dreamt that a woman visitor, who claimed to be a friend but whom she did not know, came to her and in the course of the visit told her that she would commit her crime all over again. Then she would dream a whole scene in which she did exactly that. Being part of the dream and yet outside it.'

'Did she ever have such a visitor?'

'I have checked the records, but as far as I know she had no visitor like that at all. No women.'

'No visitors at all?'

'She had one visitor who came several times. But not a woman. This was a man.' She paused. 'A clergyman. A rather dear old parson.'

Sarah Caudwell

AN ACQUAINTANCE
WITH MR COLLINS

THE TRAIN HAS REACHED Reading, and I still have not decided whether to say anything to Selena concerning the late Mr Collins. It is hardly probable that anything can be proved; it is even possible that there is nothing to prove; and unwarranted investigation might cause undeserved distress. Murder, on the other hand, is a practice not to be encouraged.

I could almost wish that I had not, finding myself with an hour or so to spare before a dinner engagement in central London, chosen to pass it in the Corkscrew. Had I spent it in some other hostelry, I should now be returning to Oxford with a mind untroubled by any more disquieting burden than my responsibilities as Tutor in Legal History at St George's College. It is idle, however, to regret my decision. It was to the Corkscrew that I directed my steps, and indeed in the hope that I might find there one or two of my young friends in Lincoln's Inn.

I am well enough known there, it seems, for the barman to remember who I am and in whose company I am most often to be found.

'If you're looking for some of your friends, Professor Tamar,' he said as he handed me my glass of Nierstein, 'you'll find Miss Jardine right at the back there.' He gestured towards the dimly lit interior.

Selena was sitting alone at one of the little oak tables, in an attitude less carefree than one expects of a young barrister in the middle of the summer vacation: her blonde head was bent over a set of papers, which she was examining with the critical expression of a Persian cat having doubts about the freshness of its fish. Reflecting, however, that in the flickering candlelight she could not in fact be attempting to read them, and that in deliberate search of solitude she would hardly have come to the Corkscrew, I did not hesitate to join her.

She greeted me with every sign of pleasure, and invited me to tell her the latest news from Oxford; but I soon perceived, having accepted the invitation, that her attention was elsewhere.

'My dear Selena,' I said gently, 'the story I have been telling you about the curious personal habits of our new Dean was told to the Bursar, in the strictest confidence, only this morning, and may well not be common knowledge until the middle of next week. It seems a pity to waste it on an unappreciative audience.'

She looked apologetic.

'I'm sorry, Hilary. I'm afraid I'm still thinking of something I was dealing with this afternoon. I happened to be the only Junior left in Chambers—the others are all on holiday—and the senior partner in Pitkin and Shoon came in in rather a dither, wanting advice in conference as a matter of urgency. I'm told he's quite a good commercial lawyer, but he candidly admits to being completely at sea over anything with a Chancery flavour. So whenever a trust or a will or anything like that comes his way, he pops into Lincoln's Inn to get the advice of Counsel. And since the sums involved are generally large enough to justify what might otherwise seem an extravagance, one wouldn't like to discourage him.'

I nodded, well understanding that a solicitor such as Mr Pitkin would be cherished by the Chancery Bar like the most golden of geese.

'He's inclined to fuss about things that don't really present any problem, so I thought I'd be able to put his mind at rest quite easily about whatever it was that was worrying him. The trouble is, I wasn't, and I can't help wondering . . . It might help to clear my mind if I could talk it over with someone. If you'd care to hear about it . . . ?'

'My dear Selena,' I said, 'I should be honoured. I must remind you, however, that I am an historian rather than a lawyer—on any intricate point of law, I fear that my views will be of but little value.'

'Oh,' said Selena, 'there's nothing difficult about the law. The law's quite clear, I can advise on it in two sentences. But the sequence of events, you see, is rather unusual, and in certain circumstances might be thought slightly . . . sinister.'

The matter on which Mr Pitkin had required advice was the estate, amounting in value to something between three and four million pounds sterling, of his late client Mr Albert Barnsley. Having acted for Mr Barnsley for many years in connection with various commercial enterprises, he was familiar with the details of his background and private life. He had related these to Selena at greater length than she could at first believe necessary for the purpose of her advising on the devolution of the estate.

The late Mr Barnsley (Mr Pitkin had told her) was what is termed a self-made man. Born in Yorkshire, the son of poor but respectable parents, he had left school at the age of sixteen, and after completing his national service had obtained employment in quite a humble capacity with a local manufacturing company. By the age of forty he had risen to the position of managing director—a sign, as I supposed, that he possessed all those qualities of drive, initiative and enterprise which I am told are required for success in the world of commerce and industry.

'Yes,' said Selena, thoughtfully sipping her wine. 'Yes, I suppose he must have had those qualities. And others, perhaps, which moralists don't seem to value so highly—the ability to make himself agreeable, for example, in particular to women. His progress was not impeded, at any rate, by the fact that he had married the chairman's daughter.'

'Perhaps,' I said, 'she was anxious to be married, and he was her only suitor.'

'Far from it, apparently. According to Mr Pitkin, Isabel was a strikingly attractive woman who could have married anyone she wanted, but she set her heart on Albert Barnsley. Her father, as you might expect, was something less than delighted. But Isabel talked him round in the end, and he gave the young couple his blessing and a rather elegant house to live in. Mind you, he didn't take any more chances than he could help—he put the house in trust for Isabel and any children she might have, and when he died he left his estate on the same trusts.'

'So Barnsley did not in fact benefit from his wife's wealth?'

'Not directly, no, apart from living in the house, but that's not quite the point. I don't say that being the chairman's son-in-law would mean he could rise without merit, but it would tend to mean, don't you think, that there was less danger of his merits going unrecognized? And after her father died, of course, Isabel's trust fund included quite a substantial holding in the company, and her husband could always rely on the trustees to support his decisions. Quite apart from that, Isabel was very skilful at dealing with the other major shareholders—after all, she'd known most of them since she was a child. She was a woman of considerable charm and personality, wholeheartedly devoted to her husband's interests, and there doesn't seem to be much doubt that she contributed very significantly to his success.'

'Were there any children?'

'One daughter—Amanda, described by Mr Pitkin as something of a tomboy. The sort of girl, he says, who'd rather have a bicycle for her birthday than a new dress. Actually it sounds as if she'd probably have got both, being an object of total adoration on the part of her parents. Her father in particular was enormously proud of her. People used to ask him sometimes if he wouldn't rather have had a son, and he used to say that Amanda was a son as well as a daughter—she could do anything a boy could do, he said, and do it a damn sight better. But I'm talking of five or six years ago, when Amanda was in her mid-teens. After that things changed.'

Under Mr Barnsley's management the company had flourished, expanded and in due course been taken over by a larger company. The takeover was not one which he had any reason to resist: his personal shareholding was by now substantial, and the price offered—as well as increasing the value of the funds held in trust for his wife and daughter—was sufficient to make him, as Selena put it, seriously rich.

The terms agreed for the takeover included his appointment to a senior position in the company making the acquisition: he was an active and energetic man, still in his forties, and the prospect of retirement held no charms for him. Though his new responsibilities required his presence in London during the working week, he had no wish to sever his connections with his home town or to uproot his family. He accordingly acquired a small bachelor flat in central London and returned at weekends to the house in Yorkshire.

'That is to say,' said Selena, 'he began by doing so. But after a while the weekends in Yorkshire became less frequent, and eventually ceased altogether. You will not find it difficult, I imagine, to guess the reason.'

'I suppose,' I said, 'that he had formed an attachment to some young woman in London—what is termed, I believe, a popsie.'

'I think,' said Selena, 'that the current expression is bimbo. Though in the present case that perhaps gives a slightly misleading impression. Natalie wasn't at all the sort of girl who dresses up in mink and mascara and gets her picture in the Sunday newspapers. There wasn't anything glamorous or sophisticated about her—she was just a typist in Barnsley's office. She was from the same part of the world that he was, and it was her first job in London—I suppose in a way that gave them something in common, and perhaps made him feel protective towards her. She was young, of course—about twenty-two—and reasonably pretty, but nothing remarkable. That's Mr Pitkin's view, at any rate— he found her rather colourless, especially by comparison with Isabel.'

It occurred to me that it might have been the contrast with Isabel that Barnsley had found attractive. It was clear that his wife had given him a great deal; but if it is more blessed to give than receive, then plainly Natalie offered him ampler scope for beatitude.

'No doubt,' said Selena. 'But as you will have gathered, she wasn't the kind of girl who wanted to be given jewellery or dinners at the Savoy or anything like that. It's rather a pity really, because with a little luck and discretion Barnsley could have had that sort of affair without upsetting anyone, and they would all have lived happily ever after. But Natalie was the domesticated sort, and wanted to be married. And he couldn't give her that quite so easily.'

Because Isabel declined to divorce him. Mr Pitkin, having reluctantly and with embarrassment accepted instructions to negotiate with her on Mr Barnsley's behalf, had found her implacable. There was nothing, she said, to negotiate about: she did not want anything from her husband that he was now able to offer her; and she saw no reason to make things easy for him. If she ever found herself in a position, by raising her little finger, to save him from a painful and lingering death, she hoped (she said) that she would still have the common humanity to raise it; but to be candid, she felt some doubt on the matter. Mr Pitkin had perhaps been slightly shocked at the depth of her bitterness.

'Though it seems to me,' said Selena, 'to be quite understandable. It must be peculiarly disconcerting, don't you think, to be left for someone entirely different from oneself? Not just like going into one's bank and being told there's no money in one's account when one thought there was, but like going in and being told one's never had an account there at all. A feeling that all along one must somehow have completely misunderstood the situation.'

I asked what Amanda's attitude had been.

'Extreme hostility towards her father. It was, you may think, very natural and proper that she should take her mother's side, but I gather it went a good deal further than that. She seems to have felt a sense of personal betrayal.'

I thought that too was understandable. When a man forms an attachment to a woman young enough to be his daughter, I suppose that his daughter may feel as deeply injured as his wife; and for Amanda, as for Isabel, it must have been peculiarly wounding that he seemed to love his mistress for qualities precisely opposite to those which he had seemed to value in herself.

'At first,' continued Selena, 'she simply refused to see him or speak to him. But eventually she found that an inadequate way of expressing her feelings, and she wrote him a letter. Mr Pitkin still has a copy of it on his file, but he said rather primly that he couldn't ask a lady like myself to read it. I don't actually suppose that Amanda Barnsley at the age of seventeen knew any expressions which are unfamiliar to me after several years in Lincoln's Inn, but one wouldn't wish to shatter Mr Pitkin's illusions. It was clearly in the crudest and most offensive terms that Amanda could think of, particularly in its references to Natalie, and was evidently designed to enrage her father beyond all endurance.'

'And did it succeed?'

'Oh, admirably. Within an hour of receiving it Mr Barnsley was storming up and down the offices of Pitkin and Shoon demanding a new will, the main purpose of which was to ensure that Amanda could not in any circumstances inherit a penny of his estate. Poor Mr Pitkin tried to calm him down and persuade him not to act with undue haste, but of course it wasn't the least bit of use. So Mr Pitkin, following his usual practice, came along to Lincoln's Inn to have the will drafted by Counsel, and it was executed by Mr Barnsley three days later. The effect of it was that the whole estate would go to Natalie, provided she survived him by a period of twenty-eight days, but if she didn't then to various charities. Not, of course, because he especially wanted to benefit the charities, but to make sure that there couldn't in any circumstances be an intestacy, under which Amanda or her mother might benefit as his next-of-kin.'

'Did Amanda know that she had been disinherited?'

'Oh yes—her father straightaway wrote a letter to Isabel, telling her in detail exactly what he'd done. His letter, I regret to say, was not in conciliatory terms—it made various disagreeable comments on what he called Isabel's vindictiveness in preventing him from marrying the woman he loved and referred to Amanda as "your hell-cat of a daughter". It was written, I need hardly say, without the advice or approval of poor Mr Pitkin. Isabel didn't answer it, and there was no further communication between them for a period of some three years. Perhaps, before I go on with the story, you would care for another glass of wine?'

I wondered, while Selena made her way towards the bar, how she would justify the epithet 'unusual'. The events she had recounted, though no doubt uniquely distressing to the principals, seemed to me thus far to be all too regrettably commonplace. I recalled, however, that she had also used the word 'sinister'; and that Mr Barnsley was dead.

Returning to our table with replenished glasses, Selena resumed her story.

'In the spring of this year Mr Pitkin received a letter from Isabel. She had not written direct to her husband, she said, for fear that he might not open her letter, or if he did that he might have the embarrassment of doing so "in the presence of someone else". But there were matters which she felt they should now discuss, and she did not think that her husband would regret seeing her. She would be most grateful if Mr Pitkin would arrange a meeting.

'I have the impression that poor Mr Pitkin was rather alarmed to hear from her. Though, as I have said, he admired her personality and charm, I think that he was also rather frightened of her, and he was by no means sure that she didn't mean to make trouble of some kind.

'Mr Barnsley himself evidently shared these misgivings, and was more than half-inclined to refuse to see her. But she seemed to be hinting that she might now be prepared to agree to a divorce, and that was enough to persuade him. It would have been another two years before a divorce could take place without her consent, and Natalie was still very unhappy about what she saw as the insecurity of her position.

'He seems to have hoped at first that he would be supported by the presence of his solicitor, but Mr Pitkin very prudently said it was out of the question, since Isabel had asked for a private meeting. Besides, if her husband were accompanied by his legal adviser and she were not, it might look as if they were trying to browbeat her.

'So a week later Mr Barnsley summoned up the fortitude and resolve which had made him a captain of British industry and set forth alone and unprotected to have tea with his wife at the Ritz Hotel. He thought, Mr Pitkin tells me, that the Ritz would be the safest place to meet her— meaning, as I understand it, the least likely place for a woman such as Isabel to make a scene.'

She wanted, it seemed, to talk to him about their daughter. Amanda was now twenty, reading English at a provincial university and specializing in the nineteenth-century novel—she had formed a great passion for the Brontës. Her academic progress was satisfactory, and she was perfectly well-behaved—almost unnaturally so, perhaps, for someone who had been such a lively and exuberant schoolgirl. Of recent months, however, she had seemed to be out of spirits, and during the Easter vacation had shown such signs of depression as to cause her mother serious concern.

Isabel had questioned her; Amanda had denied that anything was wrong; too anxious to be tactful, Isabel had persisted. Amanda had at last admitted the cause of her dejection: in spite of everything, she still found it unbearable to be estranged from her father. The admission was made with many tears, as evidencing an unforgivable disloyalty to her mother.

Isabel had been dismayed. The bitterness which she had at first felt towards her husband had faded (she said) into an amiable indifference; it had not occurred to her that her daughter's feelings towards him were more intense, and that the girl was still tormented by conflicting loyalties.

It was (said Isabel) a piece of heart-breaking nonsense: when all she minded about was making Amanda happy, she turned out to be making her miserable. If Amanda wanted to be reconciled with her father, then let them be reconciled; if the fact of his still being married to Isabel was in some way an impediment, then let there, by all means, be a divorce.

'Which meant, as I understand it,' said Selena, 'that her consent to a divorce was conditional on Barnsley making friends with Amanda again. This account of Amanda's feelings is all based, of course, on what Isabel told him—you may perhaps choose to take a more cynical view of her motives.'

I remarked that one might expect a study of the Victorian novelists to have reminded her of the practical as well as the spiritual advantages of being on good terms with any relative of substantial fortune.

'Trollope,' said Selena with evident approval, 'is always very sensible about that sort of thing—I'm not quite sure about the Brontës. But be that as it may, Mr Barnsley was quite content to accept Isabel's account of things at its face value. It wasn't only that he was pleased about the divorce—he was really very touched to think that his daughter still cared so much about him. After all, it was a long time since the offensive letter, and until she was seventeen he'd idolized her. He told Mr Pitkin to put in hand the arrangements for the divorce, and wrote in affectionate terms to Amanda to arrange a meeting.'

'Was it,' I asked, 'a successful reunion?'

'Evidently, since shortly afterwards he mentioned to

Mr Pitkin that once the business of the divorce was dealt with he would have to do something about changing his will.'

'Did he indicate what he had in mind?'

'He still wanted to leave the bulk of his estate to Natalie, but to give a sufficient share to Amanda to show his affection for her—about a fifth was what he had in mind. Well, with both parties consenting and no arguments about property or children, the divorce went through pretty quickly, and he made arrangements to marry Natalie as soon as the decree was made absolute.

'Mr Pitkin admits to having felt a certain apprehensiveness about the occasion. It was going to be a very quiet wedding in a registry office, with a small reception afterwards, but it was also going to be the first time that Amanda and Natalie had met each other, and he felt Mr Barnsley's view that they would get on like a house on fire might be a little over-optimistic. He remembered Amanda's letter, and he didn't quite trust her not to do something outrageous to show her disapproval. He also had the impression that Natalie was becoming a trifle jealous of Barnsley's renewed affection for his daughter, and might have some difficulty in concealing it.

'But as it turned out his misgivings were quite unfounded. Amanda wore a suitably pretty and feminine dress and was charming to everyone. She and Natalie shook hands, and Natalie said she hoped they would be great friends, and Amanda said she hoped so too, and then they had what Mr Pitkin calls a very nice little conversation about how Amanda was getting on with her studies. So that by the time Mr Barnsley and his bride left to go on their honeymoon, which they planned to spend driving round the Lake District, Mr Pitkin feels able to assure me that everyone was getting on splendidly.

'The only slight embarrassment was the fault of Mr Barnsley himself—he judged it a suitable moment to remind

Mr Pitkin, in the hearing of both Natalie and Amanda, that
he wanted a new will drawn up. It wasn't, in the circumstances, an entirely tactful remark. But no one else took any
particular notice, and Mr Pitkin simply assured him that a
draft would be ready for his approval on his return to London.

'As it would have been, no doubt, if Mr Barnsley had
ever returned from his honeymoon.'

She fell silent, while at the tables round us there continued the cheerful clinking of glasses and the noise of eager
gossip about rumours of scandal in the City. I thought of
Mr Barnsley setting forth with his unsophisticated young
bride, and reflected that those who lack glamour are not
necessarily without avarice.

I asked how it had happened.

'There was an accident with the car. Barnsley and Natalie were both killed instantly.'

'Both?' It was not the contingency that I had envisaged.

'Oh yes,' said Selena, 'both. Something was wrong with
the steering, apparently. Well, things sometimes do go
wrong with cars, of course. But it was quite a new car, and
supposed to have been thoroughly tested, so the local police
were just a little puzzled about it. Enough so, at any rate, to
ask Mr Pitkin, very discreetly, who would benefit under Mr
Barnsley's will. But he gave them a copy of the will made
three years before, and when they saw that the beneficiaries,
in the events which had occurred, were a dozen highly respectable national charities, they didn't pursue the matter.
There are limits to what even the most aggressive fund-rais-
ers will do to secure a charitable bequest.'

She paused and sipped her wine, regarding me over her
glass with an expression of pellucid innocence. I have
known her too long, however, to be deceived by it, and I
had detected in her voice a certain sardonic quality: I concluded that I was overlooking some point of critical impor-

tance. After a moment's thought I realized what it was, for the rule in question is one of respectable antiquity.

'Surely,' I said, 'unless there has been any recent legislation on the matter of which I am unaware, the effect of Mr Barnsley's marriage—?'

'Quite so,' said Selena. 'As you very rightly say, Hilary, and as Mr Pitkin discovered for the first time this morning, when he instructed his Probate assistant to deal with the formalities of proving the will, the effect of the marriage was to revoke it. I'm afraid a great many people get married without fully understanding the legal consequences, and in particular without realizing that when they say "I do" they are revoking any will they may previously have made. But there is no doubt, of course, that that is the position under English law. So Mr Barnsley died intestate.'

'I fear,' I said, 'that I have a somewhat hazy recollection of the modern intestacy rules. Does that mean that his estate will pass to Natalie's next-of-kin? There is a presumption, I seem to remember, where two persons die together in an accident, that the younger survived the older?'

'That's the general rule, but actually it doesn't apply on an intestacy if the people concerned are husband and wife. In those circumstances neither estate takes any benefit from the other. But even if Natalie had survived her husband by a short period, her next-of-kin would take relatively little—the widow's statutory legacy, which is a trifling sum by comparison with the value of the estate, and half the income arising from the estate during the period of survival.'

'In that case,' I said, finding myself curiously reluctant to reach this conclusion, 'I suppose that the whole estate goes to his daughter?'

'Who, if her father had died before his marriage, would have taken nothing, and if he had lived to make another will would have taken a comparatively small share of it. Yes. she is, as Mr Pitkin was careful to tell me, entirely ignorant of legal matters and will be even more astonished than he was to learn that that is the case. So naturally he didn't want to give her such momentous news until he'd had it confirmed by Chancery Counsel, and that, he said, was why he'd come to see me. But the question that was really troubling him, you see, was one he couldn't bring himself to ask, and which it would have been outside my competence to answer. That is to say, ought he to mention to the police how very advantageously things have turned out from the point of view of Miss Amanda Barnsley?'

It now for the first time occurred to me that I possessed an item of knowledge of possible relevance to the events she had described. Uncertain whether or not I should mention it, and having had no time to weigh the consequences of doing so, I remained silent.

Selena leant back in her chair and gave a sigh, as if telling the story had eased her mind.

'Well,' she said, 'it's lucky that Amanda's reading a nice harmless subject like English literature. If she'd happened to be reading law it might all look rather sinister. But nonlawyers don't usually know that a will is revoked by marriage, and I wouldn't think, would you, that it's the sort of information she'd be likely to come across by accident?'

The hour of my engagement being at hand, I was able to take my leave of her without making any direct answer. During dinner I put the matter from my mind, thinking that during the journey back to Oxford I would be able to reach a decision. But the train has passed Didcot, and I remain undecided.

It seems extraordinary and slightly absurd that I should find myself in such a quandary on account of an item of knowledge which is not, after all, in any way private or peculiar to myself. Indeed, if the work of the late Mr Wilkie Collins were held in the esteem it deserves, the plot of his admirable novel *No Name*, in which the revocation by marriage of her father's will deprives the heroine of her inheritance, would no doubt be known to everyone having any pretension to being properly educated. As it is, however, I suppose that relatively few people have any acquaintance with it—unless they are studying English literature, and specializing in the nineteenth-century novel.

Elizabeth Ferrars

CUSTODY

RAY BAGSTOCK DID NOT murder Mrs Moira Crane. The crime that he had in mind was something quite different. Not that he thought of it as a crime. He regarded it simply as the righting of a shocking injustice. Murder was something that he had never contemplated, even during the long days which he had devoted, whether working or idle, to hating Lucille. Yet when Mrs Crane was found dead by one of her lodgers from upstairs there was enough circumstantial evidence against Ray to frighten him very horribly.

Mrs Crane owned a house in a narrow back street of the small town of Dillingford, which is about fifteen miles from Oxford. She lived on the ground floor with a notice in her window saying Bed and Breakfast. Neither the beds that she offered nor the breakfasts were particularly attractive, but they were cheap and they were in a locality which Ray had believed would fit in with his plans. She was a stout, red-faced old woman who took an interest in her lodgers and liked having them in to her room to have a drink with her.

That was how it happened that the police found Ray's fingerprints on a glass on her table and also on the poker that had been used to smash her skull. The true explanation of that was that while he was having a drink with her she had asked him to poke her fire, for in spite of the stooping that it entailed she still preferred coal to gas or electricity in her room, though there were gas fires in all her lodgers'

with greedy meters that swallowed ten-pence pieces. And it
had been the opening and closing of her door which had
been heard by Mr Patel, the Indian who lived in the room
above hers, and which the man had sworn had been the
sound of Ray entering the room when in fact he had been
leaving.

Leaving in a very exasperated state of mind, because he
had thought that while he had the drink with his landlady
his plan for the afternoon had been ruined. However, that
had not been what had been significant about Mr Patel's
error. It was simply that it misled the police as to who had
been with Mrs Crane when she was killed. This had actually
happened after Ray had left the house and not while he had
been in her room. The time of her death was thought to
have been 2.27, because that was the time when the clock
on her mantelpiece had been smashed, together with a good
many other things in what was assumed to have been a
frantic search for the money which the lodger who found
her body, an elderly retired schoolteacher who had lived in
the house for fifteen years, told the police that she knew the
old woman kept hidden there.

Certainly there was no money to be found when the
police searched the room. There were only Ray's fingerprints on the glass and the poker and the sworn statement
made by Mr Patel that he had heard Mrs Crane's door
opened and closed at ten minutes past two.

If it had not been for the murder Ray's delay in leaving
the house would actually have been very fortunate for him.
He would normally have regarded it as incredible good luck,
for if he had left the house at a quarter to two, as he had
intended, he would not have had the glimpse that he did of
Lucille crossing the end of the street outside. And to find
Lucille was the reason why he was in Dillingford. He had
traced her from Finchley to Birmingham, then to Oxford,
and there had been given fairly reliable information that she
was probably in Dillingford. But if he had not seen her for

that instant as he was strolling towards the market square, it might have taken him days or even weeks to find her.

She had been on her way to the supermarket on the far side of the square. He hurried after her. But at the entrance he stood still, wondering whether to follow her in or to wait for her in the street. It was important that she should not know that he had found her. In the end he put on his dark glasses, turned up his coat-collar, and relying on the beard that he had grown since she had left him to help disguise him, went into the store. After all, it might have some other exit by which she could leave and he might lose her. Picking up a wire basket and trying to look as if he was intending to buy something, he edged his way through the crowd inside, looking for her.

Because it was a Saturday, the place was very crowded, but after a minute he saw her at the vegetable counter, gathering onions, carrots, a cauliflower and apples into the trolley that she was pushing. Then she bought a packet of detergent, bread, pork pies, long-life milk and a large bag of frozen chips. Then, near the exit, she bought two bottles of whisky. So she's still at it, he thought. Two bottles of whisky for a weekend was a good deal, even for her.

But it might be her supply for the whole week. Perhaps she came out shopping as seldom as she could because of the problem of finding someone to look after the children while she was out. If she troubled to find anyone. That was one of the things that he would have to find out. It would have been like her to lock the door on them and trust to luck that they would not set the house on fire and be burnt to death while she was gone. He wondered what she was using for money.

He was only three or four people behind her at the check-out counter. It was taking a risk, standing so close to her, but she did not look round. She had changed very little since he had seen her last. She was still as slim as ever and still wearing the overcoat that she had worn on the day when she had been granted her divorce with custody of the

children, though her splendid red-gold hair then had been
curling loose on her shoulders and today was covered by an
old headscarf. He knew that the scarf was old because once
it had belonged to him. So perhaps, in spite of the two
bottles of whisky, she had not really much in the way of
money. Certainly what he paid to her lawyer, and sometimes failed to pay, would not go very far. Of course, she
might have a job. But in that case, what was she doing
about the children? It always came back to that. That was
what he had to find out. What was she doing about them?

She pushed her trolley through to the entrance. Ray
had a moment of panic then. What she had bought was
plainly too much for her to carry, so perhaps she had a car
waiting outside, in which case he would lose her again, since
there was not much hope of his being able to find a taxi in a
hurry close to the store. But then he saw that she was packing her purchases into a shopping-trolley which she had left
by the door. She was going to walk home and he would be
able to follow a little way behind her and find out where she
was living. He paid for the two or three things that he had
bought so as not to be conspicuous and went out into the
street.

He saw her walking along the pavement and pause to
look into the window of a small dress shop and stand gazing
there for a little while, but she did not go in. But then she
did go into a chemist's that was next door to it. This time
Ray did not follow her. There was no crowd inside and no
risk that she might vanish. In about five minutes she came
out again and strolled on along the pavement. She came to
a stationer's and went in and Ray, gazing through the window, saw her buying a packet of envelopes. As she went to
the counter to pay he withdrew quickly so that she should
not see him when she came out.

After that she went into an ironmonger's. He could
not see what she bought there, but when she came out she
crossed the street and almost immediately took a turning to
the left, now making, he was sure, for home. But this street

had only a few people in it, so he stayed further behind her than he had in the busy main street. Now that he had tracked her so far he did not want to risk her turning and suddenly seeing him. He was close enough, however, to see at which door she stopped.

The moment she opened it the children came rushing out at her. The younger one clutched her convulsively as if he had been afraid that she might not return. The elder one seized the trolley, delving into it to see if she had bought anything interesting to him. Lucille went into the house and closed the door. The event had taken only a minute, but it had told Ray something that he wanted to know. As he had thought likely, she left the children alone in the house when she went out shopping, or to whatever work she might have been driven to do since she had lost touch with her lawyer and given up drawing the money that Ray occasionally sent her.

That this might be dangerous for them was something to which she had probably never given a thought, and though it filled Ray with anger for the moment, at the same time it pleased him. If he could discover when she had a habit of going out it would make it all the easier for him to carry out his plan. And if Saturday afternoon was her usual time for shopping, it would be very convenient, for it would give him now a whole week in which to make the necessary arrangements.

Thinking this over as he walked slowly back to Mrs Crane's house, he was filled with deep satisfaction. It had not been easy to trace Lucille from the flat in Birmingham where she had gone to live for a time with a friend after the divorce and from which she had taken flight after his first attempt to kidnap the children. But a neighbour there had talked to him rashly of her having mentioned Oxford, so he had looked for her there and in one of the pubs after two or three weeks of useless inquiry, he had happened to get into conversation with an elderly man who remembered some chats that he had had with a young woman with curly, red-gold hair who had asked him a number of questions about Dillingford, as she was finding living in Oxford too expensive. Ray had had one photograph of her and the man had thought that was who it might have been. And now, due to the glass of beer with Mrs Crane that Ray had not wanted and that had delayed him, he had seen her walking ahead of him within only three days of starting to look for her. Seen her and seen the children. It was going to work out this time.

But why was there a police car standing at Mrs Crane's door and why were there several uniformed policemen as well as two men in plain clothes, who could only be policemen, going in and out of it?

Ray stood still for a moment, then walked hesitantly forward.

When he paused just before reaching the open doorway one of the policemen moved as if to make room for him to pass, then had second thoughts and stood in Ray's way, looking at him questioningly.

'What's going on here?' Ray asked.

'Who are you?' the constable countered.

'My name's Bagstock,' Ray said. 'I'm staying here.'

'Is that so?' The constable turned towards the door and shouted, 'Sir, there's a man here who says his name's Bagstock and he's staying here.'

One of the men in plain clothes, who had just gone into the house, re-emerged.

'Your name's Bagstock?' he said.

'Yes,' Ray answered.

'And you're staying here?'

'Yes.'

'How long have you been staying here?'

'Three days, but what's that got to do with you?' Ray asked.

They took him inside and made him look at the old woman.

He was nearly sick on the spot, for he had never been

able to stand the sight of blood and Mrs Crane's shattered skull and the old purple cardigan that she always wore were sodden with it. The rest of the room was in chaos, chairs tipped over, cushions slashed, drawers pulled open, their contents spilled on the floor, most of her cheap little ornaments, including her clock, swept on to the carpet, and the cupboard where she kept her clothes broken open. The poker with which Ray had stirred the fire for her, with some thick dark stains on it, was lying near her. Only two empty beer cans and two glasses stood undamaged on the table.

The man in plain clothes who appeared to be in charge introduced himself to Ray as Detective-Inspector Standish and edged Ray right into the room when he tried to turn in the doorway and flee back into the street. He was holding his handkerchief to his mouth because he thought the vomit was coming. But somehow he swallowed it back and let himself be pushed forward near to the fireplace, though the room was swimming round him and when they asked him what time he had been in the room he could only answer in total confusion that he did not know.

'But you were in here, weren't you?' the detective said.

'Yes—oh yes, sometime not long after I had my lunch,' Ray said. 'Fish and chips, that's what it was, I brought it back from the pub on the corner. They'll remember me. I had quite a chat with the girl there.'

'It's later than you did that that we're interested in,' Standish said. 'We've been told by Mr Patel, who lives on the first floor, that he heard you talking to Mrs Crane in the passage at about ten minutes past two and then you went into her room with her.'

'No, no, no, that's when I was leaving,' Ray said. 'She came into the passage with me after I'd had a drink with her and we said a few things—the front door's always left open except at night, so of course no one could have heard that open or shut—and I went out and she went back into her room. I'm sure of it because I wanted to get away and kept looking at my watch to see how the time was going. If she was killed after that you'll realize I couldn't have had anything to do with it.'

'Where were you in such a hurry to go?' Standish asked.

'Nowhere special,' Ray said. 'Just out for a walk. But I—I'd had a drink with my lunch and I didn't really want another, only I didn't want to be rude to her, she was a nice old thing, so I went in for a quick one with her and I only stayed about ten minutes. Someone else came into her room, I mean, that's obvious. Anyone could have got in through that open door.'

'And you've been staying here three days.'

'Yes.'

'Where d'you come from?'

'London, but I've been travelling about a bit lately.'

'What brought you to Dillingford?'

'Just an idea I had that I'd like to live in the country and I thought this might be a good place to stay while I looked around for somewhere that'd suit me.'

'And what's your occupation?'

'I'm a journalist.' Then as Ray saw the detective preparing to ask him for what paper he worked, he added hastily, 'Freelance.' After that he went on in a pleading tone, 'Look, if you want to ask me any more questions couldn't we go upstairs to my room. It's on the second floor. And it's so awful in here. I—I don't feel very well.'

But the police thought that the best place for him, whether or not he was feeling well, was the police station, where they told him that they hoped that he might be able to help them with their inquiries.

The story of the murder was in the local evening paper that day, but it was stated that though no one had been charged yet a man was being questioned. Ray's name was not given, so even if Lucille read the evening paper she would not know that Ray had again been on her trail and when he was freed, as of course he shortly would be, he could still carry out what he had come to Dillingford to do.

But there were more questions in the police station,

questions that he had already been asked and which were repeated over and over again while he sat in a small room with the two detectives whose tones varied from being almost kind and comforting to suddenly fierce and ferocious. He began to wonder if he ought to have a solicitor here to help him, but the only one he knew was in London and was the one who had tried to defend him when Lucille sued him for divorce and who had made such a hopeless mess of it. It had been the man's fault, Ray believed, that she had been given custody of the children. It was true that he had been given access to them once a week and it had only been Lucille's sudden removal to Birmingham, from which she had come in the first place, which had upset the arrangement and made Ray determined to get possession of them somehow.

He had begun to save money after that, in preparation for the flight to Spain where he had managed to borrow a small villa from a friend. He was not really a journalist, he worked in the accountancy department of a big firm of builders and he had managed to embezzle a reasonable sum from them without being discovered before his sudden departure. He could manage on what he had, he thought. But if he brought in that solicitor now, might he not find himself letting on more about his plans to him than would be advisable? The man might want a coherent story from him about why he had been in Birmingham and Oxford, so close on Lucille's heels. He might get Ray to tell him more altogether than would be helpful. He decided to go on answering the questions the police were asking him until they had the sense to let him go.

They wanted to know, of course, where he had put the money belonging to Mrs Crane which they believed that he had stolen. They searched him and they searched the room in which he had been staying in her house, but naturally found nothing. They also took his fingerprints and presently told him that they matched those that they had found on the empty glass on her table and on her poker. It was when they told him that that he began to feel the beginning of fear, but he still would not believe that anything could be proved against him.

'Where d'you suppose I could have put that money if I'd taken it?' he asked. 'Banks are shut on Saturdays. Anyway, I've no account in Dillingford. And the post office is shut too, and I couldn't have posted it to myself unless it was a very small packet that would go into a letter-box.'

'We still don't know where you went this afternoon,' Standish said.

'Oh, here and there, I can't remember exactly where,' Ray answered.

'You said you did a bit of shopping.'

He had his plastic carrier-bag from the supermarket, which showed that he had been there.

'Yes, I went for a few minutes into the supermarket in the square,' he said. 'Just bought a Cornish pasty and some tomatoes for my supper.'

'And you were in there only a few minutes?'

'That's right, though I had to wait some time in the queue at the check-out counter.'

'Anyone know when you were there?'

'The girl at the counter, d'you mean?'

'Or anyone else?'

Slightly to his horror, Ray realized that he was hesitating. Then he said firmly, 'No one that I know of.'

'Where did you go next?'

'I just strolled along the street for a little way. I remember looking in at the window of a chemist's, but I didn't go in. And then I thought of going into a stationer's near it.'

'What did you want there?'

'Just some envelopes, but I didn't bother.'

'So there's no one in there, or in the chemist's, who would remember you.'

'No. And I passed an ironmonger's along there too, but I didn't want anything.'

'Still, that girl at the counter in the supermarket might remember when you were there.'

'Well, I suppose it's just possible.'

'It could be useful to you, you know, if someone saw you.'

At that moment Ray suddenly found himself wanting to laugh. It would have been slightly hysterical laughter, but still there was something very funny about the thought that if he had not taken such care not to be noticed by Lucille, she could have given him an alibi now. As it was, he would have to manage without any help from her.

'And where did you go next?' Standish asked.

'Oh, just along the street,' Ray said. 'I didn't notice what it was called. I went on for a bit, then I turned back and walked along to Mrs Crane's house and saw all your chaps there.'

'How long were you out altogether?'

'Didn't I tell you I went out at ten past two and I didn't notice when I got back? You'll know that better than I do.'

'That was at five to three. That means you were gone, according to your story, for about three-quarters of an hour.'

'That feels about right.'

After that they brought him a cup of tea and left him quite alone for nearly an hour.

It was long enough for him to start to brood and to lose his earlier optimism, which no doubt was why they left him to himself and was just what they intended. Thinking over the questions that they had asked and the expressions on their faces as they had asked them, he found himself becoming more and more convinced that they believed that he was guilty of the murder. He began to shiver a little though the room was not really cold. Perhaps they were out now questioning the girl in the supermarket and even the chemist and the stationer in case they had caught a glimpse of him outside their windows. But that would get them nowhere. All the same, if things should go really badly for him, he thought of how he could quite easily produce an alibi. He did not want to do it, but it might in the end be the only thing to do.

It was at about eight o'clock that evening that he began to think of it seriously. The girl at the check-out counter had been questioned by then and as they told him when they came back to the room, she had no memory of having seen him. Nor had a number of other people who had been in the store at the time that he claimed he had been there, or loitering outside while Lucille had got on with her shopping. And why should they? Beards were common enough nowadays and he was not a very noticeable sort of man.

'Now,' Standish said, 'suppose you tell us where you really went.'

He was in one of his friendlier moods and it was easier to respond to this than it would have been if he had been red-faced and shouting. Ray drew a deep breath. He felt that it would be the lesser evil to tell them the truth, or at least some of it.

'As a matter of fact, I haven't told you everything,' he said.

'Surprise, surprise!' the detective responded heartily. 'We didn't think you had, you know. Might have saved us some trouble if you had, but we thought you'd come to it sooner or later. Now where were you really?'

'Oh, I was in the supermarket,' Ray said, 'but it seems to me I've got to explain what I was doing there. I didn't want to. It's kind of a private thing. I was there, like I said, and then I was outside the chemist's and the stationer's and the ironmonger too, but my reason, you see—well, it's difficult to talk about it, but I was following my wife.'

'Didn't know you had a wife,' Standish said. 'It's the first you've said about her.'

'Because I thought it would strike you as absurd me doing a thing like that,' Ray said. 'You see, we're divorced, but it was never I who wanted that and I had an idea, only an idea, you know, it was never any more than that, that if I tried again now that she's had time to think things over, she might be ready to think of trying again. And I heard by chance that she'd come to Dillingford and then I saw her again by chance just after I'd come out from Mrs Crane's, going into the supermarket and I followed her in.'

'So she can tell us where you were a few minutes after ten past two,' Standish said, sounding exasperated. 'Why in hell couldn't you tell us that straight away?'

'Because she won't be able to tell you anything.'

'How d'you mean she won't? Can't she recognize her own husband when she sees him?'

'You see, I was taking care she shouldn't notice me,' Ray said. 'I didn't want to speak to her there, I only wanted to find out where she lived. And I've grown this beard of mine since we separated and I had on some dark glasses and I always stayed a little way behind her, so I'm sure she didn't see me.'

'I see.' Standish rubbed a hand along his jaw and stared at Ray thoughtfully. 'And you were following her only because you thought you might make things up with her.'

'That's right,' Ray said.

'You hadn't any more—well, violent ideas about her, like revenge for ruining your life, or something like that? You didn't make an afternoon of it? We aren't going to find another body somewhere, beaten to death?'

'Christ, no!' Ray exclaimed. 'She's as right as rain. Once I'd found out where she lived I went home. I never even got to talk to her. I wanted to think out how I was going to handle things, you see. Wanted to think out just what I was going to say to her.'

'But if there's any truth in all this, she'll be able to say if she was really in the supermarket when you say, and where she went next.'

'Yes, of course. Actually she went into the chemist's, but I didn't follow her in, then she went into the stationer's and the ironmonger's, and then she went home.'

'So if she says she went into all these places at the time

you say, it'll be almost the same as if she'd seen you follow her.'

'Yes, yes, that's just what I thought.' Ray nodded vigorously. 'Only do you have to say . . . ? I mean, do you have to explain to her why you're asking these questions? Oh, I suppose you do. Pity. It'll upset the way I'd thought of things, but I dare say it can't be helped.'

'Don't see what harm it can do. Come on, give us her name and address. Still calling herself Bagstock, is she, or has she gone back to her old name?'

'I think she's still Bagstock. And I think the street was called Harkway Terrace, or something like that. And the number was 37.'

'All right. Come along, Bob.' The two men went to the door. 'Mind you, Mr Bagstock, the evidence of a loving wife doesn't always go down well with a jury.'

The irony in his tone gave Ray a nasty jab. Then he was left alone again.

When they came back about an hour later it was with Lucille. She was still in her old overcoat but had taken off her headscarf and her wonderful hair was loose about her shoulders. Ray stood up when she came in and muttered, 'Hallo.'

She gave him a long look and said nothing.

'Do you identify him as your husband, Raymond Bagstock?' Standish asked.

'My ex,' she said.

'My mistake, sorry, your ex. And can you tell us if you saw him this afternoon?'

Her face was cold, as if she were looking at a stranger.

'I haven't seen him since the divorce,' she said. 'That's over a year ago.'

That was a lie. She had seen him in Birmingham when she had managed to prevent his futile attempt to take off with the children. It prepared Ray for what might be coming next.

'Can you tell us what you did yourself this afternoon?' Standish asked.

'Why should I tell you that?'

'It might help us.'

'Well, I went out shopping.'

'In the supermarket in the square?'

'No, I hardly ever go there. I can't stand the crowds.'

'Where did you go, then?'

'I went into Marks and Spencer's and bought some ready-cooked things, that's all.'

Ray felt sure that it would turn out to be true, but that probably it had been on the day before, and if anyone there remembered her they would not be sure on what day she had been in. And if the detectives searched her lodging they would find some ready-cooked food in the refrigerator.

All the same, he tried to shout, 'I tell you, that's a lie!' But his voice came out a croak. 'She was in the supermarket and she bought some vegetables and bread and things and two bottles of whisky. See if there are two unopened bottles of whisky in her house.'

'You'll find one that I bought at the pub at the corner yesterday, along with one for the old man who lives upstairs, though I only took it up to him this afternoon,' she said. 'What would I be doing, buying two bottles of whisky for myself?'

'Did you go into the chemist next to that dress-shop?' Standish asked.

She was on less certain ground there, because she might have been remembered in the chemist's. People tended to remember her hair. But that had been covered by Ray's old scarf. She shook her head and said, 'No.'

'Or into the stationer's or the ironmonger's?'

'No.'

'So you only went into Marks and Spencer's?'

'Yes.'

Standish turned to Ray and gave him a sardonic smile, as if it amused him to see his alibi go up in smoke.

'Well?' he said.

Ray said nothing. Looking at Lucille, he wondered how he had managed to keep his hands off her all those years except just that once when he had come home unexpectedly and found the children locked into the house, alone and hungry, and presently she had come in from the pub where she liked to go at lunch-time for a drink and a chat. He had bashed her jaw then and she had fallen against the corner of a cupboard and fractured two ribs and that was what had got her her divorce and custody of the children whom she did not love nearly as much as he did. A man given to atrocious violence, he had been called.

'It's all lies, I've told you the truth!' he shouted.

She gave a slow shake of her head. There was no more expression on her face than when she had come into the room.

'Not a word of it.'

'Lucille, for God's sake—!'

Again the slight shake of her head. Was there a twitching at the corners of her mouth, as if it were the beginning of a smile? But the shake of her head was repeated.

At that point, for some reason, Standish muttered, 'Excuse me,' and he and the other detectives went out. Ray felt fairly sure that they would only be where they could hear what the people in the room would have to say to one another when they thought that they were left alone. He tried desperately to think of the right thing to say for them to overhear. Was there any way that he could trap Lucille into telling the truth?

But before he could speak she leant on the table between them and thrust her face towards him.

'They'll do you for this, Ray, whatever lies you tell,' she said clearly for the men to overhear. 'You won't get away with it. And when you come out the children will be grown up and I'll have nothing to fear from you.'

'Why do you want them so much?' he asked. 'You're not a good mother.'

'But they were given to me,' she said. 'They were given to me because of what a rotten man you are. And now I'll be able to spend the next few years in peace without watching for you to snatch them. They needn't even know they've got a father, wasting his life away in gaol.'

'But, Lucille, don't you understand, you're letting a murderer go free?' he cried. 'Don't just think of me. Someone came into that house through the open door and the poor old soul let him into her room and he smashed her skull and stole her money. And he'll do it again! Don't you understand, Lucille? He'll do it again!'

He was wrong. The murderer was caught that evening. A woman who lived opposite to Mrs Crane and who at last overcame her reluctance to get mixed up with the police, telephoned them and told them that she had seen a man go into and leave her house at the time that mattered. He lived in a house next but one to Mrs Crane's and when he was interrogated was unable to account for the unusually large amount of money he had in his possession.

But Lucille did not know that Ray was wrong and she only smiled at what he said. Perhaps, but for that smile, she would have left the room in safety. The detectives were not there to see the smile, but they heard her scream and when they burst in they found her sprawling on the table with Ray's hands throttling her. Her neck was broken. So they had a murderer. Ray would never be able to flee with the children now to that villa waiting for them in Spain.

They were taken into care.

Anthea Fraser

NEMESIS

ALL OUR MARRIED LIFE we'd been haunted by Harry Pell. Haunted, that is, not by his physical presence but by the threat of him, hanging over our lives like a menacing cloud. I felt I'd known him as long as my husband, since Jeff spoke of him at our first meeting. In fact, it could be said he was the reason we came together in the first place.

I can remember it very clearly, that April day five years ago. I worked in the local library, and Jeff was waiting outside when I unlocked the doors. I noticed him particularly because he was carrying a small suitcase—and also, I admit, because of his thin-faced, nervous good looks. Naturally he didn't even glance at me. He walked purposefully down to the Reference section, where he laid his case on a table while he selected several books from the shelves. Then, returning to the table, he settled down with his back to the main part of the library and extracted some papers from his case.

'Susan!'

I spun guiltily back to face my colleague.

'I asked if the books we ordered from Langham have come in?'

'Sorry,' I mumbled, 'I'll just check.' And dismissing the stranger from my mind, I turned my attention to my work.

During the course of the morning quite a number of people visited the Reference section. Some seated themselves at the table where Jeff sat, checking through books, making notes, then leaving again. He sat on, seemingly mo-

tionless, though during a snatched glance I thought I saw
his shoulders shaking, as though laughter or even tears had
moved him.

At lunch-time I came upon Anna, the Reference librar-
ian, in the cloakroom. 'You seem to have acquired a lodger,'
I commented, combing my hair.

'Oh? I hadn't noticed.'

'That chap in the grey jacket. He came in first thing
and hasn't moved since.' Like most libraries, we had our
long-stay visitors but they were mostly down-and-outs who
came in out of the rain or cold to doze and read the newspapers. As long as they caused no trouble we didn't disturb
them. But Jeff, smart in blue shirt and grey flannels, was no
down-and-out and I couldn't help being curious about him.

I did my modest shopping, ate my sandwiches, and
returned to my desk. He was still there.

It was quiet that afternoon, and since Barbara was on
hand to deal with any queries I wandered down to the Reference section, edging my way round the solitary figure under pretence of searching for a book. His elbows were on
the table, his head resting on his hands; from behind or
either side, he appeared engrossed in the papers spread before him. But when with studied casualness I turned to face
him, I received a shock. His eyes were not on the papers but
fixed unseeingly on the desk, and his face was chalk-white. I
had never before seen an expression of such utter despair.
Instinctively I bent forward and touched his arm. 'Are you
all right?' I asked.

He jumped at my touch, and I moved quickly back.
For a moment he stared at me blankly. Then he nodded.
And as I still stood there, he said defensively, 'Not in any-
one's way, am I?'

'No, not at all. But you've been here so long. I wondered if something was wrong?'

He really looked at me then, as a person, not just someone who had disturbed him, and I braced myself, resigned
to the inevitable fading of interest. At thirty I had no illu-

sions about my pale face, my spectacles and mousy brown hair. But to my surprise he smiled, the kind of smile, I thought in confusion, that a man gives a woman he finds attractive. I felt myself flush, and stammered awkwardly, 'I—didn't mean to intrude.'

'It's kind of you to be concerned.' He hesitated. 'I wonder, could I ask you—are there any rooms to let around here?'

'You've nowhere to stay?'

'No. I only arrived this morning.'

Then why, I wondered, had he wasted all day in the library? I thought for a moment, assessing the implications of my reply. 'The lady in the flat below mine has a spare room. She lets it out in an emergency.'

'Would I qualify as one?' Again that smile.

'I could ask her,' I said weakly.

Behind her desk Anna pointedly shuffled papers, letting us know that even though no one else was in this section and we were speaking softly, silence was the rule.

Jeff leant across the table. 'What time do you finish here?'

'Five o'clock.' It was then three-thirty.

'I'll wait for you,' he said.

'What was all that about?' Barbara asked curiously when I returned to my desk.

'He needs somewhere to stay and I offered to help.'

Barbara said with a sniff, 'This is a library, not the social services.'

I did not reply.

At two minutes to five Jeff gathered his papers together and put them back in his case. I wondered if he'd added anything to them in the last seven hours. Then he rose, a little stiffly, and replaced the books he had taken from the shelves. I shrugged on my coat and was waiting for him when he reached the door.

Out in the street, he turned towards me. 'This is awfully good of you. I do appreciate it.'

'It's no trouble,' I muttered with lowered head. I was aware of Barbara and Anna behind the plate-glass window, watching us.

'I don't even know your name. Mine's Jeff Martin.'

'Susan Smith,' I said.

'Smith. What a lovely safe name!'

'Safe?' I echoed, surprised.

'Safe and anonymous, blending into the background.'

'Yes, that describes me pretty well,' I said, disappointment rancid in my mouth. He probably smiled at everyone. I was too old to indulge in daydreams.

But he caught my arm. 'No, no, that wasn't what I meant at all. It's just—well, you don't know how lucky you are. I wish my name was Smith.'

'You're welcome to it,' I returned, only slightly mollified.

Sensing my withdrawal but not, I hoped, the reason for it, he said no more and we walked in silence along the High Street where the last customers were coming out of the shops, and turned into the narrow, tree-lined road where I lived.

'This is it,' I said, trying to see the familiar three-storeyed house with his eyes. And instead of letting us in with my key, I pressed Mrs Bunting's bell. She came to the door and looked at me in surprise.

'Miss Smith! Is anything wrong?'

I said quickly, 'This gentleman's just arrived in town and wonders if he could rent your spare room?'

She looked assessingly at Jeff, sizing up character and credit-worthiness. 'For how long would it be?'

'I really don't know. Say a month to start with, if that would be all right?'

'Payment in advance,' she said firmly. 'You'd better have a look at the room, then.'

'I'll leave you to it,' I said, and with a quick smile at them both, hurried upstairs to my first-floor flat. As soon as I reached it, I regretted my precipitate retreat. It looked as though I'd abandoned him, and if he decided not to take the room I might never see him again.

In an agony of indecision I stood in the middle of the floor, still wearing my coat. Then I caught a glimpse of myself in the mirror and derision came to my aid. What a state to be in because a man had smiled at me! But I was too plain to be blasé, too unused to attention to take it lightly.

A tap on the door spun me round and I almost ran to open it. Jeff stood there, smiling. 'All done and dusted. I'm most grateful for your help—how about dinner this evening to celebrate?'

And it was that evening, in the Chinese restaurant in Sundown Road, that I first heard the name of Harry Pell. We had talked rather stiltedly during the first part of the meal; I learned Jeff was a pharmacist by profession and that he'd travelled down from Glasgow.

'You've been offered a job in Dalton?' I asked him.

A pause, then he shook his head.

'Then why did you come here?'

He lifted his shoulders. 'It seemed a nice, safe little place.'

That word again. 'Safe from what?'

He looked at me oddly. 'It's a long story, but the short answer is, safe from Harry Pell.'

No warning bells rang. I simply asked, 'And who's he?'

'Harry Pell,' he said slowly, 'is someone I've known all my life. When we were boys we were inseparable. We lost touch later, but I still thought of him as my friend. Until two years ago.'

'And then what happened?'

'And then,' he said flatly, 'he murdered someone.'

I thought I'd misheard. After a moment, with a nervous laugh, I said, 'You'll never guess what I thought you said.'

He looked up, holding my eyes. 'I said he murdered someone.'

At a table across the room a group of people suddenly

burst out laughing. The door opened on a rush of cool air, and more diners came in. But we were no longer part of the general light-heartedness. I thought: I don't want to hear this. I wish I'd never asked. But I heard myself say, 'What happened?'

He picked up the pepperpot, turning it over and over in his fingers, regardless of the fine yellow dust that fell to the cloth. He said, 'I've no right to burden you with this.'

'If I can be of help—'

His free hand briefly pressed mine. 'You already have. More than you can know.'

'But is this man after you?' I persisted fearfully. 'Is that what you've been worrying about all day?'

He nodded, avoiding my eyes.

'But why?'

'Because,' Jeff said slowly, 'I was there. I saw him do it.'

'And he thinks you'll go to the police? But if you haven't over the last two years—' I broke off, swallowing painfully. '*Why* didn't you go to the police, Jeff?'

'Don't you think I've asked myself that question? At first I suppose I was scared, in a state of shock. I couldn't believe it had happened. Harry just wasn't the sort who'd do something like that. Then, as I said, I'd known him all my life. How could I shop him?'

The silence rang in my ears; a selective silence, since around us our fellow diners still laughed and talked. I made myself ask, 'Who did he kill?'

'A woman he'd been having an affair with.'

'Then surely he'd have been a prime suspect?' My brain was filled with half-memories of thrillers I'd seen on TV.

'He would if anyone had known about it,' Jeff said drily, 'but no one did.'

'Except you.'

'Exactly. I was the only one who could tie him in with it.'

'But you haven't done, so why is he still worried?'

'Because,' Jeff said softly, and a note in his voice chilled me, 'I have something he wants. Something that could link him with the crime.'

'What?' I whispered fearfully.

'You like dessert?' inquired a voice above and between us, making us both jump. 'Lychees? Ice-cleam?'

Jeff seemed not to have registered the question. I said hoarsely, 'Just coffee, please.'

'Jeff!' Unconsciously I laid a hand on his arm. 'What have you got that he wants?'

He hesitated for a moment, then shrugged, abandoning caution. 'The murder weapon, that's what.'

My heart jerked painfully and was still. I said with an effort, 'Tell me what happened.' It didn't occur to either of us to question our sudden intimacy; incredibly, it seemed quite acceptable to be discussing murder with a man I'd met only hours before.

He moved restlessly, still fingering the pepperpot. 'As I said, Harry and I were boyhood friends. We went on fishing holidays together, sometimes fancied the same girls. But when we left school we drifted apart. I went to college, Harry's family moved away, and we lost touch.'

There was a long pause. Our coffee arrived in fragile blue and white cups. At a table by the door, a man was telling a long and involved story which brought forth regular bursts of raucous laughter.

'Until two years ago?' I prompted.

'Yes. I was on a bus in a south London suburb when I suddenly saw him, walking along the road. I could hardly believe it. I jumped up and rang the bell, but the driver insisted on going on to the next stop. I stood impatiently on the platform, craning out, and was just in time to see Harry turn into a gateway. As soon as the bus stopped, I jumped off and hurried back the way we'd come. It took quite a while to find the house. I went to the wrong one first; an old lady came to the door and when she finally understood what I wanted, she said there was no one there. I was beginning to think I'd lost him when at last I saw the house, and I remembered then the white bush at the gate behind which he'd disappeared.

'So I went up the path, rang the bell and waited, imagining how surprised he'd be to see me. But no one came. I rang again, and though I listened, I couldn't hear the bell ringing inside the house. So I knocked, several times. Still no response. It was beginning to look as if I was mistaken again. I decided to try round the back, and if I'd no luck, I'd give up and go home. I tried the side-gate; it was unlocked, and I went through. One of the rooms at the back had French windows.'

He stopped and took a quick sip of coffee. 'Which was how I found I wasn't mistaken. This was the house, all right. God!' He slammed his hand on the table, making the cups dance, and my own untasted coffee slopped into the saucer. '*Why* did I go round the back of that house? If I hadn't, my whole life would have been different.'

My throat was dry, but I gave an encouraging little nod.

'There were two people in the room, a man and a woman. The man, of course, was Harry. I couldn't hear what they were saying, but it was obvious they were arguing. The woman was waving her hands about and her face was flushed. Harry's face was set and angry, but there was a kind of desperation there too. He suddenly caught hold of her arm and tried to pull her towards him, but she twisted free, and as he came towards her again, her hand lashed out across his face.' Jeff's voice cracked. 'Then, as I watched, he caught up a pair of embroidery scissors that was lying with some sewing on a table and—and stuck them into her throat.'

'What did you do?' I whispered, horror-stricken.

'Damn-all. I was frozen to the spot. Blood spurted out and she slumped to the floor. Then, like a man in a dream, Harry turned slowly and saw me. For what seemed an eternity we stood and stared at each other. Then he came forward, still holding the dripping scissors, and unlocked the window.'

He straightened and took another sip of coffee. 'Well, to cut a long story short, I took command. I had to—he was in a state of complete shock. I got out my handkerchief and took the scissors from him. I had a quick look at the woman, but there was nothing I or anyone else could do for her. While Harry stood immobile in the middle of the room, I did what I could to tidy things up. Surprisingly he'd only a splash of blood on his shirt, and when he put his jacket on, it was covered. I wiped the window handle and key to get rid of prints. There was no way of knowing if he'd touched anything else in the room, but he hadn't been there long, and she must have admitted him herself. I didn't think about what I was doing, that I was making myself an accessory after the fact. All I knew was that Harry was in trouble and seemed incapable of helping himself.

'Within minutes we were out of the house—having wiped the door handle as we left—and walking rapidly away. We walked briskly and in silence for about twenty minutes, then we went into a pub and had a brandy each. I gathered Harry'd been involved with the woman for about a year. Her name was Julie Murray and she was married. It seemed she'd been cooling off for some time and he'd been frantically trying to hang on to her, but that evening she finally ended it. He said that when she slapped his face he saw red, but he hadn't meant to kill her. He seemed to have forgotten about the scissors, and I didn't mention them. Once he said, without any expression, "You're the only one who knows what happened."

'Before we parted he asked where I was staying and I told him, though we agreed it was best not to contact each other, at least for a while. But the next evening he phoned in a fine old state, asking what had happened to the scissors. I told him I had them, and he asked for them back.' Jeff reached for his empty cup and I topped it up from the porcelain pot.

'But by then,' he continued, 'I'd had time to work things out a bit. Harry'd changed since I'd last seen him, become hard and bitter. Though I'd automatically helped him, there were no longer close ties between us. And it was obvious he'd feel safer if there were no witnesses. He might decide to arrange an accident for me. Whichever way I looked at it, the scissors were my insurance; he wouldn't know where I'd put them, and as long as I had them, he couldn't harm me. He became very agitated when I wouldn't agree to hand them over, and I knew he'd come round to the digs. So I packed up and left that night.'

He gave a twisted smile. 'And I've been packing up and moving on ever since. Several times over the last couple of years I've caught sight of him, in towns where I've happened to be living. It *could* be coincidence, but I don't think so. I'm convinced he's still looking for me and my incriminating evidence. He won't feel safe till he has it back.'

As we walked home through the crisp spring dark, it was impossible to believe we had met only that day. Jeff's terrible secret, which he had so trustingly confided to me, had formed a strong bond between us. I think we were aware of it even then, and as the days passed and we spent evenings and weekends in each other's company, it steadily strengthened. He seemed somehow to need me, to depend on me, which no one else had ever done. It was not surprising that I fell deeply in love with him, and when, only weeks later, he asked me to marry him, I was overjoyed.

'Darling Susan,' he said, 'I feel so safe with you.'

'Because I'm called Smith?' I teased him. 'Perhaps you should take my name instead of my taking yours. Then you can come under the Smith umbrella.' Which, though I'd been half-joking, was in the event what we did.

So we were married and moved into our first home. But 'Smith' wasn't the answer to everything, as became clear when Jeff insisted on renting a house rather than buying one. It wasn't for financial reasons; I'd been surprised to find he had several bank accounts, all comfortably in credit.

But, he patiently explained, we must be free to leave at short notice should Harry track us down.

'He won't be looking for a married couple,' I'd protested, 'let alone one called Smith!'

Jeff put his arms round me. 'Bear with me, Susan. I'm probably being paranoid, but surely our being together is all that really matters.'

And of course I agreed. Jeff found himself a job with the local chemist and I continued at the library. I was happy and fulfilled as never before, loved as I'd never expected to be; a married woman.

But just over a year after our wedding, I came home from work to find Jeff unexpectedly there before me. His face was white and drawn.

'Darling, what is it?' I hurried to him in alarm and his arms closed convulsively round me. I could feel his heart crashing against my breast. And I think, with a sense of dread, that I knew what he would say.

'I've seen Harry. He came into the shop this afternoon.'

I stared at him aghast. 'Are you sure?'

'Am I likely to make a mistake like that?'

Privately, in his state of anxiety, I believed he might. I said instead, 'Did he see you?'

'No, I was in the dispensary. I caught sight of him through the hatchway as I was preparing a prescription.'

'Well, it can only be coincidence. He's probably just passing through.'

He said in a low voice, 'You know I can't take the chance.'

'But Jeff,' I wailed, gazing with suddenly accentuated love round the room we had so happily decorated together, 'we *can't* leave here—it's our home! And what about my job?'

'There are other libraries,' he said.

There was no reasoning with him. In a daze of misery I packed up our belongings, helped Jeff load them into a self-drive hired van, and left the little town which had been home to me.

And that became the pattern of our lives. We'd find a pleasant house to rent, settle ourselves into new jobs, and be happy for an indeterminate number of months. Then, inevitably, Jeff would catch sight of Harry—or think he did—and the whole thing would start again. I formed a deep and implacable hatred of Harry Pell, not only for Jeff's pitiable insecurity but for the disruption of my own life too.

One Saturday afternoon we had been shopping; it was just before Christmas and already darkness had fallen. As we came out of a brightly lit store, Jeff suddenly grabbed my arm, forcing me to turn into an unlit alleyway and run full-tilt into its gaping blackness. Gasping, panting for breath and precariously clutching my purchases, I'd no breath to ask the reason for our flight. But no need to, either. That evening we spent barricaded into our little house, with no radio or television to betray our presence or mask the sounds of attempted entry. And the next day we were on the move again.

Only once in all those upheavals did I demur at our peripatetic life, and that was after a stay of barely three months. But Jeff simply said, 'Susan, I must leave, either with or without you.' And I knew despairingly that, like him, I had no choice.

'Go to the police!' I begged him, time and again. 'They'll understand. After all, Harry could be dangerous to others as well as you. He's killed once, he could do it again.' But always he shook his head.

'Then let me!' I cried at last, exasperated by his stubbornness. 'I could explain—'

But at that his head came up, and an expression I'd never seen before crossed his face. 'If you ever attempt to contact the police, Susan, I swear you'll never see me again.'

It became clear that our constant moves, unsettling though I found them, took much heavier toll of Jeff. As the years slipped by he became thinner, paler, more jumpy. The nights when he woke me with his shouts and cries, thrashing about in the bed, became steadily more frequent. Useless to suggest he see a doctor; we both knew what was wrong with him, and the only cure, dreadful though it was to think it, was the death of Harry Pell.

Looking back, I suppose those last few months were leading inexorably towards what happened. After our last move, Jeff had not bothered to find himself a job and spent his time in the house, seemingly too nervous to venture out. There was little left of the man I'd fallen in love with, just a pitiful shadow.

So came that terrible day when I returned from shopping to find the house empty and a note on the kitchen table reading simply: 'I'm sorry, Susan.'

In a frenzy of fear I rushed out of the house just as the police car drew up outside. Jeff had thrown himself off the railway bridge into the path of an oncoming train. A gas bill in his pocket provided identification.

When the first numb despair had worn off, I went to the local police station and asked to speak to someone in charge. A pleasant-faced inspector took me into his office. He knew who I was and what had happened.

'My husband didn't really kill himself,' I told him, 'he was murdered by Harry Pell.' Not literally, of course; I knew that. There was no doubt Jeff had taken his own life—someone had seen him jump and raised the alarm. But at last I could tell the story Jeff had told me five long years ago in the Chinese restaurant.

The Inspector listened intently. A few minutes' consultation with the computer confirmed that Julie Murray had been stabbed to death at her home in Wimbledon seven years before, and the case remained open. There'd been no evidence against her husband, who was the original and only suspect.

But when the Inspector asked for details of Harry Pell, I could tell him nothing. I realized for the first time that I didn't even know what he looked like, this man who had so dominated our lives.

'And the scissors, Mrs Smith. What did your husband do with them?'

I didn't know that, either. 'There is a deed box I never saw opened,' I said. 'I've been looking for the key, but I can't find it.'

'If you'd like to bring it in, we'll try to open it for you.'

I was driven in the police car to the little house from which I should soon, and mercifully for the last time, be moving. The driver waited in the car while I collected the heavy steel box from the top of the wardrobe which was its habitual place. When I reached the Inspector's office he had an assortment of keys ready, together with other instruments to force the lock if necessary.

After several minutes' tinkering he gave a grunt of satisfaction and raised the lid. In silence we both looked at the contents: a blood-stained handkerchief wrapped round a small, thin object and a dusty old passport. With gloved hands he lifted the gory bundle and, laying it on his desk, began to unwrap it. We both knew what it contained. Averting my eyes, I picked up the passport which was lying face down in the box.

I must have made a sound, because the Inspector looked up, but I was incapable of speech. My eyes, my whole being, remained locked on the passport. For the name on the front was Mr H.J.M. Pell.

For a moment longer I fought it, recoiling against the significance of those initials. But I had to know. With sudden clumsy haste I fumbled open the booklet and my horrified suspicion was confirmed. The photograph inside, staring straight into my eyes, was of my husband. For the last five years I'd been Mrs Harold Jeffrey Martin Pell.

Reginald Hill

A SHAMEFUL EATING

REGINALD HILL is a Cumbrian who lived for many years in Doncaster, the mid-Yorkshire setting of his immensely successful series of crime novels featuring Superintendent Andy Dalziel and Peter Pascoe, who was a mere detective-constable in the first, but has now risen to the rank of Chief Inspector.

Reginald Hill has also written non-Dalziel and Pascoe crime novels, thrillers and general novels, including historical ones (under the name Charles Underhill) featuring Captain Fantom, of which this compellingly macabre story is a reminder.

A SHAMEFUL EATING is better than a shameful leaving, my dear old gramma used to say as she urged me into a second circuit of her groaning table. And I never saw any need to disagree with her, not until the start of my third week in that wallowing lifeboat.

The *Needle's Eye* had gone down fourteen days earlier, split apart by a squall so sudden that only the three of us on deck at the time had any hope of surviving. The youngest was Perkin Curtis, a fresh-faced lad on his very first voyage, with a fine tenor voice whose rendition of *A poore soule sate sighing by a sicamore tree* brought tears to the rheumy eyes of those same grizzled tars who lusted after his pink and white flesh. Three of them would have had him across the long cannon on the poop deck during the dog watch one night if I hadn't come up for a breath of air from the afterhold which I was using as a sickroom during an outbreak of Yellow Jack. I swear the boy was so innocent that he thought it no more than a bit of boisterous fun. I told him to pull his britches up, ordered two of the men below with a promise that they'd be up for captain's punishment in the morning, and kept their ringleader beside me. This was Josh Gall, the bosun's mate, a small plump man whose surface of placid amiability had scarce been touched by half a century of evil habits and riotous behaviour. But he was a fine seaman, none better for anticipating and dealing with a nautical emergency.

I should have remembered this as I savaged him with

my tongue, promising him the extremities of the law for his
assault on young Curtis. But I took no notice of a sudden
change in his expression from abject contrition to active
alarm, save to congratulate myself on having pierced his
carapace with my threats.

'Sir,' he tried to interrupt, 'will you listen—'

'Too late for excuses now, Gall,' I shouted him down.
'This time it's the lash for you!'

Alas, it wasn't his excuses he wanted me to listen to,
but that change in the wind's note which gave him warning
of the fury that was almost upon us.

'For God's sake, bring her round!' he yelled suddenly,
trying to spring by me towards the wheelhouse. Still deaf-
ened by my own rage, I caught his arm and held him fast.

Then in a trice the wind shifted from west to south,
from light airs to a near-tornado, which hit us like a man-o'-
war's broadside. The *Needle's Eye* went over till her masts lay
parallel with the sea, then a wave like a giant's fist struck her
amidships, and the poor old tub folded in two and turned
submarine.

Somehow a lifeboat was ripped free, and somehow Josh
Gall with his instinct for being in the right place at the right
time came up alongside it and scrambled in. I surfaced half a
furlong away and saw him quite clearly, for despite the fury
of the wind there was not a cloud to be seen in the huge
starry sky. I shouted, then went under again, so deep that I
saw as in a dream the bow section of the ship with its figure-
head of a full-breasted mermaid drifting downwards to its
eternal rest. Perhaps I did dream that I could see desperate
hands clawing at the foc's'le ports, but the image gave me
strength to kick upwards one last time, and when I broke
the surface I saw the lifeboat bobbing past within a couple
of feet. Gall lay sprawling over the gunwale. His eyes met
mine. I called for help but he regarded me indifferently and
made no move, and the boat would next moment have been
beyond my reach had there not been a line trailing behind.

This I seized and with my last strength hauled myself along it till I could grasp the stern and drag myself aboard.

I had no strength or breath to express my contempt for Gall, but lay there, giving God what proved premature thanks for my deliverance. Then I became aware Gall was standing upright in that rocking cockleshell with a sailor's ease, pointing and shouting.

'Over there,' he cried. 'Do you not see?'

I forced my head up and looked. About fifty yards away in the surging sea I glimpsed a wooden cask with a man clinging to it by one arm.

'Quick!' urged Gall. 'I can't manage on my lone!'

He was trying to paddle towards his shipmate, using a length of wood ripped from the shattered thwarts. I pulled free another piece and taking my place on the opposite side of the boat, joined my efforts to his. I confess I felt a little shame at my recent condemnation of Gall for his apparent failure to offer assistance to me. And my shame grew when I saw that it was no special crony of the man's we were trying to rescue, but young Perkin Curtis.

We would probably not have reached him had the storm not abated as suddenly as it came and the ocean rapidly deflated from Pennine peaks to Lincolnshire levels. But as we drew alongside Curtis, my new respect for Gall died like the wind.

He reached out, seized the boy's arm, prised it loose from the cask—then thrust the unhappy youth down into the sea!

For a second I believed he had merely lost his grip. Then I realized that what Gall was concerned to rescue was not the boy, but the cask he was clinging to!

'For God's sake, man!' I cried. 'Will you let a fellow human perish?'

'Without water, we all perish,' he snarled. 'Give us a hand to get this aboard.'

There was no point in cutting off my nose to spite my face, so I helped him drag the cask over the gunwale. Then as I stared sadly into the ocean which I thought had closed over the unfortunate youth for ever, to my joy and relief I saw Curtis's head break the surface only an arm's length away. He was clearly *in extremis,* perhaps even past relief, but I reached out my hand and grasped his shock of corn-blond hair.

'Help me!' I screamed at Gall, who regarded me with a sneering indifference for a moment. Then perhaps his cunning mind took into consideration that if we survived, my evidence to an Enquiry might yet do him some harm, and he leaned out to take Curtis by the collar and between us we pulled him aboard. He collapsed in a heap in the bow, looking for all the world like a dead man, but I have had plenty of experience of dealing with men snatched from the deep and knew what to do. Rolling him on his back, I knelt beside him and pressed hard against his stomach. A great gush of water issued from his mouth but he did not start to breathe, so I used a technique I had learnt from the savages of the Carolinas and, putting my mouth to his, filled his lungs with air from my own, then expelled it by pressure to his chest. This I repeated three or four times till of a sudden he retched, bringing up more water, and I turned him on his side, seeing that he could now breathe on his own.

I looked up to catch Gall's twisted smile.

'It's a strange world, Mr Teasdale,' he said. 'Less than thirty minutes ago you were threatening to have the skin off my back for little more than what you've just been doing.'

'You're a foul creature, Gall,' I said contemptuously. 'You sit there sneering when you should be giving gratitude to God for sparing this boy's life.'

'Oh, I'm grateful enough, Mr Teasdale, sir,' he said. 'God moves in mysterious ways, and the lad is certainly well fleshed.'

I thought his mind was simply dwelling on its usual vile carnal obsession, but perhaps already his undoubted seaman's nous was anticipating the trials ahead and providing his own unthinkable answer to them.

Now he turned his attention from me to the cask. The way it had floated told that it could be no more than half full but if that half were water, then it was indeed a priceless discovery. Gall gently twisted the spigot till a thick liquid started to ooze out. He let it touch his fingers, sniffed, tasted, and laughed his grating laugh.

'God's good to patriots, it seems,' he said. 'We can drink the King's health afore we light our pipes tonight. This here's our late lamented skipper's best rum!'

I reached over and tasted. He was right. It was one of several casks which Captain Danby had insisted on taking on board in Jamaica despite my advice that we would do better to cram our limited storage space with fresh fruit and vegetables.

'At least we can wet our whistle and die merry,' said Gall.

'Die you will if you take too much of this, Gall,' I said sternly. 'Alcohol dries up the blood and redoubles a man's thirst. But yet it is a good restorative and may help this poor boy.'

So saying, I caught half a gill in the palm of my hand and gently poured it into Curtis's mouth. It set him coughing and spluttering once more, but when the fit was passed, he had some colour in his cheeks and was able to struggle upright. He looked all around him. The sea was smooth as his own unrazored cheeks and the moon lacquered it with light so that he could see for miles in all directions. Save for a few spars from the wrecked ship, we were the only thing to trouble that polished surface. I think it was only now that his desperate plight struck him, for the tinge of colour the rum had restored drained from his cheeks once more and he cried, 'Mr Teasdale, where are the others? Where is the *Needle's Eye?*'

'Sunk, lad,' I said. 'And all your shipmates with it, God rest their souls. But do not despair. The Almighty has seen fit in His infinite mercy to spare us the full measure of His wrath, and I cannot believe that He has preserved us from the deep but to watch us perish in plain air.'

My words of comfort had but little effect, I fear. Young Curtis collapsed to the bottom of the boat once more, sobbing and howling, and his eyes gushed forth as much water as his belly had after his submersion.

Gall meanwhile had settled himself comfortably against the tiller on the one unshattered thwart in the stern. I glared at him angrily. As the one surviving officer of the *Needle's Eye*, it was time to assert my authority.

'Gall,' I said coldly, 'will you be good enough to move? It is the captain's place, I believe, to be at the helm.'

For a second I thought he would defy me, then he grinned and said, 'Aye, aye, *Cap'n* Teasdale, sir,' and shifted down the boat.

I took his place on the stern thwart and grasped the tiller. It moved in my hand like a twig on a sapling. I peered over the stern and saw that the rod linking tiller and rudder had shattered.

'Shouldn't worry about that, Cap'n,' said Gall. 'No great loss not being able to steer when we've only the currents to carry us.'

He was right. There were no oars, no mast, no sail.

'We can paddle, with the broken thwarts,' I said with a show of authority. 'Come, best make a start before the sun comes up and the heat saps our strength.'

Gall grinned again, picked up the length of broken wood and said, 'Aye, aye, Cap'n Teasdale. What's your course, Cap'n?'

I saw his game. He knew well that, as ship's doctor, my expertise lay in charting the course of men's ailments, not the ways of the sea. But with the stars showing in their full refulgence, I at least had no problem in finding directions out.

'West,' I said, pointing. 'We will head west.'

'Back to the Americas?' he said. 'Well, 'tis certainly a large target, sir, and one that would be hard to miss. Trouble is in these waters, west's the direction the prevailing winds came from and also the great currents, and while I dare say two men paddling hard might hold their own for a while, yet I do not see how they could hope to make any progress.'

'You would have us go east, then?' I asked, swallowing my pride.

'East? Now certainly that would mean we had wind and water in our favour, but betwixt us and Africa there is nothing but the Azores, and they are such a tiny target I doubt that we could hit it even if our strength held out that long.'

'So what do you suggest, Mr Gall?' I demanded. 'Bob around here, doing nothing?'

'What point in doing anything else?' he asked. 'We are as like to meet with a ship here as anywhere else. We are close to the main lanes to and from the Indies. Here let us rest, and the Lord have mercy on our souls.'

And so our ordeal began. We pooled our resources. They were poor enough in all faith. All I could supply was a tinder-box which lived up to its claim to be waterproof, a clay pipe broken in three pieces, a pouch of sodden tobacco and, most useless of all, a few silver guineas in a wash-leather purse I kept hung round my neck. Gall had even less to offer: a piece of twine about four feet in length and a broad-bladed knife such as butchers use for the dressing of meat. Young Curtis's pockets provided the best trove. Clearly he had a boy's endless appetite and out came two apples, a block of treacle toffee, a wedge of cheese, and a hunk of bread turned by its immersion in the sea into a grey and glutinous putty which nevertheless I spread out to dry, foreseeing that a time would soon come when we would be ready to eat anything.

These, with the cask of rum, were our provisions. I took charge of the rum, doling it out in the smallest of measures, fearful of the effect it could have on our weakened frames and also eager to save some in case we had to signal a distant ship. I discovered that the strong fumes given off by the heavy treacly liquor were readily ignitable by the flint from my tinder-box, and though fire is a dangerous companion on a small boat, yet it would be worth the risk if it meant a chance of rescue.

Water we had none, but God soon sent the mixed blessing of rain, which slaked our thirst while drenching our skins again, for we had no means of shelter either from clouds or the sun.

Despite my utmost parsimony, our small store of rations did not last beyond a week. Some of the cheese we sacrificed on a hook made from a shoe buckle tied to the end of Gall's piece of twine, in an effort to catch fish, but without luck. Gall slashed wildly with his knife at the occasional seabird which curiosity brought near our craft and though he once disturbed a feather, he got no closer.

We passed the second week chewing salty tobacco, sipping minute quantities of rum, and moistening our lips with rainwater. I think that I possibly suffered the most. The other two were well fleshed but I was ever lean and bony, and while they fed on their own fat, I became skeletal. But it was young Curtis who suffered the worst in his morale. Despite all my efforts at comfort, he would weep for hours on end, raving of his mother and his sisters, till finally he had no strength to weep or talk, and would not even have roused himself for his ration of water and rum had I not forced it through his flaked and bloodless lips.

'It's a waste,' said Gall one day as he watched me.

'A waste,' I said. 'Why? Do you think if you took his share it would prolong your miserable life by more than a miserable minute?'

'No, I meant it's a waste that we starve when there is victuals aplenty before us,' said Gall.

It took me a long moment to get his meaning and when I did, I looked at him aghast.

'What new depth of foulness is this?' I cried in disbelief.

'Don't preach at me, you poxy quack,' he snarled. 'The

lad's good as dead. Why strive to keep him alive just so that we can all die together? Let's make an end of him now and save ourselves. You're a surgeon, you should know best where the most nutrition lies in human meat!'

He had his knife in his hand and on his face was a look of madness which warned me I must be careful how I interfered.

I said, 'Let me have the knife, Gall. Come, you said I was the surgeon and thus best fitted to do the carving. The knife, if you please.'

He looked at me doubtingly, then slowly he handed over that dreadful weapon. I drove it into the thwart beside me.

'What? Do you betray me then? Will you not do it?' he cried.

'I am a doctor, Gall,' I answered. 'I have taken vows to preserve life, not to destroy it.'

'That's all I'm suggesting we do,' he answered with the cunning logic of insanity. 'Save two lives at the expense of one. Like you said to Curtis at the start, God won't have saved us from drowning at the bottom of the ocean just so's we can starve on top of it!'

'No,' I cried. 'Thou shalt not kill! God is just testing us. He will provide. He will show us another way.'

'Then He'd better show it quick, Cap'n Teasdale,' mocked that vile and villainous creature. 'Else, if He waits another few hours, He'll be able to tell us what we ought to have done face to face!'

I think my faith in a loving God died at that moment. I turned the spigot on the rum cask and filled the wooden cup which Gall had roughly fashioned from a piece of the useless tiller. When I handed it to him he looked at me speculatively, then downed the lot. I refilled the cup and poured the liquor down the unresisting Curtis's throat. Then I passed another brimming measure to Gall.

'Mr Teasdale, sir,' he said. 'I see you're a true gent after all. If a man must die, then let him die merry. Here's health.'

He downed the rum in a single draught. In his weakened state his old capacity for hard drinking was of no avail and I could already see the fiery liquor taking effect, while after a single draught the boy was almost unconscious.

I filled the cup again.

We were picked up ten days later by a Portuguese brigantine hauling copra from the Leeward Islands. She had sprung a seam and was making heavy weather to the Azores, and our new conditions were but little improvement on those we endured in that open boat. Yet the Promethean spark at the heart's core is most obstinate against extinction, and my two companions were carried ashore at Ponta Delgada on San Miguel with breath enough still to mist an eyeglass. We were taken to the town's infirmary, run by Father Boniface, a Catholic priest more skilled at steering his patients to the next world than keeping them in this. He expressed great amazement at our survival, especially as we were all three Protestant, but his admiration for me as a fellow doctor was unstinted.

'Gangrene, you say?'

'Aye, gangrene,' I replied indifferently.

'And with a carving knife?'

'Aye, a carving knife.'

'And how did you cauterize the arteries?' he asked eagerly.

'With the lees from a keg of rum which I then fired with my tinder-box,' I said wearily. 'Enough of these questions. They are in your care now, Father. My responsibility for them is done.'

'*Non nobis, Domine,*' he proclaimed. 'Not unto us, my friend. They are in God's care and always have been, for truly His hand must have guided thine.'

'Your care, God's care, take the credit who will,' I cried

wildly. 'Only they are out of my care. And if they now die, as seems most likely, it cannot lie at my door!'

He put my outburst down to a hysterical fever and mixed me a filthy potion which I poured down the jakes after he had gone. It did not seem possible that my companions who had no such strength to resist could long survive such divine ministrations.

I slept well that night and felt stronger in the morn, and when I learnt that the brig which had brought us here was now repaired and ready to resume its voyage to Lisbon, I announced that I purposed to sail with her. Some money from the purse I wore about my neck I gave to the good Father.

Perhaps it was the clink of the coins which penetrated Gall's ears, for he opened his eyes and spoke the first words he had uttered since our arrival.

'What? Are you leaving, Mr Teasdale? Nay, you are right not to delay on our account. God speed. And rest assured young Curtis and I will never forget what you have done for us.'

His voice was low but every word fell on my ears like a bell-note. Then he closed his eyes once more.

I made for the door, pausing only to shake hands with Boniface.

'You have two friends forever here, I think,' he said, smiling. 'Let us pray they survive.'

'I know you will do your best for them, Father,' I said. 'Be not sparing of your prayers. Nor your potions either.'

And with that I hastened down to the harbour where the brigantine was already hoisting her sails to catch the freshening western breeze.

I gave up the sea after that and went back north to my native Derbyshire, where I set up practice in the wild country of the Peak. Here distances were long, weather was wild, and payment was as like to be in eggs and vegetables as coin of the realm. Yet it was a comfort to me even as I laboured through the wildest storm to taste no tang of salt in the rain, and to know that the nearest sea was three days' hard riding to east or west. My patients apart, I saw little company for I proved far too abstemious for our hard-drinking, hard-eating, hard-hunting squire, and far too contentious for our prating parson. Once a week I would ride the seven miles to the Black Tor Inn which stood high on an edge overlooking the road from Buxton to Sheffield and learn what news the mail coach had brought in. Occasionally there might be some respectable company to talk to, but usually I made do with John Farley, the landlord, swapping local gossip over a pint of his sour ale. Then, after a plain repast of bread and cheese, with perhaps a bowl of vegetable broth if the weather were chill, I would take my leave. At my first coming to those parts, the landlord had tried to press me to a joint of meat or a bowlful of beef stew, convinced as such men are that flesh is necessary to human health. But my continual refusal, and I dare say my continual survival, persuaded him in the end that a man might live on cheese and vegetables alone, though he begged me not to recommend such a diet to my patients and his customers.

'There's little profit to be made in such plain fare,' he confided. 'For when a man can see exactly what he is eating, he can add up the cost of the parts and complain bitterly if he thinks a poor innkeeper is seeking too much profit. But once let there be meat in it and gravy and spices and herbs, though it be but in truth three parts vegetable water, then is he more willing to pay what I ask without quarrel!'

He spoke thus familiarly with me only after long acquaintance, and also because he was convinced by my frugal method of life that I lived up to the old reputation of my profession and loved gold as much as he did.

I smiled and thereafter joined him in long plaints about the rising cost of things and the parsimony of our shared customers, and on such plain fare for the stomach and for the mind, I existed quite happily for near on ten years.

Happily, I say. Well, it is a question of degree; and

though I oft-times felt that I would be as well out of this world as in it, yet it is a brave surgeon who can practise on himself, and an unbroken pattern of life can come to be pleasant though no single part of it has much power to please.

So my life passed till this bleak November day. It was a wild dark morning with the promise of winter's first snow in the blast and I almost abandoned my customary ride to the Black Tor. Yet, perhaps because I knew such a break in the pattern of my existence would make me feel unsettled, I saddled my patient old mare and set out. The stage had been and gone when I reached the inn. Some passengers had alighted, I was told, but they were resting after their long bone-shaking ride and had left orders not to be disturbed till their dinner was ready, so I went and sat alone in the upstairs parlour till John Farley came to join me.

'It's blowing up a real hurricano out there,' he pronounced. 'Feel how it makes the old timbers shake. You'd almost think we were out at sea.'

I smiled thinly, thinking how little he knew of what it really felt like to be in a storm in the Atlantic's bubbling cauldron. But he was right about the rising wind for I could hear it singing in the chimney and round the shutters, and from time to time it did indeed seem as if the boards beneath my feet vibrated like a ship's deck.

'It will be good for trade, John,' I joked. 'Those who are here will not be able to leave for home.'

'Nay,' he said gloomily. 'You mean those who are at home will not set out to come here.'

So we talked of nothing in particular, and smoked a pipe, and supped our ale, till there came a knock at the door, or rather a thud low down, as if someone had kicked it.

'Who's there?' called Farley.

'Doctor's dinner,' came back a voice I recognized as belonging to Willie Bell, a slow-witted youth who worked in the kitchen.

'Well, fetch it in, you great lubbock!'

'Can't open the door, maister,' replied Willie.

With an exasperated groan, Farley rose and pulled the door open.

It was immediately apparent why Willie could not turn the handle himself.

Instead of the usual small tray with a loaf and a wedge of cheese, he was carrying a huge pewter salver with a great domed lid.

He staggered forward and deposited it on the table in front of me, then waved his hands in the air, saying, ''Tis hot.'

'Hot? What's hot?' cried Farley. 'What's this you've brought, you idiot?'

And so saying, he snatched the lid off the salver.

A great cloud of aromatic steam arose, obscuring what lay there for a moment. Then as the morning mist is sucked up the fellside by the reddening sun, it cleared to reveal two mountainous joints of roast meat, one a leg of pork, the other a shoulder of mutton.

My first thought was that this must be some monstrous joke of mine host's, and I leapt to my feet, ready to vent my indignation upon him. Then I looked into his face and saw that his amazement was as real as mine.

'Numbskull!' he yelled, raising his fist threateningly above the pot-boy's head. 'What stupidity is this? Have you not been working here long enough to know what manner of vittles his honour prefers?'

Willie cringed away, crying, 'Aye, maister, but the missus told me as he wanted this here today.'

'The missus?' Farley looked at me with wild surmise. 'Doctor, I'm sorry. Clearly this fool has got more muddled than he usually is, if that's possible. We'll have this sorted in a trice. Dora!'

His bellow shook the room almost as much as the storm without, which was increasing in intensity with each passing minute.

A few moments later Mrs Farley, a stout good-natured woman whose natural generosity when it came to loading plates brought her into frequent conflict with her husband, appeared in the doorway.

'This idiot says you gave him this as the Doctor's dinner,' said Farley, pointing at the steaming salver.

'That's right,' said his wife. 'Is something wrong wi' it?'

'Wrong? A leg of pork and a shoulder of mutton, and you ask if something's wrong?' cried Farley. 'When did you know Dr Teasdale let a morsel of meat pass his lips? What are you thinking of, woman?'

'I'll thank you not to *woman* me,' said his wife with spirit. 'It was the Doctor's friends as told me to send it up.'

A blast like a giant's hand struck the building so that it seemed that at the very least it must tear the chimneys off, and for about half a minute speech was impossible. Then the wind subsided to a steady roar, and I moistened my lips with beer and asked faintly, 'What friends, Mrs Farley?'

'The two gentlemen who got off the coach,' she replied. 'They ordered a roast leg and a roast shoulder as soon as they arrived and naturally I thought it was for them, though a lot it seemed for just the two of them. But when they came down just now they said, no, it weren't for them, it was for their friend, Dr Teasdale, and would I send it straight up? I hope I didn't do wrong.'

Farley was looking at me. What he saw in my face must have assured him that these men were no friends of mine, for he said, 'Right, wife. Let's you and I have a talk to these two gentlemen who make themselves so pleasant with decent folk.'

'Oh, it's too late for that,' said his wife. 'They've gone.'

'Gone?' said Farley, looking aghast at the loaded salver. 'Did they pay their reckoning?'

'Oh aye. They paid in full. For their room, the food, and the other things they bought. I asked 'em if they didn't want a word with the Doctor, and they said no, they'd likely see him at home later.'

'Well, this beats cock-fighting,' said Farley with undisguisable relief at learning that this jape was not going to cost him money. 'What do you make of it, Doctor?'

'Mrs Farley,' I said with difficulty. 'What did they look like, these two men?'

'Oh, if it's a description you want for the constable, I'd know 'em again anywhere,' she cried. 'They were the oddest pair. Him, the older one who did the talking, he had one of them peg-legs and walked with a crutch. And the other, the younger one, who never opened his mouth, poor lad, he had his sleeve pinned across his chest like he had no arm to go in it.'

I could speak no further but Farley's curiosity was bubbling over.

'You said they bought some other things, wife. What manner of things did they buy to carry out into this terrible storm with them?'

'The oddest set of things you can imagine,' she replied, shaking her head in puzzlement. 'But they did not carry them off with them. No, they said they was sure the Doctor, understanding their disabilities, would oblige them by fetching them along hisself. And they left them on the kitchen table.'

'Left *what*, for God's sake, woman?' cried Farley in desperation.

But I did not stay for her answer.

Rudely thrusting her aside, I clattered down the narrow stairway to the kitchen, and flung open the door.

There on the great oak table, in a miasma of smoke and steam and the reek of roasting meat, stood a cask of rum; a tinder-box; a carving knife.

Charlotte MacLeod

A STICKY BUSINESS

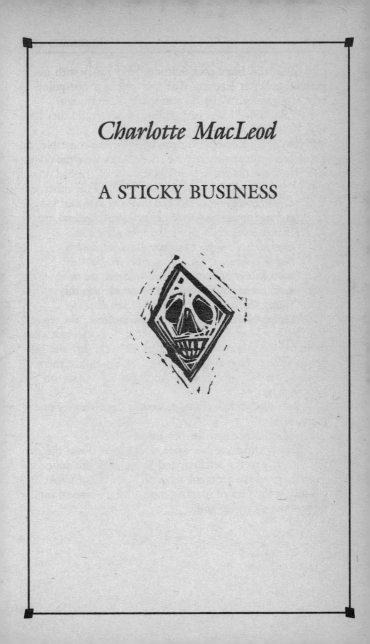

MRS HYPATIA KELLING, relict of her late and little regretted fourth cousin once removed Waldo Kelling, was like other Kellings in having married within the clan. In her day, everybody had been expected to marry somebody and naturally nobody wanted to see the money go outside the family. In other respects, however, Hypatia was not at all like the rest of them. Other Kellings were clannish. They sent cards on birthdays and holidays, they showed up at weddings. They particularly enjoyed funerals, where they could inventory the faults and sometimes even the virtues of the departed in exhaustive detail. Hypatia had no use for small talk.

Hypatia was a scholar. She had taken an advanced degree in classical Greek at a time when few young women of her class aspired to anything beyond an MRS. Throughout a long lifetime, she had continued her close acquaintance with Aeschylus, Euripides, Sophocles, Thucydides, and others of their ilk, though she despised Aristophanes as overly given to frivolity and thought Plato an old gasbag. During the past decade, however, she had been greatly hampered in her studies by failing eyesight. Medical treatment had not availed; by now she was barely able to distinguish light from dark, much less alpha from omega.

Still, Hypatia was not without her pleasures nor yet without her Kellings, the ones whose company she could best endure and even relish. These were ten charming little figurines who stood mute and motionless in a locked glass-fronted cabinet at the left of the fireplace in her otherwise austerely albeit handsomely furnished dining-room.

Waldo's father had been the author of their creation. Hypatia had never liked her father-in-law. In fact she hadn't thought much of Waldo, either, but that was beside the point. But she did have to give the old man credit for the imaginative enterprise he had shown back before the turn of the century when he'd commissioned a then unknown young artist to replicate some of the more interesting Kelling ancestors in porcelain.

Whatever his other faults, the elder Waldo had been no fool when it came to judging objets d'art. He might have been perspicacious enough to realize that the obscure modeller would one day be not only recognized but acclaimed, that the amusing poppets Miss Burne-Millais pinched so deftly out of fine white clay and tinted so sweetly with fine-haired brushes would become the quarry of cognoscenti with fortunes to spend.

The Kelling collection was unique; collectors would no doubt have been beating on the doors had they known it existed; but few of them did, and that was fine with Hypatia. The last thing she wanted was a pack of slavering outsiders waving cheques under her nose. Her own income was more than sufficient for her modest needs. She never cared to travel because she was already there. The Chippendale and Hepplewhite that had served her and Waldo's ancestors would surely last out whatever might be left of her lifetime. She had all the clothes she'd ever need, the old Reo was still running well enough for occasional afternoon airings. Her simple daily needs were adequately dealt with by her cook, her maid, her chauffeur who doubled as houseman and gardener, and the various workers who came in to assist.

No servant was ever allowed to handle the Kellings, of course. From the day she'd entered this house as a bride, Hypatia had taken upon herself the agreeable duty of caring for Miss Burne-Millais's masterworks. Had anybody ever hinted that Mrs Kelling took the same pleasure in the figurines that she might have taken in her dolls if she'd been that sort of child, she would no doubt have repudiated the notion with one glance of frozen scorn; but she would not have given up her cherished task.

Once a month, on the first Friday, Hypatia washed the Kellings one by one in a china basin half-filled with warm soapy water, rinsed them in a second basin of clear water, and dried them on soft linen towels kept for that particular purpose. Once a week between washings, she dusted each one with a tiny sable brush. Only the best for the Kellings.

Sometimes Hypatia even caught herself smiling, as when she ran her brush over the rose-garlanded embonpoint of the long-ago Ernestina whom Romney had painted as a middle-aged Venus accompanied by a white dove, he and God alone knew why. Romney had pulled off his opus with a straight face. Miss Burne-Millais must have been, Hypatia thought, a bit of a minx.

In truth, the artist had poked sly fun at every one of her subjects. The black-garbed Puritan carried his Bible clutched to his bosom and his jug of rum half concealed by his coat-tails. The doughty sea captain bestrode his frigate's quarterdeck looking awfully green around the gills. The Revolutionary Minuteman crouched behind his stone wall holding his powder horn wrong way around and regarding his flintlock rifle with an expression of mild puzzlement. The stately China merchant dressed up as a Mandarin seemed unaware that a butterfly had perched on his moustache. A Victorian bridal couple stood under a fig tree around whose trunk twined a bright green serpent; the bride was offering the groom a shiny red apple.

There were five more: the bluestocking Cassiopeia who'd once called Margaret Fuller a flibbertigibbet to her face; the madcap Prudence who'd been so calamitously misnamed; Petrie, who'd gone to Egypt to look for mummies, being frightened away by a scarab; frugal Theophilus in his counting-house counting out his money, his rotund wife beside him eating bread and honey. Dashing Serapis had been very young, alive, and kicking over the traces when the artist modelled him in his frock-coat, yellow gloves, and top hat.

Serapis was the only one of the models still extant by the time Hypatia took charge of the figurines. She'd last seen him at Waldo's funeral, an old man trying to be young and not fooling anybody. She hadn't cared for Serapis in the flesh, but found his miniature effigy agreeable to wash.

Nowadays Hypatia had to pursue her delicate avocation solely by touch. She could no longer enjoy the exquisite colours or the infinitesimal brush strokes that had so deftly brought forth a knowing look or a curling lip, but her enjoyment in the Kellings was not thereby greatly lessened. Memory's eye was as sharp as ever; as she ran her fingertips over their charmingly convoluted shapes, Hypatia could still visualize each minute detail, down to the all but invisible bee atop Theophilus's wife's honey jar.

Every one of the porcelains was exactly as it had come out of Miss Burne-Millais's kiln; not a crack, a chip, or a flaw anywhere. Nor would there be one, not while the set remained in Hypatia's care. Acknowledging the restrictions imposed by her infirmity, she took greater care than ever to lift each piece out of its cubicle without knocking it against the cabinet, to ease it in and out of the basin as though it had been a live baby, to dry it with meticulous care and return it to its appointed spot before she locked the cabinet and hung the key back on the gold chain she wore around her neck night and day.

That the lock was a flimsy thing which anybody with a modicum of deftness and determination could crack in a wink never entered her mind. Why should it? Her house servants had been with her forever, the cleaners who came in by the day were never allowed within joggling distance of the cabinet. Hypatia had never cared much for visitors; now that she could literally see nobody, she never invited anybody. Since she lived far enough from other Kellings to make uninvited dropppings-in impractical, they seldom dropped. The only one who made the effort to visit her on a regular basis was James, and he wasn't even a Kelling.

James wasn't much of anything, really. His mother had been Waldo's stepsister, acquired through a misguided second marriage between Waldo's father and a much younger woman whom he'd been calling his secretary for a number of years while Waldo was away at school and Waldo's mother off exploring the Upper Zambesi. The latter had finally succumbed to a native spear thrust, no doubt for good and sufficient reason as she had been a particularly exasperating person, even for a Kelling.

Upon receiving the news of his first wife's demise, Waldo's father had immediately married the secretary, learning only after the wedding that he had thereby saddled himself with a nineteen-year-old stepdaughter, the alleged result of a short and tragic marriage with a handsome Canadian army officer who had lost his life in the Boer War performing some heroic deed about which the ex-secretary was none too clear, Bloemfontein being so far away.

The stepdaughter had not been underfoot for long; she'd seized the first possible opportunity to elope with Waldo's father's handsome young coachman. The amorous pair had fled to Syracuse, New York, in Waldo's father's new Hupmobile with which they'd started a limousine service and from subsequent reports done quite well.

James might or might not have been the sole fruit of this impetuous union. He himself had never said and Hypatia's stepmother-in-law had not been around long enough to ask. After only a year or so of lawful wedlock, the second Mrs Waldo Senior had also taken off for the Upper Zambesi. Hypatia had thought this a sensible and considerate thing for the woman to do and had thus been favourably disposed towards young James when he'd presented himself at her door some years later with a volume of Euripides under his arm, wondering whether Hypatia could help him construe a difficult passage from *Iphigenia in Tauris*.

From *Iphigenia* it was but a step to the *Orestes* and a

bond of sorts had been formed. James was accorded the privilege of sitting at Hypatia's tea-table on first and third Thursdays, eating Hymettus honey on his crumpets as a tribute to the ancient Greeks. Over the teacups, the two continued their scholarly explorations. If Hypatia did most of the talking and James most of the eating, that was only proper considering their respective ages and conditions.

And so it had gone, while months slipped into years and years into decades; while Waldo stepped into Charon's ferryboat and glided away down the Styx almost unnoticed; while Hypatia's brown tresses turned to silver and pudgy young James became fat middle-aged James. What he did between alternate Thursdays James never said and Hypatia never bothered to ask. She assumed he was teaching Greek somewhere. Perhaps he had a family; if so, he never mentioned them and it never entered Hypatia's head to wonder.

Her servants were under the impression that their mistress doted upon the faithful James; in fact she cared far less for him than she did for the dashing Serapis, who was her least favourite of the Kelling porcelains. James would not have given Miss Burne-Millais much in the way of inspiration. His features were nondescript, his form unprepossessing. His manners were deplorable: he slopped his tea, gobbled his food, and got honey all over his fingers. His clothes were shabby, although Hypatia had thought nothing of that even when she could still see them. She herself would have looked like a walking ragbag were her devoted Maude less diligent in mending, sponging, and pressing the garments Hypatia absent-mindedly donned day after day, year after year.

Nor was James a sparkling conversationalist. If he did venture an opinion, it was always one which Hypatia herself had voiced at some previous tea-time. The only point she would grant in his favour was that he had a retentive memory. She gave James no credit for being a patient listener, she never considered the possibility that he might have kept

showing up so punctiliously all these years because he was
fond of her. Why should he be? Serapis certainly wasn't.

It was Serapis who at last forced Hypatia to think of
James as a human being. First Fridays were always the Kellings' bath days. This particular Friday, Agnes the cook had
brought in the oilcloth sheet as soon as she'd cleared away
Hypatia's breakfast. She'd spread the sheet over the dining-
room table; she'd set out the two china basins, one with
warm soapy water, one with clear; she'd fetched the small
stack of soft old linen towels. Then she'd gone back to her
kitchen and stayed there.

Left to herself, Hypatia had taken the key from the
chain around her neck, opened the cabinet, and set about
washing the Kellings in strict order of precedence: first the
Puritan, then the captain, third the Minuteman, and so on
down through family history. She'd had no reason or incli-
nation to hurry, she'd spent a long time on each piece. Her
well-trained fingertips had served her well, she'd picked out
every last detail, relating it to her clear mental picture,
dwelling pleasurably on Miss Burne-Millais's witty interpre-
tations of past family worthies and unworthies.

Hypatia had never quite made up her mind whether it
was Prudence or Serapis who deserved the title of most unworthy. Prudence had got her bath between Cassiopeia and
Theophilus; at last it got to be Serapis's turn. The old
woman bent stiffly, for her joints were no longer what
they'd been sixty years before, and slid her hand across the
bottom of the lowest cubicle on the right-hand side of the
cabinet; expecting to encounter a round porcelain base on
which rested, light as the butterfly on the Mandarin's moustache, one spatted foot in a pointy-toed black patent leather
boot. She felt only the shelf.

This was not possible. Refusing to believe her senses,
still taking pains to be gentle, Hypatia moved her hand
around the space Serapis should have been occupying. But
there was no way she could have missed him. The space was
too small, the narrow cabinet had been built expressly to

hold the Kellings, with just five shelves not more than a foot long divided down the middle so that each figurine had its own cubbyhole. To keep them from squabbling, Waldo's father had maintained; Hypatia had always found his whimsies particularly annoying.

Was it humanly possible that Hypatia had set Serapis down somewhere outside the cabinet when last she'd dusted, and forgotten to restore him to his proper place? She'd been interrupted in her weekly routine, she remembered with a frown of annoyance, by Mrs Apollonia Kelling, who'd driven all the way from Cambridge to cheer her up. Hypatia had not wanted to be cheered up, she'd wanted to get on with her work.

But Apollonia could be stickier than honey. She'd gabbled until Hypatia had in desperation started quoting Euripides at her in Greek. One could always count on Euripides.

Alone at last, Hypatia had gone back and finished her dusting, she was sure she had. Knowing full well that she'd never have left Serapis out of the cabinet, couldn't possibly have squeezed him in with one of the other figurines, nevertheless she went back and searched the other nine compartments. Every Kelling was in his or her proper place, each was alone. Then where was Serapis?

Never once in her life had Hypatia panicked. She was at a loss to understand the horrible feeling that came over her now: the cold sweat that trickled down her armpits, the constriction in her throat, the sudden queasiness in a portion of her anatomy it would have been indelicate to name.

Until this moment Hypatia had refused to think of her blindness as a handicap. Knowing she must cope with it, she had concentrated on developing compensatory skills and reorganizing her lifestyle to conquer this new challenge, much as she'd reorganized and conquered Waldo once they were married. That she'd reorganized him into an untimely grave was not something that had ever occurred to her, she was certainly not thinking about Waldo now. Standing by the open cabinet, feeling her scalp crawl, she was gripped by the horror of her own utter helplessness.

Hypatia had believed herself, all this time, to be totally self-sufficient. What a fool she'd been to think so! She'd relied absolutely and unquestioningly on Maude to get her dressed, to fix her hair, to make sure her toilet articles, her writing materials, whatever she might want at any given moment would be ready to hand in its appointed place. She'd prided herself on going straight to where they were and picking out the correct item without hesitation. But it was Maude who laid them out, Maude who put them back, Maude who followed the cleaners around nagging at them to leave each piece of furniture exactly where it had always been so that the mistress could cross a room without tripping over a chair or bumping into a table. What if Maude should start mixing things up?

Hypatia relied on Agnes to order the food, to check the grocery bills, to prepare the meals, even to arrange the serving so that the mistress could feed herself without getting into a mess. She relied on Watts to take care of the car and of herself when she rode in it, to take her where she wanted to go and bring her back in safety. She trusted him to take care of the garden, to clip the shrubs as she wanted them clipped, to set out the annuals she told him to buy, to maintain the paths well enough for her to take her exercise without risking a fall.

And she was taking all this, Hypatia realized in her moment of truth, literally on blind faith. How did she know Maude was keeping her clothes clean and her hair tidy? How did she know Agnes wasn't cheating on the grocery bills? How did she know Watts was planting chaste white petunias instead of hideous magenta? How did she know everything in the house was where it had always been?

Waldo's great-grandparents had been the first of his line to live in this house; the generations had succeeded them as a matter of course. All had fancied themselves patrons of the arts; the Kelling figurines were by no means the only objects of value distributed about its many rooms. Hypatia had never been much interested in paintings, prints, bibelots, or first editions that had nothing to do with the ancient Greeks, but she'd recognized their worth from the aesthetic as well as the monetary point of view and been content to leave them where they were.

And where were they? Hypatia was further horrified to acknowledge that even in this room where she spent so much time eating her meals and tending the Kellings, she couldn't recall which of the Paul Revere serving pieces should be standing on the buffet, which Sèvres vases belonged on the mantelpiece. How easy it would be to replace a precious object with an inferior one of similar shape, an original painting with a copy or even a coloured photograph. Would Maude or Agnes or Watts notice the difference? Would they tell her if they did?

Robbing me blind! Waldo's father had been wont to employ the expression in his frequent fulminations against the Inland Revenue. Little did he know.

This would never do, she must pull herself together. Perhaps Agnes had come in while the mistress was still preoccupied with Theophilus and his wife, set Serapis on the table thinking to save her the trouble of taking him out, and slipped out without letting her know. Agnes did not always show much in the way of acumen, though Maude always insisted she meant well and Hypatia had been willing to concede the hypothesis. How could she go on believing that anybody meant well?

Hypatia began feeling her way all over the tabletop, the chair seats, the mantelpiece, the sideboard, the long, narrow hunt table where sat the great Rose Medallion bowl which the Mandarin had brought back from the Orient in one of his ships. What if this bowl she now explored with shaking hands was not the one she'd been accustomed to seeing while her eyes still functioned?

She had no tactile memory to guide her, she'd never been in the habit of handling those many possessions she'd acquired through marriage and widowhood. The Kellings were her sole concern, the rest of the dusting had for many years been Maude's responsibility. Presumably Maude was still punctilious in her duty; Hypatia's by now hypersensitized fingertips detected no film of dust. She got down on her knees and began feeling her way inch by inch across the floor.

This was no job for an old woman. Hypatia was absurdly fearful lest Agnes come in and catch her in so undignified a position. Why was she doing it, anyway? Surely she'd have heard the sound if, dreadful thought, Serapis had fallen out of the cabinet. Maybe her hearing was less acute than she believed it to be; could she even trust herself?

At last Hypatia hauled herself to her feet, clambering slowly by means of the table-leg like an old, lame lizard. Serapis was gone, that was the long and the short of it. She had not carried him off and left him somewhere, she wasn't that far gone in senility. Then who had?

Maude was the obvious suspect. Maude could so easily have slipped a different key on the chain while she was dressing the mistress, and put the right one back at bedtime. Hypatia picked it up, she'd laid it to the left of the soapy water basin as she always did on bath days. This had to be the right key, or it wouldn't have unlocked the cabinet. Besides, she knew its feel too well to be mistaken.

Rubbing her finger over the wards, Hypatia realized for the first time in all these years what a simple thing it was. How could she have trusted so negligible a lock for so long? Anybody who knew how could probably open the cabinet with a bent hairpin.

Hypatia herself never used hairpins, she'd had her hair clipped into a shingle bob back in 1926 and kept it that way ever since to save fuss. As far as she knew, though, Agnes still clung to her old-fashioned pug; and Agnes was more deft with her hands than she was with her brains. As for Watts, he had tools for the garden, tools for the car, tools for doing odd jobs around the house; he must have one that could force the cabinet door. But why should he want to? And why pick Serapis out of all the Kellings?

Why pick the Kellings at all? The servants knew how often their mistress handled the ten figurines, how impossible it would be for her not to perceive that one was missing. There were so many other valuables around, things far easier to steal, things Hypatia might never miss. Or had everything else been stolen already?

She must try to recall what and where the more precious and portable objects might be, and whether they were still around. It would be no good asking Maude, Agnes, or Watts. One of them must be the thief, there was nobody else. The cleaners who came by the day were dogged every step by Maude. Hypatia herself always made a point of being around, letting them know there was a higher power than the maid to be reckoned with even though she never interfered with their work. She'd heard them often enough warning each other in whispers to watch their step because the old lady never missed a trick.

Hypatia had taken a grim satisfaction in being perceived as still formidable. Thank God none of them could see her now, shivering and sweating, no doubt dishevelled from that ignominious crawl around the floor. She smoothed her skirt and hair as best she could, washed her hands in the soapy basin, and used one of the damp linen towels to sponge her face. Agnes would be coming to tidy up, Maude would be waiting upstairs to help her out of this aged relic she wore on the Kellings' bath days and into her wrapper for the usual lie-down after her exacting and fatiguing task was done.

What would she do without Maude? Or Agnes, or Watts? The three knew her ways, they anticipated her needs, they seldom got sick or asked for extra time off. They never turned surly and threatened to quit. They didn't even bicker among themselves, at least not where Hypatia could hear them. At her age and in her state, how could she adjust to anybody new, assuming she could find someone even half-way suitable? She didn't live so entirely out of the world that she hadn't heard tales of woe about the servant problem, though it had been many years since she'd had to cope with the distasteful business of interviewing, weeding out the possible from the impossible, and getting them trained to suit her.

She'd never made a bad choice, she'd never mishandled her staff. She'd raised wages in proportion to years of service; by now the three incumbents were all quite handsomely paid. She'd given them comfortable quarters, she was not stingy about food, she never interfered with their leisure time or scolded them for no good reason. She certainly never nosed into their personal lives, if indeed they had any. On balance, Hypatia decided that she was now and always had been an exemplary employer. How could they repay her with such rank ingratitude?

How could she charge them with their malefactions, even if she succeeded in finding out which of them was to blame? What if all three took umbrage and walked out, leaving her to manage as best she could? Where could she turn? What would become of her?

For one craven moment, Hypatia thought perhaps it would be best simply to ignore what had happened. Let them steal. What difference would it make to a blind old woman who didn't even know what she was missing?

But she did know. Serapis was missing. Would Themistocles have taken such an affront lying down? Perhaps she would die soon; what if she should meet the original Serapis cavorting through the Elysian Fields in his spats and patent leathers? He'd been disgustingly cocky about having his place in Waldo Senior's cabinet; he'd surely ask whether he was still there. How could she lie to a fellow shade?

No, she must deal with this important matter promptly and firmly. Should she call the police? Unthinkable! Should she engage a private detective? Preposterous! She would keep her own counsel, eschew the defeatism of Socrates, and apply the practical wisdom of Solon. Hypatia rang for

Agnes to take away the basins and went upstairs to change her dress.

Throughout the following week, she spent most of her waking hours going methodically from room to room, handling whatever objects she encountered, stretching her memory. Sometimes it worked. A filigreed box, a jade statuette, a heavy bronze, an embroidered textile, one of the bibelots Waldo and his father had prized out of all proportion to their aesthetic worth, in her opinion, would trigger a reminiscence.

The big drawing-room was so far her most productive hunting ground. There had always been far too many such trinkets displayed here, clustered in groups on fussy piecrust tables, set out by categories on massive étagères. She located the various pieces of furniture with little difficulty, she discovered bric à-brac in abundance, but not in the extravagant profusion she remembered.

Pieces were missing, there was no doubt about that; one here, one there, so as not to leave conspicuous gaps in the various collections. Hypatia familiarized herself with the different groups and counted the pieces, storing the information in her well-trained memory. When she was sure Maude, Agnes and Watts were all occupied elsewhere, she'd go back and count them again. To her annoyance, the numbers kept coming out right. On Friday, she went through her customary routine of dusting the Kellings, taking them one by one beginning with the Puritan as always, hoping against reason that the bottom right-hand cubbyhole would not be empty when she got to it, willing Serapis back into his appointed place. He was not there. She locked the cabinet for whatever good it might do, and went back to prowling and counting.

At least this gave Hypatia something to do. She was surprised to find how stimulating she found her explorations: entering rooms where she had not found occasion to set foot in years, coming across forms and textures she was puzzled to identify as any possessions of hers. The days passed more quickly; almost before she knew it, the third Thursday of the month rolled around.

As Agnes brought in Hypatia's unvarying breakfast of black coffee, one boiled egg, and two slices of toast to be eaten with honey, she inquired as she always did, 'Will Mr James be coming to tea this afternoon, Mrs Kelling?'

'I expect so,' Hypatia replied.

Then she stiffened, not that Agnes would notice because Hypatia had never been one to slump, but enough so that she herself could feel her spine grow rigid as a steel bar. How could she possibly have been so dense? She had automatically left her one steady visitor off her list of suspects because James was always met at the door by one of the servants and shown directly into the drawing-room. Having submitted his flaccid hand to his hostess's vigorous shake, he took his customary place in the wing chair across from hers and stayed there.

Agnes would serve the sherry, bring the tea, and stay to pour out now that Hypatia chose not to risk overfilling the cups. After James had eaten his fill, which generally took at least half an hour, Agnes would push the trolley back to the kitchen. In a little while, Watts in his role of houseman would fetch James's hat and coat and show him to the door; unless Watts happened to be digging in the garden or ministering to the aged Reo, in which case Hypatia would ring for Agnes or Maude. Never was James left free to roam the house alone.

Or was he? Hypatia considered the facts. James always arrived punctually at four o'clock and stayed until half past five, sometimes as late as six. Agnes would bring in the tiny glasses of sherry as soon as he and Hypatia had got settled into their chairs, say at ten minutes past four. She would then go back to make the tea. At this time Maude would be in the kitchen ostensibly doing some of Hypatia's mending and pressing, more probably having her own tea with Agnes. It was never until a quarter to five that Agnes wheeled the tea-trolley into the drawing-room. During that interval, James would be engaged in conversation with Hypatia.

Wrong. Hypatia would be expounding her thoughts on some passage from the *Antigone,* perhaps, or the *Trachiniae.* James would have nothing to contribute, he never did. How long would it take him to slip his feet out of his shoes and pad silently over to one of the tables or étagères; to slip some easily concealed objet d'art into his pocket and sneak back to his seat in time to say, 'That's very insightful, Mrs Kelling'? James's pockets always bagged anyway, at least they'd always used to as far as Hypatia could recall. Not that she would have thought the fact worth retaining, but her mind was turning out some oddly cluttered corners these days.

Looking back over James's previous visit, she remembered that she'd been rather wound up that day over the *Phoenissae.* While she was declaiming Jocasta's prologue, he'd have had time enough to scuttle into the dining-room and rob the Kelling cabinet by means of a skeleton key or a picklock. Hypatia supposed he might even have snatched one of Agnes's hairpins while she was serving the sherry.

As an explanation for Serapis's disappearance, this made better sense. Maude, Agnes and Watts all knew how deep an interest their mistress took in the Kellings. Only James could have supposed she was involved with Greek literature to the exclusion of all else. Having been successful so far with his thievery, he'd have employed the same tactic, taking one piece from a group and trusting it wouldn't be missed.

Why should he think otherwise? He knew Mrs Kelling couldn't see the empty compartment. The servants might notice, but he'd gamble on their not saying anything for fear they themselves would be accused of taking or breaking the delicate object, or because they'd assume she'd broken it herself and done away with the pieces. And he'd have been right. So far none of them had said one word about the missing Serapis. He could make off with the lot, and they still wouldn't utter. What was she to do?

Finish her breakfast, for one thing. Attempting a stoicism she did not feel, Hypatia reached for the honey jar. Then she paused, the little wooden scoop half way between the jar and her plate, spinning a sticky thread down to the placemat.

Agnes would be in the kitchen now with Maude and Watts, the three of them eating their breakfast together. She would not be coming back for another twenty minutes or so; she knew her mistress never liked to be rushed or observed at breakfast since softboiled eggs and honey could be awkward things for a blind arthritic to manage. Hypatia got up and unlocked the cabinet. Working as fast as she dared, she smeared a thin glaze of honey over each of the Kellings. Then she washed her sticky hands in the finger bowl Agnes always brought in with the breakfast, dried them on her napkin before closing the cabinet so that she wouldn't leave sticky fingerprints on the glass, and got to work on her egg. She was sipping the last of her coffee when Agnes came in.

'Oh, I'm sorry, Mrs Kelling. I thought you'd be done by now.'

'That's all right, Agnes, I've just finished. I've eaten rather a lot of honey as you may notice, so I shan't want any served at tea-time. You can bring in some jelly instead.'

'Jelly, Mrs Kelling? For tea?' One might have thought from Agnes's tone that the mistress had been talking classical Greek.

'Yes, of course,' Hypatia replied impatiently. 'There is jelly in the house. Is there not?'

'Oh yes, Mrs Kelling, plenty of jelly. There's that guava you got for Christmas, and currant and grape and—'

'Guava will do. But remember, no honey.'

'Yes, Mrs Kelling.'

Agnes gathered up the dishes and went away muttering to herself. 'No honey. Guava jelly for tea. Well, I never!'

As soon as she'd found out her eyes were going, Hypa-

tia had got hold of as many Greek texts in Braille as she
could. She was thus well equipped to plan a programme that
would enable her to hold the floor for as long as might be
necessary to the success of her plan. When James arrived on
the dot of four, she greeted him with what might have
appeared to be unwonted cordiality but was in fact pent-up
excitement.

He allowed his limp hand to be shaken, he took his
assigned place, he commented in detail on the weather outside (bleak and chill, with a gusty north-east wind). He
thanked Agnes for the sherry or perhaps for the hairpin;
how could Hypatia know? She took over the conversation,
straining her ears above her nonstop monologue for any
untoward sound. She heard only the wind in the chimney.

Agnes brought the tea. Hypatia took guava jelly for her
crumpet; presumably James did, also. He emitted small
grunts as he ate, he managed to get in a timid word about
the tettix, or grasshopper. Hypatia corrected his pronuncia-
tion and again took up her monologue.

It seemed to her she'd been talking forever. Was Agnes
never coming back for the trolley? Impatient for her de-
nouement, Hypatia nipped off her lecture and stood up.

'I'm sorry, James, but I feel a sore throat coming on.
You will excuse me.'

'Oh, what a shame.' James spoke thickly, he must have
crammed the last bite into his mouth as he rose. 'I'd better
be getting along, then. I hope you're not coming down
with a cold.'

'So do I.' She held out her hand, and felt him take it.

''Fraid I'm a bit sticky,' he mumbled. 'Honey always—'

'Aha!' Her ruse had worked, her bird was snared.
'James,' she said, 'there is no honey.'

'But—but there is, Mrs Kelling. Right here in the little
blue pot, same as always. See? I mean—'

'Do not attempt to deceive me, James. Honey was not
served today.'

'But—darn it! Here, smell.'

Hypatia hated having things thrust under her nose. She put up a hand to thrust the object away. The shape was familiar and sticky, like the hand that held it. The cloying fragrance was unmistakable. What could she say?

'Very well, James, I stand corrected. Agnes will show you out.'

And Hypatia would have terse words with Agnes. She touched the bell and stood rigid until she'd heard the door close behind James and footsteps return to the drawing-room.

'Now then, Agnes, explain yourself.'

'It's not Agnes, Mrs Kelling.' The voice was that of Watts. 'If it's about the honey—'

'It is. Send Agnes to me.'

'But she didn't do it. I put the honey on the tray myself.'

'Indeed? Would you care to tell me why you took it upon yourself to disobey my explicit order?'

'Well, see—'

'Speak up, Watts!'

'Yes, Mrs Kelling. How it happened was, I found a leak in the laundry-room this morning. I didn't like to bother you at your breakfast, but you said we should always—'

'I know what I said. Go on.'

'Yes, Mrs Kelling. So anyway, I stuck my head in at the dining-room door and noticed you over by the cabinet with one of the Kellings in your hand. I didn't want to startle you and maybe make you drop it, so I thought I'd better wait till you put it back. Then I saw what you were doing.'

'And assumed I'd gone out of my mind, I suppose.'

'No, Mrs Kelling, I'd never think that. I had a fairly good idea what you were up to, so I went back down the cellar and shut off the laundry-room stopcock, then came up to get my breakfast. When Agnes brought back your breakfast tray and told Maude and me about the guava jelly, I knew I'd guessed right. So this afternoon when Agnes set out the tea I added the honey because I knew Mr James would go for it and you'd have him. We knew he'd been taking things, Maude's been worried sick about it. We all have.'

'Then why didn't you tell me?' snapped Hypatia.

'We didn't dare, if you want the truth. Him being family—'

'James is the grandson of my late father-in-law's second wife by her first marriage. That does not constitute a family relationship, Watts.'

'No, Mrs Kelling. But still—'

'I can understand your dilemma, Watts.' Hypatia wished to be fair, but she could not help being bitter. 'Couldn't you have overcome your scruples before you let him get away with Serapis?'

'Oh, but he didn't!'

Watts poured out the words in a gush of relief. 'Serapis is safe in the butler's pantry. I put him there myself, I figured that was the only way we'd ever get you to notice what was going on. I can't tell you what a relief it was when I watched you putting honey on the rest of the Kellings. That was a great idea, Mrs Kelling. And it would have worked if you'd given me a chance to get the trolley out of the room before you gave Mr James the bum's rush. Excuse me, I didn't mean to—'

'No matter, Watts, our mutual purpose has been achieved. Take away the trolley and tell Agnes to set out the basins. Maude is to draw up a list of the missing articles, I shall decide what is to be done about them. And bring Serapis back to the dining-room at once. Oh, Watts, one more question. How did you manage to unlock the cabinet?'

'Easy enough, Mrs Kelling. That's not much of a lock, if you'll forgive me for saying so. If you really want to know, I used one of Agnes's hairpins.'

'Thank you, Watts. That will be all.'

Once Hypatia knew the extent of James's pilferings, which numbered fourteen small pieces, all taken from the drawing-room, she had no reason to continue exploring the house. Nevertheless, she found herself roaming here and there, picking things up and putting them down, unable to concentrate even on Euripides. She was not eager for a distasteful scene, but she did want to get the matter over and done with. She would have sent for James in advance of his scheduled time, but she had no idea where he lived. When he did come, Hypatia received him as usual and waited until Agnes had served the ritual tot of sherry. Then she handed him Maude's list.

'Would you care to explain this, James?'

James explained, and explained, and explained. His was a dull, sad tale of mediocrity sliding into failure and despair. He had taught, yes; not Greek but arithmetic, in an elementary school where wages, standards, and morale had none of them been high. He had been declared redundant, his wife had come down with a terrible, lingering disease. His pension was not enough for them to live on, he'd taken a part-time job bundling papers at a newsmonger's. It paid little, and the work was hard.

Down through the drab, dragging years, James's only hours of glory had been those spent in Mrs Kelling's drawing-room, sipping tea like a gentleman, talking Greek like a scholar. His wife had understood. She'd never begrudged him a luxury she could not share, but it made him feel selfish. One day when her pain had been bad and he'd skimped the housework to come to Mrs Kelling's, he'd got to feeling so guilty he couldn't stand it. He had no money to buy something for his wife on the way home, not even a single flower. He couldn't steal one from the park, the frost had killed them all. He'd sat staring around this elegant room, he'd seen all those wonderful ornaments sitting there, enjoyed by nobody. He'd tiptoed over to a table while the maid was gone and Mrs Kelling was talking, and pocketed a tiny jade bird on a spun-silver nest. He'd told his wife the bird was a gift from Mrs Kelling. She'd cried.

Since she could no longer hold a pen, much less write a note, she'd begged James to tell Mrs Kelling how grateful she was. He'd come back from his next visit with a cordial message and an ivory elephant. It had been so easy, and his wife was so much happier. The stolen items were on a little table beside her bed where she could look at them and sometimes, when she felt strong enough, reach out and touch one. He would bring them back and never darken Mrs Kelling's door again.

Hypatia had heard him out in silence, now she spoke. 'I find it remiss of you, James, not to have told me sooner that your services were available. Henceforth I shall expect you at two o'clock instead of four on Tuesdays, Thursdays and Saturdays. You will read to me in Greek until half past five. Your accent is regrettable, I shall coach you. That will come to ten and a half hours a week for which you will be compensated at the rate of twenty dollars an hour plus a weekly gift of my choosing to add to your wife's present collection. We will take tea together as usual. With honey. Now please be good enough to fetch the *Septem contra Thebas* from the third shelf of the small bookcase and begin reading at the top of page six. We have frittered away quite enough time in idle conversation.'

John Malcolm

THE CISTERNA

'OVER HERE it's a recognized method of committing suicide,' Johnny Campos said, staring into the depths. 'Old women, mostly. Take care of this edge, it's crumbling. The local sandstone—*mares*—does after a while. Wouldn't want to lose you, Tim.' He grinned wolfishly. 'Not just as you're getting better.'

I peered cautiously over the waist-level sandstone parapet into the deep gloom below me. Still water glinted thirty feet beneath my shoes. Wet cavern smells made me shiver. A cisterna is a huge rock bottle that goes right down into the earth, gently swelling outwards from its funnelled well-neck at ground level, where we were standing.

'Eels,' Johnny said, with some satisfaction. 'They say they—the Mallorquins—put an eel or eels down in it to keep the water clean. Clear up the bugs and the larvae. I don't like to think of a body down there with eels about.' He paused and sniffed the dank smells. 'It's the impact that kills them, of course.'

'Kills what?'

'The women. Old ones, especially. Hell of a drop if it's fairly empty, which this one is. Must have a fault in it down there somewhere. A crack. Usually they're quite full about now.' He squinted up at the broken piping that led to the well-head. 'Maybe that's the problem. Plenty of rain in the first four months of the year. It's by the end of summer, usually, that it's all used up. Not much to drown in, then.'

I shivered again and looked up with him at the flaking

walls of the old finca, where broken clay gutters and down-pipe hung cracked from the eaves or gaped, missing. 'Just rainwater collection? That's all it is?'

'Sure. They all are, out in the country. The island has no rivers or lakes. Tons of water fall on it but it goes mostly underground, into wells and so on. Every finca has a cisterna, not many as big or as deep as this but this is a big finca, or was. The converted ones put in a pump and take the water back up again, to a tank on the roof. Modern plumbing, at a stroke.' He grinned again and I got a whiff of the property-tycoon Johnny that he was. 'Come on, 'Tonia's got the key. The girls will be mad keen to look inside.'

He turned away from the well-head, where a broken pulley testified to the countless buckets of water that had been hauled from the depths. The cisterna was on the edge of the group of buildings and the view from it, over the broken rocky landscape of northern Mallorca, was spectacular. Below us were lemons belonging to a neighbour and, next to them, an orange grove with deep green ranks of trees. To our left, the scrubby grey ground was dotted with gnarled and neglected olive stumps of great age, gradually clogging the view with their intermittent and inexplicable planting pattern. Johnny clapped me on the back.

'Come on, Tim. Never keep a lady waiting, eh?'

I smiled at his suggestive expression and turned into the bright sunshine with relief. The visit was less tiring than I had feared it might be and Sue appeared to be getting on well with Antonia. At last, I thought, she's seeing a bit of the real island, not the nasty tourist-crust caking the south and gradually encasing the coast-edges like a concrete skin disease.

I had been ill, after an unpleasant interlude I won't describe, that had left me operated-on and immobile in hospital. Gradually I had recovered and was now almost well. A lung had been repaired; it was said to be near-perfect but in need of careful treatment. A holiday had been prescribed and I had chosen the north coast of Mallorca because it had been convenient, in May and out of season, to make a quick booking. I felt that I might be able to show Sue parts of the island unknown to the general tourist but until that day we had done little about it. The journey had tired me more than I had bargained for. The first week was spent at the hotel, where we sat under high umbrella pines, watching the sands. It was an odd time of year and the holidaymakers varied from the old and retired to young couples with small children not yet of school age and, here and there, a mature solitary lady who might have wandered in from the pages of a novel by Anita Brookner. I felt no tension of any sort and I knew that Sue was happy. Everything was going well.

It was at the end of the first week that, while we were breakfasting on the sunlit terrace, a shadow fell across our table and a cultured masculine voice boomed into my ear.

'Good God! I don't believe it! Tim Simpson?'

I looked up quickly from my tea to find, standing next to me, a dark, strong figure that looked powerfully down. I gaped at him.

'Johnny? Johnny Campos? What on earth are you doing here?'

The brown, broad face grinned at me. Next to it stood a dark, attractive girl. I got to my feet and stared at both of them rather impolitely. It was a surprise. I had not seen Johnny Campos for nearly ten years, perhaps not since I had left College. He was an old friend and had shared part of my boyhood at St George's, Buenos Aires. Johnny was the son of an Argentine father and a Scots mother, both of them wealthy and sophisticated, members of the set that has kept Buenos Aires the most European of South American cities. His father was a great sportsman and had brought Johnny up in a British tradition, ensuring that Johnny became a great rugby player, fast and mercurial like the French but also rather hot-tempered. When he came up to Cambridge, a year after me, he had got his trial cap straight away. He was not in the same College but we had kept in contact with each other, cracking jokes and swearing during

rugger matches in the appalling River Plate accent that is to
Spanish what Australian is to English, only rather worse.
After the match we would sing *Adios Muchachos* in the show-
ers together, juvenile stuff, or get maudlin after the occasional sporting-club dinner when we usually ended up in
Johnny's rooms listening to *La Violetera* and *Adios Pampa
Mia* in the late hours while drinking malt whisky. Johnny
missed his home country. For all his impeccable English
style and his gentlemanly manners Johnny was really only at
ease in the clubs of B.A. or out riding on one of his father's
estancias. England cramped his style; he often teased me
about my ability to live on such a small domestic scale.
There was much to admire about him; I had heard that he
had been over to play for a touring Argentine side later but
I was away somewhere and missed him. Then there had
been the embarrassing business of the Falklands.

I pulled myself together. 'I'm sorry. You'll think me
utterly rude. But what a surprise! It's great to see you. Sue,
this is Johnny Campos, an old friend from Argentina; he
was at school with me, and knew the worst.'

Johnny gave a shout of laughter and kissed Sue's hand
gallantly before turning to his companion. 'Antonia, you
must meet one of my oldest friends, from school and Cambridge. Tim Simpson. A full rugby blue, you know, a
legendary one. And Sue.'

I took Antonia's hand with pleasure. She was dark, as
I've said, and very attractive in an Irish way, with brilliant
eyes and a clear, pale skin. Johnny winked at me.

'Antonia's a latino too, Tim. From Colombia. Medel-
lin. Antonia Riley, would you believe? She knows all about
people like us.'

She laughed at him, rich and wide-mouthed. 'All about
you, yes. Too much.' And she also winked at me as I took in
her English accent, an accent tailored surely by Roedean or
Cheltenham or the like. Johnny always had sophisticated
tastes in girlfriends, I remembered, being capable of charm-

ing the pants off any female susceptible to a dash of South American attention.

'Please join us.' I gestured at the spare chairs round our table. 'We're just finishing breakfast; some coffee, perhaps?'

'Great.' Johnny held a chair for his companion before stretching himself out on another beside her, big and muscular, unchanged from my memories of him. 'Although we have to move on soon, we're going to look at a finca. Are you staying long?'

'Another two weeks.'

'Two weeks! You lucky devil! I wish I had that long. I've just come over for the week. 'Tonia's been here two weeks already. How does one get away at this time of year?' He grinned a mocking challenge at me. 'No business to attend to?'

'Ah. Well, actually, Johnny, I've been unwell. So I'm convalescing, you see.'

'Really?' The mocking grin disappeared and he gave me a concerned look. 'I hope it's nothing serious? I thought you looked quite well but—somehow—not quite the robust old Tim of my youth.'

I shook my head. 'Nothing serious. An operation. After a—an accident.' I was unwilling to elaborate. 'But I'm almost myself again. Thanks to Sue's ministrations and this place.' I smiled at Sue and she gave me a look of complicity.

'Oh.' Johnny nodded and tactfully asked no more. 'I'm glad to hear it. Actually I've dashed over to look at a property 'Tonia's sorted out for us.'

'Here? In Mallorca?'

'Yes. It's a finca, inland. Completely run down and in need of restoration. 'Tonia and I want a place we can relax in and—' he grinned at me ruefully—'with all due respect to your delightful country we need the weather as well as the culture. The Spanish, I mean. I have to spend more and more time in Northern Europe on business and I can't dash back to B.A. every weekend. So we decided to buy a place here. 'Tonia's been over finding one and this sounds great. I tell you what—' he brightened—'why don't you come with us? It's about forty minutes' drive from here, inland.' He glanced round the terrace. 'The seaside's too hectic and we need peace and quiet, so we're having a go at a place we can fix ourselves before everything's sold or becomes too expensive. I'd value your opinion. Why don't you come? 'Tonia's got a good hire car.'

I glanced at Sue and saw a look of concern on her face. 'That's kind of you. But I'm still a bit of a crock, Johnny. Perhaps I'd better not.'

'Oh, come on, Tim! Please? You look OK to me. Sue, you can't persuade him, can you? The drive will do you good. We'll take a picnic—some chorizos, just like old times —you won't have to walk far. I promise. Will he, 'Tonia?'

She shook her head and smiled a dazzling smile at me. 'No, you won't. You can drive right up to the house. I got the directions from Ramón, the estate agent, when I got the key. It sounds absolutely super. Has Sue seen the interior of the island at all?'

That settled it. My resolve to show Sue the rural part of Mallorca reasserted itself. I thought of the palm trees and the olives, the orange groves, almonds, loquats, persimmon and carob bean trees—algarrobas—cracking down under their own tortured weight. 'All right,' I agreed. 'It sounds great.'

Johnny was delighted. Antonia looked just as pleased, indeed she looked even happier than Johnny as she beamed at me. I put it down to female company. A woman needs another woman to talk to on these holidays, something to dilute the sexual concentration, someone to release the tension with. I suppose that's a chauvinist view, but that's the way it always seems. We tend to become too much responsibility for a girl.

Sue and Antonia fussed about after breakfast, getting themselves ready and organizing the picnic. It had been late when Sue and I had got up, so by the time we left it was after eleven. Johnny told me quite a bit about himself while we waited. He was a director of the family property company and used service flats when over in Europe. The economic situation in Argentina was no better than it had ever been; if anything it was worse. Like most South Americans, Johnny was intent on securing assets in Europe and North America. His father and mother had foreseen all that, of course; in such situations wealthy people develop a sense of ruthless self-preservation, of cut-and-run, that we soft, secure folk do not have. A company had been set up to manage their assets abroad. Johnny had a flair for it, was a clever property man on an international scale with a nose for what people like himself, people with money detached from their home country, wanted. He had done well.

'And you,' he said, as we whirled along in the saloon that Antonia had hired, 'you work in a bank, then?'

'Yes. A merchant bank. White's.'

'White's! I know them well! James, in Brazil, especially. And let me see, the new one—Jeremy?'

'I work for Jeremy.'

'Splendid! Tim, what a small world! So you're one of Jeremy's whizz kids? Perhaps we can do business together?'

'Why not?'

'Great! But enough. I can see 'Tonia pouting. No business, eh? We are on holiday, I promise.' He patted her knee. 'We are going to see what might become our—what—our love-nest?'

Antonia laughed and poked him in the ribs, making him swerve dangerously close to one of the rocky walls along the road. She screamed and giggled for a moment, changing the suave public-schoolgirl into a creature I had only half-apprehended so far. That Johnny was dead keen on her was obvious; while she and Sue were preparing things, away from us, he had dropped his voice as he spoke of her.

'Two years,' he said, hoarseness creeping in. 'It's been two years. You remember me, Tim. Easy come, easy go. Not this time. It's not money, either, not on either side. We're both independent. Her old man made a bomb in emeralds and salted it away in New York. Cunning old Irish gringo. She's impulsive and self-willed. Well—what can you expect? An Irish Latin—fireworks, eh?' He winked at me again embarrassingly, the wink and the remark conjuring up visions I quickly suppressed. His face changed. 'Your Sue, now, I can see what's got you there. Charming. The best sort of English girl. You make a couple. No question.' He made it sound deadly dull as his eyes burned towards Antonia in the distance.

The finca was off a small metalled road that wound up the mountains. We bumped up a rocky track that made me wince as the car springs squeaked and the tyres cannonaded chunks of stone up under the chassis with loud bangs. At the top we stopped by a pair of weedy overgrown gates and Antonia sprang out.

'I'll open up,' she said. 'Wait here, Johnny.'

She left the gates open and rejoined us. Johnny drove up a long, neglected rocky track rather than a drive, on which faint tyre marks showed the impression other potential buyers must have made earlier. At the top the track turned by a low wall and Johnny stopped.

It was magnificent. A group of large, half-ruined buildings clustered round a big palm tree that shaded a weed-covered courtyard in front of the main door of the house. The roof of the residential part was still relatively intact but a vast wing at right angles had lost all its covering and tangled saplings sprouted out of the small windows, even on the second storey. Brambles heaped up to ten feet high on the floor. Another large palm tree shaded a barn.

'That was where the olive press stood,' Antonia said, getting out of the car. 'I've seen several of these old fincas now. You can see the remains of it—the press, I mean. Isn't it romantic? What a setting!'

I eased myself carefully out of the car and sniffed. The sun was high above us and the air was full of fragrance. High mountain spaces soared around me. About a mile away were the workings of an old quarry; in the north, Mallorca is a stone island, terraced, walled and built of stone, a lot of it the damp *mares* sandstone that matures to a soft yellow and can be cut to architectural shapes with ease. It is a bit like the west of Ireland in the sense that so many fields have had to be cleared of stone before they could be worked, so many walls built, so many terraces constructed painfully up the sides of the mountains by the Mallorcans, the Catalans, the Moors, Romans, Goths and God knows who that I wondered if some long-hidden Irish soul in Antonia was responding to this rocky, historic panorama.

'It's beautiful,' I said, looking round and smiling at Sue, who was staring in wonder. 'Does it have any water, though?'

'A pantano higher up and a cisterna,' Antonia said. 'Why don't you and Johnny look at it while Sue and I poke around? The place has nearly a hundred acres with it; we should see where to put a swimming-pool, not too far from the house. Eh, Johnny?'

I blinked as Johnny nodded and then beckoned to me. We could see the well-like rim of the cisterna against the edge of the escarpment, beyond which the valleys dipped and the ridges piled to edge the sky.

'A hundred acres?' I queried as we trudged across the rocky ground. 'Isn't it very expensive? I mean—I'm sorry—but—'

He shook his head. 'The land has very little value. It's not up to much agriculturally and you'd never get permission to develop here. The house is ruined; we'll look at it in a moment. They want twenty million—that's a hundred thousand pounds—for it as it is. They may come down a bit, but Ramón, 'Tonia's estate agent lad, says not much. He thinks you'd need another hundred thousand to do it up. Says he has good contacts.' He cocked a dark eye at me. 'This is an expensive place by Spanish standards but what would you get in southern England for that?'

'Well—not much—'

'Nothing! And you won't get much for that here, soon. A flat in Palma Nova maybe. No, I see this as a great place for 'Tonia and me to come to when it's done. Now here we have the cisterna; let me tell you all about it.'

As we walked back from the broken edge of the circular well-wall Antonia ran prancing under the great palm tree in the courtyard, waving her arms. 'Come on!' she called. 'We think we've found a place for a pool. Now let's see the house. I've got the key. Isn't it super?'

Marvelling at her restraint—a woman surely likes to look into a house before she looks at anything else—I smiled as we got up to the walls. A key was hardly necessary. The front door might look solid but the long French-style windows were all distorted and broken, the frames eaten by woodworm or crumbling with wet rot. Inside the panes the long inner shutters were closed but bleached and split, or hung erratically on hinges that had rusted and would now fail to work. A vigorous shove and the whole lot would collapse inwards. The place had not been lived in for years. I pondered for a moment on the strange economic cycle of life that made large, once-prosperous farms like this fall into ruin and which now, all over the island, was gradually leading to their restoration. Antonia opened the front door with a flourish.

'Dark, isn't it?' she giggled, as a gust of damp air flowed past us like an escaping spirit. 'It's a smashing hall, though. Don't you think?'

The hall was the main room of the house, two floors in height. A dark beamed ceiling with bobadillo tiles between heavy wood joists hung high above us. At one end a broken staircase led to a door into the upper storey rooms. Various doorways punctured the severe plaster and stone walls, which were dotted with occasional rusty iron hooks of sinister function. The floor was a mixture of tiles and stones on which broken pieces of furniture, mainly splintered chairs, stood forlornly. Behind the hall was an unadorned kitchen with a huge chimney, inside which stood an ancient iron cooking range. We crunched our way across the hall through a well-proportioned doorway into a high, square room.

'Good heavens,' Johnny Campos said, his white teeth grinning in the half-gloom. 'The master bedroom, eh?'

It was true. Long broken shutters let in shafts of intense sunlight which revealed thick peeling walls, dirty flooring and a large double bed with a pedimented mahogany headboard and high posts at each corner. Damp had disfigured whatever decoration had been let into the figured wood but it was a restrained design, elegant, almost Sheraton but foreign. Inlaid stringing lines and some sort of motif were let into a panel in the headboard.

'Gracious,' Antonia said coquettishly. 'What on earth is it? What style is that?' She cocked an eye at Sue and me.

'I think it's a local version of Empire,' I said. 'The nearest thing for us would be Sheraton. Around 1810 or 1820 perhaps. It must have been quite handsome once. Fancy leaving it behind.'

Johnny grunted. 'Probably didn't think much of it. It's pretty dilapidated. There's been a monogram of some sort in the panel but it's all so bad—veneer, I see, not solid— that it's hard to make out.'

'J.M.G.' Antonia said absently, peering at it. 'I suppose José and Maria are inevitable in this country but I wonder what the G was for. Gonzalez? No, that's more Spanish than Mallorcan or Catalan.' She shrugged and pressed the dusty mattress, making the springs creak. 'I think this is the dining-room. Upstairs is the place for bedrooms. Come on, let's go up that staircase.'

'Coming,' Johnny said absently. He had switched his gaze to the floor, to the junction of the wall, where a skirting might have been. 'It's as damp as hell in here. No Mallorcan house ever has a damp course. They just build straight on to the ground and hope things will dry out in the summer. They seem to think it will all go away.'

'A bit like the British, really.' Antonia's voice receded as she guided Sue towards the staircase. 'They've only just found out about central heating.'

The departure of the girls somehow lessened the light in the room. Johnny put his head back to stare at the stained ceiling and then lowered it slowly to stare at the bedhead, the dusty mattress and, lastly, the gritty floor.

'What's up?' I asked him, feeling unease. A twinge in my lung gave me a throb of warning, as though for the rest of my life it was going to act as a harbinger, whether in objection to damp air or to some other, more emotionally unacceptable condition it was too early to tell.

He brought his dark eyes up to meet mine. 'Nothing. Just thinking. Shame, isn't it, to lose your property and leave your ancestral bed behind? The bed of generations, gone forever. Old folk, I suppose. An old lady possibly, left behind.' He turned to look at the undisturbed, shuttered windows, caked with dust, and I wondered if he was thinking of the cisterna. 'Come on,' he said, moving with sudden, muscular precision, 'let's go and see the rest.'

We clambered about the old building until we were thirsty with dust, checking lofts and outhouses before locking the front door again. We looked briefly at the demesne before finding a shady spot slightly away from the house to have our picnic. Antonia got a rug from the car and spread it on the rough dry grass, full of stones, where there was a flat surface. She was excited. She got out the food and made Johnny open a bottle of cold white wine she'd kept carefully insulated in a plastic box.

'Come on, you old trout,' she pouted at him. 'Stop stalling. It's wonderful, isn't it?'

'Oh yes,' he replied, brushing away some bits of twig and grass that had got into the rug. 'It's a beautiful spot. The house is in terrible shape, though.' He turned a bit of wood between finger and thumb carefully. 'Needs a lot of money spending on it.'

'I know that. I told you.' Antonia threw back her glass of wine impetuously. 'But it's super, isn't it? It's just what

we were looking for. I love it.' She stared at him challeng-
ingly. 'I love it,' she repeated.

He smiled his dark smile, putting the fragments to one
side. 'It's a good investment. I can't fault buying it from
that point of view. This place will go through the roof when
it's done up.'

'Ha!' She threw her glass in the air and caught it deftly
before holding it out for more. 'That's it! That means he'll
buy it! Johnny gets so *Scottish* when he's about to spend
money. All caution and care. Darling! Wonderful! What a
relief!'

She put down her glass and bounded across to kiss
him. Sue smiled at me. I wondered jealously whether she
was thinking what it would be like to have a partner who
bought such expensive but lucrative toys, like Johnny, and
said, perhaps a little sharply, 'Won't it be very time-consum-
ing to do this place up? I mean, how will you supervise it to
get what you want?'

'Oh'—Johnny's voice was half-muffled by the presence
of Antonia, wrapped fondly round him—'Tonia will do
that. She's great at managing restorations like this. With an
architect, of course. That fellow Ramón said he could put
us on to a good one. You said he could recommend someone reasonably priced, didn't you, darling?'

'Oh yes.' Antonia squeezed him fondly. 'But that's a
long way off yet.'

'Sure. We have to buy the place first.'

I pondered the wisdom of leaving a girl like Antonia to
stay unaccompanied in these romantic surroundings, engaged on restoration while Johnny travelled on business. I
was restrained from saying anything by the thought that I,
too, had travelled much, leaving Sue to herself. We finished
the bottle of wine in celebratory mood.

'We should take a longer look at the layout,' Johnny
said eventually. 'The land, I mean. Not all one hundred
acres but the part nearest the house. Tim?'

I shook my head. The wine and the sun had made me

soporific. I tapped my chest significantly. 'My old war wound,' I said. 'I'll take it easy if you don't mind. Enough for one day. I'll wait here while you lot go.'

Sue shook her head and put her hand in mine to indicate that she would stop. I knew what she was thinking: let them celebrate this together, it's important for them.

'Well, I want to spend a penny first,' Antonia said. 'I'll go over behind the house. Then we'll take a look, Johnny, OK?'

'OK.' He grinned at her and watched her pick her way out of sight with an intent stare before turning to me. 'She's pleased, isn't she? Bubbling, in fact.'

'Oh yes. You lucky beggar. This is a great place. I can imagine what it will be like done up. Quite a project, though.'

He shrugged. 'The company will provide the funds. We'll set it up in a tax-efficient way.'

Suddenly I didn't feel he was so lucky. I felt that acquisition that comes as a matter of business somehow could not have the sharp pleasure that a personal acquisition brings. Yet where did one separate the two? Personal acquisition from savings or income comes from business, so why the psychological difference?

Johnny stood up, brushing crumbs and grass carefully off his clothes. He put his hands almost delicately into his pockets. 'I'd better go after 'Tonia. See you soon.'

'OK, Johnny. No hurry. We'll wait here. *Hasta pronto.*'

He sauntered off, leaving us in the shade. Sue leant over and kissed me gently. 'Are you all right? It's funny to see you being a sort of latin. People always say you're so English, Tim. As I think of you.'

'Very few English Englishmen live in Britain any more. What about you? Do you like it?'

She nodded brightly, her eyes shining. 'It's been wonderful. What a day we've had! We'd never have seen this if— oh look! A hoopoe!' She pointed excitedly at a brightly-coloured bird that had swooped past. 'Tim! How super! What a wonderful place! Lucky Antonia!'

'Yes.' I took a panoramic stare round. It was idyllic. In the far distance I could hear sheep-bells clocking continuously from a flock behind the olives. Odd distant sounds, even a car or van and a tractor engine boomed softly across the valley. Then there was a call like a cow or horse, vaguely throaty and human, from far off.

Sue frowned. 'What was that?'

'Dunno. Some animal somewhere. Any coffee left?'

She nodded and got out a flask. We sat together contentedly sipping a rather strong brew until Johnny came round the side of the finca. He looked a little breathless and hot.

'I say—hasn't 'Tonia come back here?'

'No. Did you split up?'

He frowned as he got closer. 'No. I couldn't find her. She wasn't behind the place. I went off into the groves to look for her. Then I assumed she'd cut back here.'

Sue shot me a glance, making me sit up. 'She can't be far away,' I said. 'Where was it you decided to put the swimming pool, Sue? Perhaps she went there.'

Sue got up and brushed herself quickly with her hands. 'I'll show you,' she said to Johnny. 'Come on, it's up that rise.'

He nodded. His face was rather more irritable than concerned but something made me decide to contribute. I got up, too. 'I'll look around the house,' I said. 'In case she went to look inside again or something.' An image of the dark flaking bedroom came to mind and my lung gave a warning twinge. 'Perhaps she expected you in there.'

'Are you sure? Not too tired?'

'No, no, I'm fine.'

'Thanks, Tim. I can't think where she's got to.'

The house was still locked. I walked carefully round its silent crumbling walls alone as Johnny and Sue went out of sight away among the olive stumps. At the corner of the main wing of the house I turned to look over the distant land from the escarpment and saw the ringed wall of the cisterna-well with a huge chunk missing. Fresh broken sand-stone like snapped yellow biscuit powdered the ground. A terrible stab of pain went through the scar on my chest, deep into the lung.

'Johnny! Johnny!' It hurt to shout so loud.

The soggy bundle of clothes at the bottom hardly rose above the dark water level. The black smell of damp fun-nelled up the long well-neck like old, horrible breath. I thought of eels. My lung stabbed me again as I straightened to shout louder.

'Johnny! Johnny! Johnny!'

I had to drag him away from the edge, screaming for a rope. I had to stop him from jumping in. I had to hold Sue tight while he ran crazily to the car and drove down the scattered rocks, crashing from side to side with shrieking engine until he got to the tractor ploughing under the nearby olive groves. Other stocky Mallorquins appeared be-side the driver, materializing from the empty landscape. Three of them came back with him, carrying a rope. The smallest and stockiest man went down the cisterna like a fearless monkey while we held the rope which we had tied to the car axle. We hauled and drove while he signalled. Antonia's body came out wet, sloppy, inert, difficult to han-dle, lifeless. A huge bruise disfigured the side of her face. Johnny yelled and shouted while I tried mouth-to-mouth resuscitation, my lung strangely sound and strong now, working for me as well as I ever remembered it. When I stopped Johnny took over and I was then conscious of the smell of old water on my face. After a while I heard him whimpering, his face in his hands. One of the Mallorquins took the car to the nearest telephone and those of us left around the broken wall of the cisterna fell silent.

Later, much later, when we had all made statements, and Johnny was lying sedated in a clinic in Palma, the local police inspector came to see me. He was calm and wise and shrewd as well as sympathetic. In his eyes I saw the experience of many investigations, crimes of passion, puzzlement at why a pretty lady should lean so hard on a doubtful cisterna wall. He did not infer or insinuate. He asked his questions quietly and I answered them all. After a time we had a beer together and he insisted on paying as he stood up to leave.

'A tragic accident,' he said, holding his dry firm hand out to shake mine.

'Yes.'

'My sympathies to your lady. If, by any chance, anything should occur to you, any small thing that comes back into your memory—shock produces strange effects—I hope that you will contact me?'

'Certainly.'

He nodded, regarded me carefully, and left. That night Sue made me make love to her, careless of my semi-convalescence, as though life was about to end and she wanted me to prove that it could not, to verify my substance. My lung had no feeling of unease; it was as though it had tested itself and was satisfied, would work from now on without complaint. Afterwards Sue fell asleep holding my hand so tightly that it was almost painful. I lay beside her, listening to her harsh hot breathing, my mind and eyes wide open.

I was thinking unworthy thoughts. I was thinking of the dark damp bedroom at the finca, with its sagging shutters, the mouldering Empire bedhead and Johnny's intent face as he stared at the floor. I could still see the peeling plaster on the tidemarked walls and feel the crunch of the tiles under my shoes as we admired the high ceiling and the long, rotten casements. Some people in Mallorca suffer from arthritis because, contrary to popular image, there is a lot of damp in the winter months. Damp that seeps up the unprotected walls. Damp that loosens the glue holding the veneers to the head of an old bed that has been left in a dark room for years, so that pieces of the mahogany flake off, taking bits of inlay with them. So many bits of inlay that parts of the carefully scrolled letters proudly monogrammed into the pediment at the top of the bedhead had fallen out and you couldn't decipher properly what the initials had been.

Perhaps Antonia had simply guessed them. Perhaps she had decided for reasons of her own what initials should be attributed to that proud conjugal couch. It would be unworthy to think otherwise, unworthy in a latino, macho sort of way. The only way she could have known for certain would be if she had seen them before they fell off, on an earlier visit. But Antonia had never visited the finca before. Had she not said so? Ramón had given her directions with the key. Ramón the estate agent, who had been helping her to find a property in that wonderful landscape. Who could help her to find contractors to do the place up. Why had Johnny stared at the floor like that? Was it because pieces of fallen veneer and inlay were visible there? Fresh pieces? Pieces that might have been in their proper place earlier, before some violent, some muscular, carefree activity had shaken the ancient frame and caused the pieces to rain down, the feeble glue at last unable to withstand the sudden movements?

No, such thoughts were not worthy. They were the product of a masculine, suspicious identity, one which had just himself—No, that was not the way to think. Such worldly-knowledgeable, shallow ideas only came to people like me.

Or Johnny Campos, of course.

Sue tightened her grip on my hand. It was ridiculous to think that a girl like Antonia would engage with an estate agent, however young and handsome, on a neglected dusty mattress like that. All her education and upbringing were against it.

Unless she had taken a rug from the car.

Into my mind's eye there now came Johnny, sitting at the picnic, idly brushing twigs and grass off the place where he was about to sit. My hand gripped Sue back, almost

painfully. I knew now what it was that he had brushed and
what he had turned between finger and thumb, what it was
that he put so carefully in his pockets as evidence when he
got up to follow and confront her behind the finca.

Pieces of mahogany veneer.

Patricia Moyes

THE MAN WHO HAD
EVERYTHING

E VERY YEAR, around Christmas time, certain very expensive stores publish gift catalogues aimed at the Man Who Has Everything. They include such useful items as vicuna underpants, solid gold paperclips and platinum-and-diamond cocktail shakers. However, Harvey Barrington was not in the least interested in any of these baubles: and he was truly a man who had everything. Well, almost everything.

For a start, of course, he was immensely rich, and he had come honestly by every penny of his fortune. While still in his early twenties, he had inherited a modest family firm which made inexpensive furniture. By sheer hard work and a business flair amounting to near-genius, he had expanded Barrington and Company into an empire. By the time he was thirty, the company had gone public and diversified into textiles, carpets and household appliances: its furniture had also become very expensive. At fifty-three, Harvey had sold out to a mammoth international concern, pocketed his millions and announced his retirement. He wished, he said, to have some leisure while he was still young enough to enjoy it.

And he had plenty to enjoy. He owned a duplex penthouse apartment on the river in Chelsea, and a very pretty Elizabethan farmhouse in Sussex. He had a chalet in a Swiss ski resort, and a 20-acre property—complete with eighteenth-century plantation house—on a small Caribbean island. He skippered his own 50-foot sailing yacht and flew his own helicopter. All seemed set fair for a thoroughly enjoyable retirement.

Even before he had inherited the business, Harvey had married a pretty but otherwise unremarkable girl called Jenny. He had met her at the tennis club in the unfashionable London suburb where he then lived with his parents. Harvey and Jenny had won the Mixed Doubles, and decided to make the partnership permanent. They had three children, all girls, who at the time of Harvey's retirement were all married with families of their own—two of them in the United States and one in Australia. Meanwhile, Jenny had put on a bit of weight, and her face had rounded out from youthful prettiness to mature amiability.

Jenny Barrington, through all the years of Harvey's rise to affluence, had remained a pleasant, unambitious woman. She spent most of her time at the Sussex farmhouse, where she had a circle of bridge-playing friends. She was not stupid, and she realized that a man like Harvey, not at all bad-looking and surrounded by the fascinating aura of money and success, was going to indulge in romantic adventures. She had no illusions about what frequently went on during his many trips abroad, or the times that he spent without her in London and Switzerland.

However, Jenny was not depressed. She knew that she could not hope to compete with Harvey's youthful beauties on their terms, so she took care never to become aware of any details about them. Instead, she concentrated on being nice to come home to. She knew that Harvey appreciated her attitude, and that he would always come home. Since Jenny disliked sailing, did not ski and was terrified of the helicopter, Harvey—what with his sporting activities and his hectic working life—spent a lot of time away from his wife: but always at the back of his mind was the comforting thought that she was there—reassuring, undemanding, restful. Home.

After his retirement, of course, things changed. The Barringtons were together a great deal more. Instead of odd days or weekends snatched on the ski slopes or the boat, Harvey found that he could take long holidays and go on extended cruises. He persuaded Jenny to go with him, but she decided that she was too old to learn to ski, she got sea-sick on the water, and she missed her bridge parties. By the time he was fifty-five, Harvey Barrington, the man who had everything, was forced to admit to himself that he was deathly bored. It was at this dangerous point in his life that he met Samantha Polegate-White.

Samantha was twenty-three, and a refugee from an impecunious upper-middle-class family. For as long as she could remember, her parents had been struggling to do something or other. First it had been the struggle to maintain the family house—an ugly Victorian edifice in East Anglia, which was far too large for a family of three. Then they had struggled to send Samantha to a very snobbish and costly boarding-school, where, not being academically inclined, she learnt virtually nothing. They would certainly have struggled to send her to University, had she been able to pass the entrance examinations. Instead, they struggled to get her into a fashionable secretarial college in London, where they hoped she would meet 'the right people', become a Sloane Ranger and make a brilliant marriage: for there was no argument about the fact that Samantha was sensationally beautiful. Not surprisingly, on her twenty-first birthday, Samantha had rebelled.

She ran away from the secretarial college and the nice little studio flat in Kensington (her parents, naturally, were struggling to pay the rent). She first joined a very curious commune squatting in an empty house in Hackney, but the poverty and discomfort soon disgusted her, and she decided to capitalize on her looks and become a model. She quickly found out that it took more than a pretty face to become one of the highly-paid girls who appear in the glossy magazines and on the cat-walks of couturiers. The only jobs she could get were poorly-paid and back-breaking, modelling cheap clothes in the showrooms of wholesale manufacturers in London's garment district.

Samantha hated the work, hated the life and hated the bed-sitter in Lewisham which was the only accommodation she could afford. However, she was in something of a fix. She was determined not to go back to her family and admit that she had been wrong—and yet she was quite unqualified for any other, more agreeable work. It was at this stage that she ran into an old schoolfriend while shopping in Oxford Street. The Polegate-Whites' struggle to send their daughter to an expensive school paid off at last.

Over coffee, the old schoolfriend professed herself devastated at Samantha's plight, and promised to find her something to do in Daddy's business. Daddy's business turned out to be a Mayfair brokerage firm which dealt in luxury yachts. Samantha was installed, on a purely decorative basis, as a receptionist. And so it was that she met Harvey Barrington, who dropped in to open negotiations in the matter of selling his boat and buying a larger one. That was how it all began.

It is not unusual for a man of Harvey's age to fall in love with a much younger girl. In this case, however, it was more than a passing fancy; it was a desperate infatuation. It might have cooled down, or even disappeared altogether, if Samantha had agreed to go to bed with Harvey. But she had had enough of dreary hard work and unpleasant living conditions, and her two years of independence had taught her a number of lessons—among them that very rich and good-looking men are accustomed to easily-bought sexual favours, and, for all their promises, have no compunction about dropping the girl when they tire of her. From the beginning, she decided that it was to be marriage or nothing. In vain Harvey offered luxury apartments, money, jewellery, clothes.

'Come back to me,' said Samantha heartlessly, 'with your Decree Nisi tucked neatly into your briefcase, and we'll talk about it then.'

Harvey was not used to this sort of reception, and it drove him crazy. Finally, in desperation, he asked Jenny for a divorce.

Jenny was amused. 'Don't be silly, Harvey. Of course not. You'd regret it in a few months. You'd want to come home—you know that perfectly well. But by then it would be too late.'

It was not long after this that Harvey Barrington came to the conclusion that he would have to kill his wife.

He went round one evening to see Samantha in the Hampstead studio apartment where she now lived (Daddy, at his daughter's insistence, was paying Samantha far more than she was worth).

'I've spoken to Jenny,' he said. 'She won't hear of a divorce.'

'Well then, there's nothing to be done, is there?' Samantha sounded practical, but she realized that she was taking a big risk. She had no intention of losing Harvey.

'Oh yes there is,' said Harvey. 'Now, listen to me. I'm going to take Jenny to the Caribbean house for a holiday. It's just possible she might have some sort of an accident. I won't say any more. Meanwhile, I want all my letters back, and we mustn't see each other at all for the time being. You can tell your boss's daughter that we've had a row. There must be no connection whatsoever between us. OK?'

'OK, Harvey,' said Samantha. She went over to her dressing-table, took a bundle of letters out of the drawer and handed it to him. 'They're all there.'

Harvey took the letters, glanced through them and nodded. Then he said, 'Whatever happens, don't try to contact me at any time.'

Samantha smiled. 'Don't call us, we'll call you.'

'Exactly.'

The next day, Harvey told Jenny that he had come to his senses and got over his ridiculous infatuation. He suggested that they should take a Caribbean holiday to celebrate—just the two of them. They flew out the following week.

The fact that the island was still a British Crown Colony had many advantages: the only minus point was that under British law there is no such thing as a private beach. Harvey could stop outsiders from walking through his property to reach the sea, but he could not prevent sailors from anchoring off his white coral sands and coming ashore for a swim. However, he did not think that this would interfere with his plan. It was summertime and so out of season, and his beach was very secluded. He felt sure that it would be quite easy to arrange for Jenny to drown.

The first few days passed peacefully enough. The sun shone, the Barringtons swam and sunbathed and watched magnificent sunsets as they sipped rum punches on their terrace. Jenny was delighted to be without the usual crowd of acquaintances—he had always been too busy to acquire real friends—that Harvey was accustomed to invite to the island.

Each morning at half past ten, the Barringtons went down to the beach for a swim. It was a charming little bay, with big grey boulders that scattered the sand and then strode out into the water, breaking the smooth blue line of the horizon.

It was a favourite sport of the local youngsters to climb up on to the top of the biggest rock, and jump from it into the water. Harvey remembered an occasion a few years back when a boy had made an awkward leap, struck his head on the boulder on the way down, fallen unconscious into the water and drowned. What had happened once, he reckoned, could happen again. In fact, it was going to happen the following day, a Wednesday.

On Wednesday, however, the sky was cloudy, with threatening rain, and Jenny announced that she wouldn't come to the beach.

'You go, Harvey,' she said. 'I'll stay here and read my book.'

Harvey shrugged, and went off to swim alone. He was quite glad to do so, as a matter of fact, because it gave him an opportunity to scout out the terrain in peace, and to find a suitable piece of rock with which to knock Jenny out before dumping her in the water. He also practised climbing to the top of the big boulder, and was pleased to find that it was quite easy.

On Thursday, Jenny came to the beach. After a short dip, Harvey said, 'Look, I want to show you something.'

He scrambled up the rock, gave Jenny a cheerful wave, and jumped into the sea. He surfaced spluttering and laughing.

'It's great fun. Why don't you try it, darling?'

Sitting on the sand, Jenny smiled and shook her head. 'Not for me, thanks. I'm too old for that sort of thing.'

'You're always saying you're too old. First it was skiing, and now this. At least come and see. The climb up isn't at all difficult.'

'Oh, very well.' Jenny got up and began to walk towards the rocks. This was important, because Harvey needed her footprints in the sand, approaching the big boulder. And, at that moment, a white sailing ketch rounded the point, came up into the wind and dropped anchor just off the beach. Her crew jumped into the dinghy and rowed ashore, chattering and laughing.

'Hi, there!' called a tall, fair young man, in an unmistakable New York accent. 'Lovely morning!'

Harvey managed an uneasy grin, and returned the greeting. At the same time, he stashed away the piece of rock which he had left hidden among the boulders, and which he had intended to use for knocking out his wife. Once more, the deed would have to be postponed.

Then it occurred to him that perhaps it was a good thing that these young Americans had shown up. They would make useful corroborative witnesses.

'We're having some good sport here,' he called out. 'Come and have a go!'

He shinned up the boulder again, and jumped into the sea. The Americans—there were four of them, two men and two girls—applauded and ran along the beach to try for themselves. Soon they were all taking turns to scramble up and jump or dive down, and so infectious was their young enthusiasm that even Jenny was persuaded to try it.

'That was marvellous!' She struck out for the shore and another jump. 'Perhaps I'll even learn to ski!'

Friday morning. Another beautiful day. Harvey and Jenny walked down to the deserted beach.

'Coming for another rock jump?' Harvey asked.

'In a minute. You go first.'

Harvey walked over to the foot of the huge boulder. His rock was where he had left it, satisfactorily camouflaged among the other grey stones. He felt a strong surge of excitement. This was it. He would make his jump, come quickly ashore and catch up with Jenny as she started to climb. It would all be over in a matter of seconds. His heart thumping, Harvey climbed the boulder. His adrenalin was pumping and his face was damp with sweat, which ran down into his eyes. That was probably the reason why his foot slipped as he reached the summit of the rock. He grabbed vainly at the air, trying to save himself, but it was no use. He fell, clumsily. His head struck granite, and he knew no more.

When he recovered consciousness, Harvey was in his bed in the plantation house, with the local doctor bending over him.

'Welcome back to the land of the living, Mr Barrington,' said the doctor cheerily. He was an elderly Englishman who had retired to the island, but had been persuaded to continue his profession for the benefit of its inhabitants. 'That was a very narrow shave you had, sir. If it hadn't been for your wife, you'd be a dead man now.'

Harvey struggled to sit up. 'What happened? I can't remember—'

'You were playing a silly, dangerous game,' said the doctor severely. 'Climbing up that big boulder and jumping into the sea. Mrs Barrington says that you lost your footing at the top and fell off, hitting your head on the way down to the water. Exactly what happened to that poor boy two years ago. Thank God Mrs Barrington was there. She managed to drag you out of the water and gave you artificial respiration. When she was sure you were breathing again, she ran up to the house and telephoned me. You're a lucky man in more ways than one, Mr Barrington. Lucky to be alive, and lucky to have a brave and resourceful wife. You should be very thankful.'

'I am,' said Harvey, and suddenly realized that it was true. Of course, Jenny had been perfectly right all along. Samantha now seemed no more than any of the other pretty faces he had encountered in the course of his life. Jenny was the only person who meant anything to him. He had come home.

There was no question, of course, of Harvey going to the beach or anywhere else for several days. The doctor insisted on complete rest and quiet. So it was that, two days later, Jenny Barrington went to the beach alone.

She felt wonderful, young and strong again. Harvey really loved her. She would learn to ski. She would go out on the boat, take pills against sea-sickness and learn to sail. So full was she of these thoughts and plans that she never noticed how far out the current was taking her. In a panic she turned for the shore, but she never made it. Her body was washed up a day later, some way down the coast.

Of course, it rated a small mention in all the London newspapers. 'Millionaire's Wife Drowns in Caribbean Paradise.' Samantha saw it, and was much impressed. A few days later, after the inquest and the funeral in the island's small church, there were pictures of Harvey flying back to Heathrow. 'Heart-Broken Millionaire Barrington Returns Home Alone.' Samantha smiled to herself.

She stopped smiling, however, when the weeks went by and she still heard nothing from Harvey. Discretion was all very well, but this was going too far. After all, hadn't it been proved beyond all doubt that this was Death by Misadventure? Harvey, it was reported, had been nowhere near the beach at the time—in fact, he was at home, laid up in bed after a nasty accident. The Coroner had made some pointed remarks about the foolhardiness of going swimming alone. This being so, Samantha could not imagine why Harvey had not contacted her. Finally, she could bear it no longer. One evening she telephoned his London number.

'Harvey, it's me. Samantha. I was desolated to hear about Jenny. Why don't you come round to my place for a drink?'

'No,' said Harvey, and rang off.

Samantha bit her lip. This was ridiculous. Well, at least she knew he was at the Chelsea apartment. She took a cab and went there.

Harvey opened the door himself. Samantha knew that he only employed a daily cleaning woman for the apartment, presumably so that he could use it as an occasional love-nest when Jenny was in Sussex.

He said roughly, 'What the hell are you doing here?'

Samantha stepped past him into the hall. 'What do you think I'm doing, darling? I came to see you, of course.'

She held out her arms for an embrace, but Harvey backed away from her. He said, 'Please go, Samantha. Everything has changed.'

'What on earth do you mean?'

'There's really no reason why I should explain to you, but I will. Jenny saved my life, down on the island. And then she drowned by accident, when I wasn't there to help her. I only realized then what she meant to me. I could never—'

'You are a fool, Harvey.' Samantha masked her dismay and fury under a thin coat of mockery. 'When shall we announce our engagement?'

'Never.'

'Really? Then I shall go to the police and tell them how you were planning to kill Jenny.'

'You can't do that. You've absolutely no proof of anything. My letters—'

'Oh, I gave you back your letters, all right. But surely you must have realized that I'd made photocopies of them, just in case. They're deposited at my bank. And whenever you visited me, I had my tape-recorder going. Including the last time.' Samantha put her beautiful head on one side and considered. 'I wonder which would be more amusing? To go to the police, or to go to the tabloid press. The press, I think. Imagine what they'd pay me.'

'You wouldn't dare!'

'I certainly would. I'm not going to let that fat old bitch get the better of me.'

It was then that Harvey Barrington strangled Samantha Polegate-White. Then he sat down at his desk and wrote a full confession, before telephoning the police anonymously to report an accident at his address.

Long before the police arrived, he had walked out of the riverside apartment building and into the dark waters of the Thames. His letter of confession did not actually mention suicide. But it ended, 'By the time you read this, I shall be home.'

Michael Pearce

THE MAMUR ZAPT AND
THE·HOUSE OF DOVES

MICHAEL PEARCE *grew up in the (then) Anglo-Egyptian Sudan, among the political and other tensions he has portrayed so skilfully in three memorable crime novels and in this story, all featuring Captain Owen, British head of the Political CID in Edwardian Cairo and the Mamur Zapt of the title. Michael Pearce later returned to the Sudan to teach and retains a human rights interest in the area. In between whiles his career has followed the standard academic rake's progress from teaching to writing to editing to administration. He finds international politics a pallid imitation of academic ones.*

WHEN OWEN ARRIVED at his office, early as was his custom, the sun had not yet reached the courtyard and the shadows were still cold on the sand. The little line of petitioners was already waiting, however.

Three years ago, when he had first come to Cairo, a line like this would have embarrassed him. He would have seen it as a manifestation of suppliance. Now, he accepted it as merely a characteristic preference for the personal. In Egypt justice was intimate, personal. It could never be the cold bureaucratic thing that Cromer had tried to make it.

He walked along the line chatting with each of the petitioners. Some he would take up to his office. The problems of others he could resolve in the courtyard.

One of the petitioners was a tall, dark-bearded man with an unusually gentle face who stood out from the others by the quality of his dress. He was wearing like them the ordinary galabiyeh and turban but his were made of better cloth and well cut.

'Effendi,' he said, 'my master has died and I am triple-bound.'

'Triple-bound?'

'Bound by service, bound by favour, bound by fear.'

'I still do not understand.'

'He is a Pasha's cook,' someone in the line explained. 'Any man who cooks for a Pasha is thus bound.'

'It is because they are afraid of being poisoned,' said someone else. 'They bind their cooks so as to be safe.'

As always in Cairo, a man's problems were something his neighbours, even if they were neighbours but for the moment, reckoned to share.

'And what is the nature of this binding?'

'I was brought up on my master's estate as my father had been before me. That is the bond of service,' said the cook.

'Anyone who cooks for a Pasha is double-paid,' said someone else in the line. 'That is the bond of favour.'

'And the bond of fear?'

'If my master dies from poison they will kill me.'

'And your master has died?'

'From poison,' said the cook. 'So they will kill me.'

The cook raised his head and looked Owen straight in the face. 'Effendi,' he said, 'I did not poison my master. It was someone else. Nevertheless, it is me they will kill. Unless you find the one who did it.'

'Have you any idea who might have done this terrible thing?'

'No. But I prepare all the food that goes to my master with my own hands and I know it could not have been done in our house.'

'In some other house, then?'

'My master frequently dined out. Especially at the present time.'

'Why especially at the present time?'

The cook shrugged his shoulders. 'I do not know, effendi. I know only that there are big things afoot. For the past two weeks my master has dined out almost every night.'

'In that case why should they look first to you?'

Again the shrug, helpless.

'I do not know, effendi. It is unjust. But they will.'

Owen's interest was caught. Looking back on it afterwards in the cool of his room, he realized that this was how things happened in Egypt: not in the shape of a cold formal communication through the post but through a warm human encounter in the streets. A personal request was made in person and required a personal response.

But he could not quite escape his Western bureaucratic conditioning. This sounded to him like ordinary police work and Owen was not an ordinary policeman.

'Have you not spoken to the Parquet?' he asked.

When a crime was reported, under Egyptian legal procedure, which was French in style and based on the Code Napoléon, the police had immediately to inform the Department of Prosecutions of the Ministry of Justice, the Parquet, which then, as under the French system, took over responsibility for conducting the inquiry.

'Effendi, I have,' said the cook.

'And?'

'The man who came to us from the Parquet was a young man dressed like an effendi and as sharp as a knife. I told him what I have told you. He listened without saying anything. Then he thought for a long time. And then he said: "Go to the Mamur Zapt and tell him I sent you." '

'I know the man,' said Owen. 'His name is Mahmoud.'

'That is his name.'

Owen could still not see why the cook had come to him. For the Mamur Zapt was Head of what in England would be called the Political CID and handled only political matters.

'What is the name of your master?' he asked.

'The Pasha Abdul Ismail.'

'In that case I will come,' said Owen.

Owen walked in past the two eunuchs named according to custom after precious stones or flowers, crunched across the gravel courtyard where a club of friendly cats dozed around a cluster of palms and went in at the great door.

Upstairs in the harem rooms women were wailing. Downstairs, however, all was calm. At the far end of the great room there was a raised dais covered with cushions on which a plump young man was sitting. He rose to greet Owen.

'C'est un très grand plaisir, monsieur,' he said. 'J'ai entendu beaucoup de vous.'

The upper Egyptian classes habitually spoke French. Nor was it just a matter of language. Their culture was French; they read French newspapers, sent their sons to French schools, dressed their wives in Paris, went to France for their holidays.

'I am very sorry to hear about your father,' said Owen, guessing, correctly as it happened.

The young man put on a sad face.

'A great loss. Not just to ourselves but to the country.'

'There will be a state funeral, of course?'

'Of course,' agreed the plump young man.

'For such a life to end in such a way!'

'Those who did it must be caught,' said the young man. 'I have, of course, a personal interest in seeing that they are not allowed to repeat their crime.'

'That is why I am here.'

'You came without being sent for. Please accept my thanks.'

Owen bowed.

'And without having read the notes of the case first,' he said. 'There is no question, I suppose, of the cause of death?'

The young man shrugged.

'It was clear,' he said. 'If you have been brought up in a family like mine you recognize the symptoms. It has been medically confirmed.'

'One thinks immediately of the cook.'

'Oh yes. He is triple-bound, of course.'

'And will suffer accordingly if the case is proved?'

'He will suffer anyway. Otherwise, successors would be encouraged in their laxity.'

'Was he lax?'

'Probably not. Mustafa has been with the family for many years and my father had strict standards.'

'Then I hope he will not suffer the extreme penalty.'

'A whipping should be sufficient.'

'You speak as if you were sure he had no hand in the business itself.'

'Oh yes.'

'Then where do you think the poison might have been administered? You have no idea, I suppose?'

'Oh yes. The French Chargé's.'

'I beg your pardon?'

'The French Chargé d'Affaires. My father was dining there the night he was taken ill.'

Owen pulled himself together.

'You surprise me,' he said. He hesitated. 'This could not be a matter of, well, ordinary food poisoning, could it?'

'The Chargé would not feel very flattered by your suggestion,' the young man said. He reached over to a tray behind him and helped himself to a large portion of Turkish Delight. 'But no. Arsenic was the cause of my father's death. Or so your Mr Cairns Grant assured me.'

'In that case I am even more surprised,' said Owen. 'I mean—the Chargé!'

'He is a good servant of France. Of course, he is paid to be.'

'But . . .' Owen fished for words. 'He must have had some motive,' he ended weakly.

'Hatred of England,' said the young man immediately.

'Well, our relations are sometimes difficult, I know—'

'It is uncertainty, you see, about the Khedive's intentions. It is rumoured that there is about to be a reshuffle. Patros has fallen out of favour. Who is to succeed him as Prime Minister? And what will be the complexion of the new Government? As you know, there are two factions at Court: those who are loyal to the Khedive and are prepared to accept the British, for the time being, of course; and those who support the French.'

When the great powers had intervened in Egypt's affairs thirty years before and had established the system of Dual Control, Egypt's finances had been taken out of the hands of the profligate Khedive and entrusted to the Controllers, one French, one English. The French had thus come to share in the government of Egypt.

They had lost that position as a result of the Arabi rebellion, when they had inclined to the wrong side. The British Army had suppressed the rebellion and since then Egypt had been governed in effect if not in name by Britain's Agent, Cromer. At the Khedive's invitation, of course.

The French did not see it like that and nor, after thirty years, did another Khedive. Might not the British be encouraged to go? They might, if the right Government was formed.

'My father has always been loyal to the Khedive,' said the plump young man. 'And to the British, of course. That is why he has been a Minister for so long. Things can change, naturally. And so when the Chargé invited him to meet some of the pro-French party for private discussions he felt it advisable to accept.'

The young man helped himself to some more Turkish Delight and wiped his fingers.

'Proposals were put to him, which, alas, he had to decline as they would have had the effect of detaching him from his true allegiances. And so they poisoned him.'

'Outrageous,' said the French Chargé. 'Infamous! You are going too far!'

He was referring not to the arsenic but to the suggestion that the meal had been less than perfect.

'You have eaten here yourself!'

'And always well.'

The Chargé was not mollified.

'I supervised the preparation myself. I always do.'

'It has the touch of the master.'

'Abdullah is good but he needs watching. Occasionally, just occasionally, mind, he leaves it that fraction too long.'

'What makes the difference between the good and the superb is just that last touch.'

'Well, yes,' said the Chargé, 'you have a point there.'

'But, Chargé, about the arsenic—'

'Shocking!' said the Chargé. 'Terrible!'

'You see, Chargé, the last time he dined was *chez vous*. So the finger of suspicion naturally points—'

'Well, yes, of course,' said the Chargé. 'That was obviously the idea.'

'You mean—?'

'It was clearly intended to incriminate us. To discredit us with the Khedive. I must tell you that I regard it as an unfriendly act.'

'You are saying you are not responsible?'

'Certainly not.'

'Who is, then?'

'Surely you don't have to ask me?'

'I *am* asking you.'

'The British.'

'The British!'

'You are well informed, I have to admit that. You knew about the dinner. You must also know, then, about what was said. So you knew that Abdul Ismail was about to defect.'

'Abdul Ismail was going to switch sides?'

'Until you stopped him,' said the Chargé.

'If Abdul Ismail was going to defect, Minister,' said Owen, 'it would not have been the British who would have wanted to stop him.'

'Of course not,' agreed the Minister. 'It would have been me. Though I doubt if I would have gone to such lengths. Abdul Ismail was hardly important enough. We were thinking of dropping him anyway. He was hardly an asset with the electorate.'

Egypt did have elections, although they did not directly affect the membership of the Cabinet, which was the Khedive's choice. All the same, he could not afford to disregard the electorate entirely.

The Minister, who definitely was an asset with the electorate, settled himself more comfortably on his chair.

'But aren't you rather on the wrong track?' he asked. 'I doubt very much whether defection was anything to do with it. You don't even know for certain that Abdul Ismail *was* actually poisoned at the Chargé's. Personally, I doubt it. The French care too much about their food to wish to distract themselves with other considerations.'

'What track should I be on, then?'

'Why search for motives when the motive is staring you in the face? Abdul Ismail was a Minister at the time of Denshewai.'

Denshewai was a village in the Nile Delta and had been the scene three years before of an incident as potent in nationalist mythology as the Amritsar Massacre in India. Some British officers out pigeon-shooting had been attacked by villagers and one had died. The villagers had been punished in exemplary fashion; so savagely as to rouse Egyptian indignation everywhere and light the fires of nationalism irrevocably.

'It has never been forgiven,' said the Minister, 'and anyone who had anything to do with it has never really been safe ever since, as of course you know. Abdul Ismail was a junior minister at the time. He was not, in fact, directly concerned but the Nationalists do not discriminate in such matters.'

'You think it may be a Nationalist group?'

'Well, terrorist groups are more in your line than in mine. All I say is that here is a possible motive. And that Abdul Ismail was not exactly an electoral asset. Speaking objectively, of course,' said the Minister, smiling sweetly. 'I was not myself a Minister at the time.'

* * *

At one end of the souk was an open space where trees gave a little shade. It was here that the cooks and boys from the big houses liked to congregate after they had bought their vegetables and take tea, black, bitter, raw stuff. They would squat in groups around the tea-man, their little enamel cups before them, chattering vigorously.

Owen, perched on a high stool at the tea-stall, could hear them behind him. There was a fat, benign-looking Greek squatting among the group nearest him.

'Fortunate the servants of a house where there is a mighty cook,' the Greek was saying.

'Less fortunate than you might think,' one of the men said tartly. 'The mightier the cook, the more fussy he is about the vegetables we buy.'

'Ah yes, but afterwards you can taste the fruit of his labours.'

'The better the cook, the more likely the guests are to eat up everything.'

'Your master served a mighty meal the other night when all the Pashas came. Was there nothing left that night?'

'As a matter of fact there was and we did very well.'

'One of the guests was taken ill, I hear.'

'It would have been because he had eaten too much, then.'

'The food was as mighty as ever?'

'I can vouch for it. For I helped myself to a sample of everything.'

'And that was before it reached the table,' said one of the other boys slyly.

A little later in the morning Owen was again sitting at a tea-stall, this time on the other side of the square. Again behind him the boys were squatting and chattering and again among the group nearest him the fat, benign-looking Greek was sitting.

'Fortunate the servants of a house where there is a mighty cook,' the Greek was saying.

'Well, we do usually dine well, that's true.'

'Your master dined too well the other night if what I hear is true.'

'Well or ill: that's the question.'

'Well or ill: that's a point!' said the Greek, laughing and slapping his thighs. 'At least he dined *out,* which is just as well from Mustafa's point of view.'

'He dined in, too, before he went to the Frenchman's. He's a greedy one, our master.'

'Dine in too? Before a meal like that?'

'As true as that I am sitting here. Some pigeons had come up from the estate that week. He's always partial to pigeons and he had a pair of them that afternoon.'

'No wonder he was ill!'

'Ah, but it wasn't that. He can stuff a great deal inside his fat stomach without it having any effect.'

'They say it was poison.'

'They say,' said the boy sceptically. 'It's my belief he died of a heart-attack.'

'None of the other Pashas suffered any after-effects.'

'That's right.'

'Maybe it was this queasy that's going around,' said the fat Greek.

'What queasy is this?'

'There's a lot of it around. I felt a bit funny myself.'

'Strange that you should say that. I felt odd myself this morning.'

'There you are then! It's probably going the rounds. Anyone else in your place been sick? Apart from the Pasha, I mean?'

'Now you come to mention it, Suleiman wasn't at all well a couple of days ago.'

The cook, Mustafa, was showing Owen how he prepared the meals. From time to time he took down a small pot from the shelves, opened it, tasted the contents and then gave them to Owen to taste. In the kitchen the heat was stifling.

Behind Owen the fat Greek was prowling about the place, poking into corners. Owen caught snatches of his conversation with the servants.

'Hello!' he said in concerned tones to an elderly, rancorous-looking man slumped in the doorway. 'You don't look too good. Is anything wrong?'

'It is the gripe,' the man said. 'I've had it for nearly a week now and can't seem to shake it off.'

'I expect it's the heat,' said the Greek. 'It always seems to make things worse. How did it afflict you?'

Suleiman began a lengthy description of his symptoms.

'That day: the day the Pasha went to the Chargé's,' Owen said to the cook. 'Did the Pasha eat anything else?'

'He's always eating.'

'But something that you prepared? Pigeons, for instance?'

The cook was silent for a moment. Then he looked Owen in the face.

'I was wrong,' he said. 'I should have told you. I remembered it afterwards but I didn't like to say because . . .' He shrugged his shoulders. 'Well, because,' he said.

'It was that day?'

'Yes. A basket of pigeons had come up from the estate at the beginning of the week. The Pasha is very fond of pigeons. He had two every day that week. Before he went out.'

'And he had two that day?'

'Yes.'

'You prepared them yourself?'

'As always.'

'Did you notice anything special about them?'

The cook hesitated. 'I thought they had a different smell. But then, all the pigeons that week had smelt like that so I thought perhaps they had been feeding on different grain.'

'They were alive and well, though?'

'Oh yes.'

'And when you chose them for the table they were alive and well?'

'That is so.'

'You chose them and killed them. Did you then cook them at once?'

'At once. They are better like that.'

'And then they were eaten at once? Who bore them to the Pasha?'

'Abdul.'

'And would Abdul have fetched the plate after?'

'He would.'

'Would he have picked the remains?'

'Those fat houseboys?' The kitchen servants laughed.

'If there had been any remains,' said one of them, 'it would have been we who would have eaten them.'

'And *did* any of you eat them?'

'No.'

'Yes.'

It was Suleiman, attending with sudden interest.

The Greek smiled at Owen.

'You picked the remains of the pigeons?' Owen asked.

'Yes. The Pasha's not the only one who's partial to pigeons.'

'Well, well.'

The cook had suddenly gone ashen. 'As God is my witness—'

'God is your witness,' said Owen sternly. 'So tell me.'

But the cook could tell nothing. He was in a state of shock. After a while one of the other boys led him away and sat him down by the kitchen wall, where he sat staring blankly into space.

The Greek, whose name was Georgiades and who was one of Owen's agents, tried to question the other servants, but they were either equally stunned or else excited beyond control and he could get no sense out of them. After a while he gave up and looked at Owen.

'Tomorrow,' said Owen.

As they went out of the door they passed Suleiman. He looked up at them.

'It was the pigeons, then?'

'Yes. Go to the English hakim and he will give you something.'

'I shall be all right,' said Suleiman. 'The pickings were small. The Pasha likes his pigeons. Nevertheless, I shall go to the English hakim.'

He walked out with them into the street. He seemed reluctant to leave them. Suddenly he made up his mind.

'If it was the pigeons,' he said, 'you will not find the answer here.'

'Where will I find it?'

'At Wad Tabbi,' said Suleiman.

The Pasha's estate at Wad Tabbi was a long way south of Cairo in the Balyana district. The staple crop of this part of Egypt was sugar cane and there were estates with hundreds of acres of unbroken sugar cane cultivation without a single road running through them.

Wad Tabbi itself was a village with a few good houses and many mean ones. The good ones were built of stone and had an upper floor reached by an outside stair. The meaner ones were made of mud brick and single-storey. They had flat roofs on which the peasants stored their grain and vegetables and occasionally brushwood.

At one end of the village was a large square tower, crenellated on top and with heavy loopholes in the sides. As you approached it you became aware of a continuous soft moaning from inside. Owen could hear it even where he was sitting, in the middle of the village outside the headman's house.

The tower was the Pasha's pigeonhouse and all the pigeons in it belonged to him. The fellahin were not allowed to have pigeons of their own. This was not always the case, for in some villages, especially in the north, the village itself possessed a pigeonhouse which was owned in common by the villagers.

In other villages, again mostly in the north, there was no central pigeonhouse but every house had a cote on its roof, usually consisting of baked clay pots turned on to their sides.

Pigeons were important to the economy of the countryside. For the rich landlords the guano collected in the large pigeonhouses was a major source of income. For the poorer fellahin the food the pigeons represented was sometimes the difference between living and dying. It was no wonder, thought Owen, that the incident at Denshewai had touched a nerve.

When you came to a place like Wad Tabbi you realized that Egypt was still essentially a rural country, moved by the things of the village rather than the things of the town. Although he had spent a year in the provinces when he had first come to Egypt, he was himself a man of the town.

He had thought long and hard about who he should bring with him to Wad Tabbi. Georgiades, even more a man of the town than Owen himself, would have been useless. And so he had brought with him his orderly, Yussuf. Yussuf was no policeman and was far from the brightest orderly in the office; but he had been born and bred in the country and knew the ways of the fellahin.

Owen could see him now, further along the street, squatting in the dust with a small circle of men, drinking tea. He had his own commission and Owen would come to him later.

The keeper who looked after the Pasha's pigeons at Wad Tabbi was working on the other side of the estate, constructing a second dovehouse. He was in any case the overseer and had had nothing directly to do with the pigeons himself. The person who actually fed and cleaned and tended the pigeons was an old woman. They brought her before him.

'Greetings, Mother,' he said.

The woman bowed submissively.

'You keep the pigeons?'

'Yes, effendi.'

'You collect the eggs, feed the birds?'

'Yes, effendi.'

'And choose the pigeons for the Pasha's table?'

Although the questions were put to the old woman, they were routed through the village headman, the omda, the male speaking for her, as was proper. And it was the omda who replied on her behalf.

'Yes, effendi.'

'Alone, or with another?'

'Alone, effendi.'

'You choose the birds yourself? And then what do you do? Put them in a basket?'

'Yes, effendi.'

'And then what happens?'

'They are taken to the boat.'

'What boat is this?'

'It is the Pasha's own boat.'

'He sends it for the pigeons?'

'Not just for the pigeons. Fruit, eggs, chickens—fresh things for the Pasha's table.'

'How often does it come?'

'Twice a month.'

'And always it takes pigeons?'

'That is correct, effendi.'

'And always you choose them?'

'Yes, effendi.'

'And thus it was the last time you sent the pigeons?'

'Yes, effendi.'

'Do you remember that day?'

'She remembers it well.'

'Why does she remember it well?'

'Because her son had been staying with her.'

'That makes it special for her?'

'Yes, effendi. He lives away from the village and only comes home from time to time.'

'So that would make it stand out. She remembers the day, then. Can she think back to the pigeons? Was there anything special about them too?'

'They were good pigeons.'

'They were not sick and ailing when they left?'

'Certainly not, effendi,' said the omda, shocked and speaking in his own person. 'We only send good things to the Pasha.'

'They were plump and juicy,' said the woman, suddenly speaking for herself. 'Just the way the Pasha likes them.'

'She knows, does she?'

'She has been choosing pigeons for the Pasha's table for a long time, effendi.'

'She chose the pigeons, then, that day. By herself?'

'As always.'

'And put them in a basket. Which was then taken to the river?'

'Yes, effendi.'

'What happened there?'

'They were given to Hussein.'

'Who is Hussein?'

'The Pasha's boatman. He stows the things himself so that they are as he likes. He lets no one else touch them.'

'And when he has finished storing the things, does he leave at once? Or wait till the next day?'

'At once, effendi. Then the food gets to the Pasha's kitchen while it is still fresh. The boat is a felucca, effendi, and sails fast.'

'Does it stop anywhere?'

'It might stop briefly at a village if there was someone who wanted to get off. Occasionally there is someone from Wad Tabbi who wishes to visit a relative.'

'Was it so on this occasion?'

The omda consulted the onlookers.

'I do not think so.'

'There was Jemal,' said someone.

'Who is Jemal?'

'Fatima's son.' The omda indicated the old woman.

'Who had been staying with her?'

'Yes, but he did not get off at a village. He went right back to the city.'

'I will speak with Hussein later, and perhaps with the son.'

Owen sipped his coffee meditatively, pondering his next question. The woman waited submissively, impenetrable behind her black veil.

'Effendi,' said the omda diffidently, 'why are the pigeons so important?'

Owen decided to tell him.

'Because it was after eating them that the Pasha died.'

For a moment there was a stunned silence.

Then the omda exploded.

'Effendi, you cannot be right! It cannot be the pigeons.'

'Why not?'

'Mustafa would have prepared them himself. I know Mustafa. He comes from this village. He is a good man.'

'He certainly seems so.'

'Besides, he is triple-bound. Think what that means, effendi!'

'I know what it means.'

'A man eats many things. In many places. Why should it be the pigeons?'

'Because it cannot be other things.'

'Then someone else in the kitchens must have done it!'

'Mustafa prepares all the food for the Pasha. You said so yourself.'

'It is still possible—it must be! Mustafa cannot have done it!'

'That,' said Owen, 'is why I am here.'

'But—' The omda broke off, clasped his head between his hands and shook it violently. 'That cannot be right either. You have spoken with us and know that we had nothing to do with it. Besides—if the pigeons were poisoned here, why did they not die at once? At any rate, before they got to the Pasha?'

'That is what I have come to learn,' said Owen, and adjourned the proceedings.

He walked up the street to where Yussuf was sitting with his new cronies. Yussuf parted from them reluctantly and he and Owen took a short stroll up a track behind the pigeon-house.

'Well, Yussuf, did you do as I asked?'

'Yes, effendi, I put the question, not as coming from you, but as my own. I spoke of my village and said I had a neighbour who had wronged me. He was a powerful man, however—' Yussuf looked anxiously at Owen—'I said he was our omda.'

'Good.'

'I said that I dare not oppose him to his face. But he had a buffalo which he greatly treasured and that I meant to poison.'

Poisoning your neighbour's buffalo was virtually a social habit in Egyptian villages and almost invariably the poison used was arsenic. Whenever a buffalo died it was assumed to have been poisoned and accusations between neighbours flew thick and fast. In his year in the provinces Owen had been called on to adjudicate in many such disputes.

Conversely, when neighbours disputed, buffaloes not infrequently died. Those who possessed relevant skills were therefore in considerable demand; and many an elderly woman, forced by circumstance to fend for herself, achieved a respected role in the local community on that basis.

'I asked if there was one in Wad Tabbi to whom I could

go for counsel, for it was best to inquire away from home on such matters.'

'Good. And was there one?'

'Yes, effendi. The old woman at the House of Doves, Fatima.'

'Fatima,' said Owen, 'I would like you to help me with a problem I have.'

'I will do what I can,' said the old woman, surprised.

'My problem is this: I have a neighbour whose buffalo has been poisoned. It is a big, strong buffalo. Now, it would take several doses of poison to kill such a big, fat buffalo, would it not?'

'I don't know why you're asking me,' said the woman, 'but yes, it would.'

'One dose would not be sufficient?'

'Not normally. You would feed it poison for several days, for with a big body the poison takes time to work.'

'Thank you. Now here is my problem. The Pasha was a big, fat buffalo. To kill him would take several doses. That is why I knew the Pasha could not have been poisoned—not by this poison—by one meal he ate at another's house. Nor, for that matter, by one meal at his own house. It had to be repeated. And that was one of the things that led me to the pigeons.'

'But, effendi—' began the omda.

Owen held up his hand.

'But here we have another problem. I do not think the birds were poisoned in the Pasha's kitchens. But if they were poisoned somewhere else, in Wad Tabbi, for instance, why did they not die before they reached the Pasha? For pigeons, you see, have a small body.'

'I do not know,' said the woman.

'I think you do,' said Owen.

* * *

For a long time the woman sat squatting in the dust, looking at the ground. Then she threw the veil on her face and stood up.

'He's dead, then, is he?' she said. 'Well, he won't be missed. That's one thing of which you can be sure.'

'Woman!' said the omda sharply. 'Enough of such talk!'

The woman ignored him.

'He's dead,' she said, half to herself, as if she couldn't really believe it. 'Well, I'm glad. Those pigeons have poisoned our lives for long enough. Now they've poisoned his. I remember my man: "Those pigeons will kill us," he said. They came and filled their crops on our beans and lentils and barley until we had nothing left.'

'That was a long time ago,' said the omda.

'One day my man could stand it no more. He went out into the fields and threw stones at them until they flew away. One was left behind, a fat, juicy one, and that night at least we ate well. The next day, though, the overseer came and took my husband and said: "We will teach you!" And they thrashed him with the curbash until he was dead.'

'There is no curbash now, woman,' said the omda. 'All that is in the past.'

'The stripes are still fresh.'

'It was wrong. The Pasha himself said so. He spoke harshly to the overseer. And afterwards he took you to help in the House of Doves.'

'I owe him nothing. He gave me nothing. I went to him once to ask him for money to buy my son out of military service but he refused me. "How will you pay me back?" he asked. "For you have nothing and will have nothing. Let Jemal go into the army. It will do him good." "You have killed the father," I said. "Why now do you wish to kill the son?"'

'Enough, woman!' said the omda.

'That is the son who was visiting you?' asked Owen.

'Yes,' said the woman. 'I have but one son.'

'And he is in the army?'

The woman smiled. 'No. I sent him to the great madrisseh in the city, El Azhar, so that he could study to be a holy man. At least they give him bread and he does not have to do military service. One day he will be a kadi and I will be proud of him.'

'Do not hold your head up too high, woman,' said the omda.

'I will hold it neither too high nor too low,' said the woman. 'The world is changing. The rule of the Pashas is coming to an end. When the British go, they will go too.'

'What sort of talk is this?' said the astonished omda.

The woman looked at Owen. 'Your time is coming too. It is nearly at an end. Great things are afoot in the city. I have heard.'

'How have you heard?' asked Owen.

'These things come on the wind,' said the woman evasively.

'These things are nothing but the wind,' said the omda.

'Are not these your son's words?' asked Owen.

'What if they are? The old can learn from the young as the young from the old. Before my son went to El Azhar he had no words and I had no words. Now he has learned them and given them to me.'

'What if the words are false?'

'I will take my chance; for there are a lot of false words about.'

She held out her hands to Owen. 'Come! You can take me. I am not afraid.'

'You poisoned the pigeons?'

'I poisoned the pigeons. And I am glad. You asked me how. I will tell you. I mixed the poison in the grain I fed them.'

'Why did not the birds die?'

'I fed it to them little by little. They would have died in the end. But the poison takes time to work. The problem was to feed them enough but not too much. They have small bodies and I did not know how much I could give them. So I tried it out on other birds until I knew.'

'It was not done suddenly, then?'

'No, it was not done suddenly. I have been wanting to do it since he refused me money for my son. But the time was not ripe.'

'What makes it ripe now?'

'Look around you,' said the woman.

'My friend!' cried the French Chargé, embracing him warmly. 'For you, this evening, we have something special!'

'Don't tell me,' said Owen.

'Pigeons. Stuffed breast of pigeon.'

'Wonderful! Although, considering where I am, I shall approach them with caution.'

'The pigeon,' said the Chargé, 'is a revolutionary bird. Did you know that? Among the complaints which led to our own Revolution the one which was the most prominent in the countryside touched on pigeons.'

'Really?'

'Yes. Every château had a pigeonhouse—you can see them today—and the birds flew far and wide over the fields of the peasants, eating their fill. The peasants could do nothing about it, for the birds belonged to the lord; nor were they allowed to own pigeons themselves. And so—' the Chargé raised his glass—'*la Révolution!*'

'*La Révolution!*' said Owen. 'But not in Egypt.'

'Amen,' said the Chargé, putting the glass down. 'But then, this affaire of yours was not in the end political after all, was it?'

'I wouldn't say that,' said Owen.

Mike Ripley

SMELTDOWN

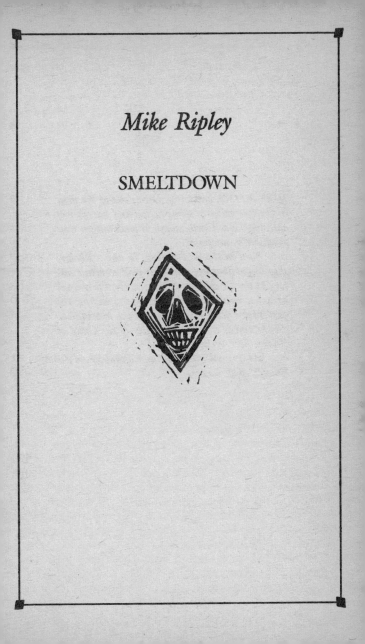

MIKE RIPLEY, *creator of Angel, one of the most distinctive voices in crime fiction and narrator of this story, is a Yorkshireman by birth but an East Anglian by adoption.*

Born in the West Riding, he won a scholarship to public school and then read economic history at the University of East Anglia. He trained as a journalist on local newspapers, but for the past twelve years has worked in the brewing industry and is a founder member of the Guild of British Beer Writers.

He lives with his wife and daughter on the Essex/Suffolk border.

THIS ALL STARTED because Taffy Duck couldn't keep his mouth shut after a few drinks even if he topped his lager with superglue, and Armstrong got belted up the backside by a diesel tanker so recently half-inched the steering-wheel was still warm.

The truck thing happened first.

I had left Armstrong parked under a street lamp in a respectable, middle-class street in Barking. (Who am I kidding? But that's what would have gone on the insurance claim form.) Now it's none of anybody's business what I was doing in that particular street at 5.0 a.m. that morning, except to say I was in the process of leaving. The lady in question has a husband who works very anti-social shifts (you're telling me—5.0 a.m.!) in the London Fire Brigade and I'm not about to cross anyone who knows all there is to know about how things catch fire.

Armstrong is an Austin black cab—the London taxi you find on postcards and biscuit tins—and although I and the Hackney Carriage licensing authorities know he isn't actually a licensed cab any more, you have to look close to tell. Which is why I can usually park with impunity on a variety of yellow lines and, in this case, probably closer to a road junction than I should.

But I'm not making excuses for the tanker-driver, whoever it was, because he simply came round the corner far too fast, lost control and over-corrected, so that while the cab unit missed by a mile, the tanker unit belted Armstrong over the rear offside wheel, lifting him a couple of inches into the air with a scrunch of buckling metal.

My first reaction was to stand where I was about twenty yards away and yell, 'You stupid son of a bitch!' as the tanker slowed to a stop at an angle across the street. But then, and I must have had the Fire Brigade on my mind, I thought: Petrol tanker—collision—fuel tank—fire. And I did the most sensible thing: I threw myself face down on the pavement and put my hands over my head.

Nothing happened, except it went very quiet.

I uncovered an ear and opened an eye. The tanker blocked the street, but it was still in one piece. So was I and so, almost, was Armstrong. So was the pair of feet doing a nifty four-minute mile round the corner. He could run, which is good, as everybody has to have *one* thing in life they're good at (Rule of Life No. 10) and he certainly couldn't drive.

There was no way I was driving Armstrong anywhere, not with the rear wheel arch caved in like that, and probably the wheel itself bent. This was a job for my old mate Duncan the Drunken; probably the best car mechanic in the world. But first I had to find a phone and generally get out of sight before an off-duty fire-engine drew up.

I also thought it might be an idea to move the tanker. People notice these things, especially when they are casually parked at right-angles to the road.

The tanker itself was decked out in the colours of an international oil company. It also contained diesel, not petrol, around 33,000 litres, which I calculated to be about £12,000 retail value. I wondered if I could claim salvage.

The driver had left his cab door open and the keys in the ignition, so I climbed up and settled myself behind the wheel. I felt quite at home as one of my driving licences is actually for Heavy Goods Vehicles, even though I'd never actually moved a tanker before.

I started her up and spun the wheel so the cab came back in line with the bowser, and began to climb through the gears trying to think of a suitable place to park the damn thing in what was after all a residential area.

It hadn't crossed my mind then to ask what it had been doing in the area in the first place. But that's what I was asked in the next street when I stood on the brakes to avoid the police Rover and two traffic cops got out.

They had to let me go eventually, although they took my fingerprints so they could eliminate them from those in the tanker's cab, promising—I don't think—to destroy them afterwards.

I could prove that Armstrong was mine and that I was really an innocent victim in all this. In fact, I told them the complete truth, missing out only the reason for being in that particular street at 5.0 a.m. Instead, I said I'd been to a party, had too much to drink and slept in the back of the cab and even had my sleeping-bag (called Hemingway) in the boot if they'd like to check—if they could get the boot open, that was. In fact, I was the one being the responsible citizen in not drinking and driving, I pointed out, claiming the moral high ground.

So they breathalysed me, but didn't get a result and had to believe me. There were a lot of questions before I was allowed to walk. Like had I ever nicked 33,000 litres of diesel before? (Armstrong ran on diesel so I was fair game.) Did I know anybody who would? Did I know a driver called Gwyn Vivian, sometimes called Taffy Duck? Where had I been the previous afternoon? Had I ever been to a transport café called Spaniard's Corner near Harwich out in Essex?

They weren't happy with all those negatives and were miffed enough not to let me use the phone on the way out, so I hoofed it to Barking station and took a tube into the City, then bus-hopped to Hackney and the house I share with assorted weirdos.

By the time I'd rung Duncan and told him where to collect Armstrong, it was early afternoon. I cooked myself some lunch, popped a can of beer and put my head down for a much-needed kip.

Duncan rang back around five and told me that it would cost up to two grand to fix Armstrong but surely the insurance would cover it. It would have, if I'd remembered to pay the last premium three weeks before. But Duncan needn't know that. I told him to go ahead and asked if he had a vehicle I could borrow in the meantime, and he said he would drop something round and put it on the bill.

I had a shower and changed into my shabbiest jeans and second-best leather jacket, having removed Springsteen from it with only a modicum of violence. He was going through a mid-life crisis (say, life number five) where he thought he was possibly not a cat at all, but some furry nesting creature.

Then it was another bus ride and another tube down to Whitechapel and, in an alley just behind the tube station, the Centre Pocket, a snooker club of ill repute where I knew I'd find Taffy Duck.

Oh yes, I'd sort of glossed over the fact that I knew him when the cops asked. In fact, I'd worked with Taffy in the past, roadying for various minor pop groups, although Taffy's heart had never been in it. He was your basic tobacconist/pub/betting-shop/back-to-the-pub man who could take two days to read the *Daily Mirror* and looked on snooker as his version of jogging. One-nighter gigs in Birmingham and then Newcastle weren't his scene.

Taffy wasn't playing on any of the tables in the Centre Pocket, he was sitting nervously on a bar stool at the corner of the bar, which had been fitted out by a carpenter who'd had bits left over from the last undertaker's he'd remodelled.

He was watching the door and was obviously relieved when he saw it was only me. He brightened when I offered to buy him another lager, but with typical Welsh foresight he said: 'I can't get you one back, you know, I'm out of work.'

'I know, Taffy, as of yesterday when you let those two lads walk off with your tanker.'

While Taffy did a double-take, the barman gave me my pint and took a fiver from me. He didn't offer any change, but as I wasn't actually a member of the snooker club, I didn't complain too loudly.

'You've picked an expensive place to be unemployed,' I said, smiling.

'Orders. I'm waiting for the boss,' said Taffy and once he was started he was difficult to stop. 'How did you know about my spot of trouble?'

Before I could answer he told me the whole story. Hired as a relief driver, he'd hitched his way to Harwich with a pair of false delivery plates under his arm, which is like a free ticket in a car belonging to anyone in the motor trade. He'd collected the tanker and stopped at the Spaniard's Corner café (pronounced 'caff' and, as one of the very few establishments remaining which wasn't a Little Chef, likely to get listed building status soon) for lunch, or 'dinner' as Taffy put it.

On his way to the toilets, in a separate block outside, he'd been tackled—yes, tackled, just like a Welsh fly-half going over the line to score—behind the knees and gone down like a sack of coal. The coal was probably Welsh too. He'd had his hands and feet tied with electrical tape, the keys of the tanker lifted from his pocket and then he'd been dumped behind the rubbish bins, to be found by one of the cooks an hour later. There had been two attackers, both in full motorbiker kit including helmets with dark visors. They hadn't said a word to him or each other, and just after he heard the tanker leave, a bike revved up.

'What could I do, Roy? I was powerless.' He said it like it was a word he'd been rehearsing. 'Anyway, how did you hear about it?'

'The Boys in Blue told me, Taffy.'

Then I told Taffy most of what had happened to me

and he rolled his eyes and tut-tutted until I'd finished, but he made no move to buy another round.

'Now, one thing bugs me, Taffy,' I said, rolling my empty glass on the bar.

'Oh yeah. What's that, Roy?'

'How much do you reckon that tanker rig was worth?'

'Dunno.' He shrugged his shoulders. 'Ninety grand? It was almost new.'

'And the diesel inside was maybe twelve grand. And when I found your truck this morning, it was empty. Now who do we know who has a central heating system that requires 33,000 litres of diesel? Or a fleet of about 600 back cabs? Or how about a garage which retails diesel? Or maybe a very thirsty cigarette-lighter for a chain-smoker?'

'What are you getting at?' asked Taffy.

'Who wants that much diesel? Who goes to the trouble of pinching your tanker, draining it and then dumping it?'

'You've got me there, Roy. But the funny thing is it happened two weeks ago to Ferdy Kyle. I was talking to him about it in here the other night. And he works for Mr McCandy as well. Good evening, Mr McCandy.'

He said it over my shoulder and I turned slightly to find most of the light blocked out by an exhibit from the *Guinness Book of Records*. (Largest dinner jacket ever made category.)

'Who's he?'

'Name's Roy Angel, Mr McCandy,' said Taffy. 'You listen to what he has to say and it'll bear me out, honest it will.'

'Sit. Over there.'

The one who'd asked who I was wasn't quite as big as the one in the dinner jacket, but it was close. He was fiftyish and dressed in a light brown suit. He had rings made out of half-sovereigns on both hands. (Rule of Life No. 85: Never trust anyone who has rings made from coins. If they do it because they think it's fashionable, then they have appalling taste. If they do it because they're good as knuckle-dusters, keep clear of them anyway.)

'I'm Donald McCandy,' said the suit. 'They call me Big Mac McCandy, but not to my face.'

I wasn't about to break the habit.

'And this'—he waved a ring at the huge dinner jacket— 'is Domestos.'

He waited for a reaction but didn't get one from me.

'That's right,' said McCandy, tempting us to laugh, 'Domestos, like the lavatory cleaner because he's—'

'Thick and strong?' offered Taffy and I winced and closed my eyes, so I didn't see exactly where Domestos hit him, but I heard it.

'Good. Now that's out of the way, the rest of the evening's your own,' said Big Mac pleasantly. 'Let's have a drink.'

We sat down, Taffy scraping his chair across the floor and staggering slightly, his eyes full of tears. I noticed that the few snooker players there were in the club had moved to the table furthest away.

The barman came to take our order. We were honoured.

'Good evening, Justin,' said McCandy. 'My usual, a Perrier for my colleague and whatever these gentlemen are drinking.'

'Large brandy,' said Taffy. He was game, I'll give him that.

'Whatever these gentlemen were drinking last,' smiled Big Mac.

'It's Julian,' said the barman and we all looked at him.

He was about nineteen, his hair fashionably short and there was a faint sneer on his lips.

'Julian,' he said again, 'not Justin.'

'Whatever,' said McCandy and let it go at that. The kid had either loadsa nerve or no brains at all.

'Now let's talk shop, gentlemen.'

Big Mac had obviously got the outline of Taffy's tale

already but he was very interested in what I had to tell him.
At the end of it, McCandy said: 'So where does that leave
us?'

I didn't like the 'us' one bit, so I kept quiet.

Taffy, of course, couldn't do that to save his life, or in
this case, mine.

'Roy's got a theory, Mr McCandy.'

'Then let's hear it, son. What did you say your name
was?'

'Angel, and it's not much of a theory.'

'Angel, eh. I don't think Domestos here has ever met
an angel before.'

'But I bet he's helped create a few,' I risked, and Mc-
Candy grinned.

'Nice one, son. Now, in your own time . . .'

'Can I just get one thing clear? What exactly is this to
do with you, Mr McCandy?' I was as polite as pie. 'And I'm
not being chopsy, I just don't get the whole picture.'

McCandy raised an eyebrow which I hoped wasn't code
for Domestos to stomach-punch me from the inside.

'Well, Mr Angel, the picture is this.' He sipped on his
'usual' which looked like *crème de menthe frappé*, but I bet
nobody ever said anything about it. 'I run an integrated
business. Garages are my core business, but also a few pubs,
this club and a couple of others. The secret is to have cash-
flow and channel it properly.

'Now, just at the moment, my garages, like most others, are having a big push on unleaded petrol. It's the in
thing. At the same time, there's a rising demand for diesel
due to the increase in private cars with diesel engines. OK?
Right. What this means is the small operator like me buys
fuel on the spot market, but because the oil companies are
running around like headless chickens supplying unleaded,
there's a shortage of tankers and drivers. I have to use what
talent is available.' He looked scathingly at Taffy. 'To top up
my regular supplies, that is. One of my garages goes
through two tankers of diesel a week, easy. Only I'm going

to run short again this week and that means I lose customers 'cos those bastard black cab drivers take their business elsewhere.'

If Taffy breathed a word about Armstrong, he wouldn't have to worry about Domestos.

'Taffy said this has happened before,' I said sympathetically.

'This is number four in two months.'

Taffy looked astonished.

'And were all the tankers recovered?'

'Yep. All bone dry. And anywhere from here to Dover, just left at the side of the road.'

'Did they travel the same route?'

'No. Ferdy Kyle got done on the M1 at Northampton.'

'At a café?'

'Yeah,' said Taffy. 'Ferdy knows all the caffs and truck stops.'

McCandy and I looked at each other. Domestos looked at Taffy, judging the distance between them.

'Ferdy's not the villain,' said Big Mac. 'He got badly hurt in the kidneys.'

'During the hijack?' I asked.

'No,' said McCandy, all matter-of-fact. 'Afterwards.'

'He wasn't too chipper the other night when he was in here,' said Taffy, thinking he was helping.

'And I suppose you discussed your route for your tanker,' I said.

'Sure. I've been out of the game for a bit, Roy. Ferdy suggested the Spaniard's Corner place as having good nosh, as well as giving me a coupla short cuts.'

'Who else was here when you and Ferdy were rabbiting?' I asked.

'Nobody. It was early on. Just me and Ferdy. No customers. Young Justin said it had been quiet all morning.'

'Julian,' McCandy corrected him softly.

'Do you find all your drivers in here, Mr McCandy?'

'Most. If not here, then in the Jubilee down the road.'

'One of your pubs?' He nodded at me. 'And do your bar staff do relief work in all your establishments?'

I thought he'd like that—'establishments'—but he just nodded silently again and then said, even quieter than before: 'Julian.'

Which is how I came to be following young Julian for the next three days. Big Mac had thought it a good idea as I was on hand and Taffy was a known face. And I had an incentive. Do it right and I'd never see Domestos again.

Duncan had supplied us with relief wheels while Armstrong was laid up, an ancient Ford Transit van which had been so badly resprayed you could still read WILLHIRE down the side. The clock said it had only done 8,000 miles and, charitably, I assumed it had only gone round once.

Big Mac had convinced himself that the spate of diesel thefts had been engineered by a rival to sabotage the legitimate parts of his business empire. To me, that seemed like putting a toothless flea on a Rottweiler but I did as I was told. Mr McCandy has that effect on people.

For two nights running he had pairs of his drivers meet in the Centre Pocket and discuss their tanker routes for the next day in earshot of Julian. I was to wait outside in my Transit until closing time and then see where Julian went and who he met. Nothing happened except I managed to get half way through Paul Kennedy's *Rise and Fall of the Great Powers,* a paperback big enough to use as a weapon in case of trouble.

Julian would usher out the last snooker players, lock the front doors, presumably wash the last of the glasses, then emerge from a side door, put three or four empty beer kegs out on the pavement, lock up and walk home. In his case, and I followed on foot twice to make sure, that was the Jubilee, one of McCandy's pubs, where he lived in the staff accommodation above the bar. Most big pubs in London have to offer rooms to their staff nowadays in order to keep them longer than a week. McCandy had leases on a dozen pubs and, by asking around during the day, I discovered he had about fifty youngish staff, mostly Irish or Australian, living in.

On the third night, I followed Julian in the van after he'd gone through his lights off, kegs out, lock up routine. He arrived back at the Jubilee and entered through the back yard, where he chatted with one of the pub's barmen who was going through the same ritual, putting out empty kegs for the delivery dray to collect next morning. Then they disappeared inside and lights came on in the upstairs rooms followed by the faint strains of a Wet Wet Wet record.

'This is getting bloody silly,' Big Mac said the next day when we met as arranged in a café/sandwich bar across the road from one of his garages in Bethnal Green. 'I've now got more diesel than I can sell and this is not helping my cash-flow situation at all.'

As my cash-flow tended to be all one way, I found it difficult to empathize, but I pretended.

'Maybe we're wrong about Julian,' I said.

'I have a feeling in my water about him,' said Mc-Candy, turning his killer look on me. 'And I told Nigel that when he hired him.'

'Nigel.'

'My son. He runs all my licensed properties.'

Well, somebody had to. With Big Mac's record he wouldn't have got a licence.

'Bright lad. Did Business Administration at university. Likes to help out his old mates and I think that's a good sign. You know, the mark of a considerate employer.'

I'd assumed that the mark of a considerate employer as far as Big Mac was concerned was leaving somebody with one good eye, but I said: 'Er . . . I don't follow, Mr Mc-Candy.'

'Nigel. And Julian. They were at university together. Julian couldn't get a job so Nigel took him on until something turned up. I have to be fair, we've had three or four of his old cronies through the firm and they've done OK. Two

of Nigel's buddies are managers in my pubs right now. And
it gives the organization a bit of class to have all those de-
grees after the names on the letterheads.'

'So Julian's got a degree, has he?' I sipped some milky
coffee and put the brain out of neutral.

'Two, as a matter of fact,' said Big Mac proudly. 'A
B.Sc. and an M.Sc. What's that got to do with anything?'

'Probably nothing.' I took a deep breath. 'Look, Mr
McCandy, we've got to think logically about this.'

'Go on, then,' he said.

'You think this is somebody getting at you. You personally.'

'Yeah,' he said slowly, thinking about it.

'But it's not—in itself—going to put you out of business, is it? Just filching the odd drop of diesel.'

'Over a hundred thousand bloody litres to date,' he
snapped. 'That's not chicken feed.'

'No, I know,' I said soothingly. 'But it isn't the way to
really screw you, is it?'

'So?'

'So that can't be the main reason for nicking the fuel,
can it? It must be because whoever's doing it actually needs
the diesel.'

I licked my lips which had suddenly dried out.

'Mr McCandy, what would you use all that fuel for
apart from putting it in engines?'

'I haven't a fucking clue.'

'I have.'

That afternoon I drove across town to Bloomsbury and
parked in a side road off Gower Street. The place I was
looking for was the rear quarter of a 1930s office block
converted into a laboratory and a small lecture theatre. It
was part of London University, but since the upsurge in the
activities of the Animal Liberationists a few years ago it
hasn't appeared on any map of university buildings and the
phone number is ex-directory.

Zoë had worked there on secondment from London Zoo for five years, lecturing and demonstrating on wild animal physiology and behaviour, but we went back longer than that. She used to get away from her parents overnight by telling them she was going badger-spotting, and even though she lived in a part of Tooting where they hadn't seen a tree since George III got out of his carriage to swap small talk with it, they believed her.

I had to blag my way past an ancient security guard who would have stood no chance against a Libbers steam team, but the key to their security was that no one knew of their existence. He reluctantly got Zoë on the internal phone and she reluctantly told him to let me in.

She was sitting in an empty lab cataloguing a tray of 35mm slides and she looked up from under huge blue-framed glasses to say: 'Well, a rave from the grave. Mr Angel. What are you after?'

'Now, Zoë darling, we had a pretty steady relationship once,' I said, showing the good teeth.

'Just remember,' she said, pointing a pencil at me, 'it was purely sexual. There was nothing Platonic about it.'

'You do remember.'

She pretended to think for a second, then smiled, swivelled on her bench stool and opened her knees so she could pull me in close. I pushed her glasses up into her hair and fumbled a hand inside her lab coat.

Between kisses, she murmured: 'So you just happened to be in the neighbourhood, eh?'

'Sort of,' I whispered into her ear, my hand trying to find the place on her lower spine which I knew was The Spot so far as she was concerned. 'And I just had a thought about that experiment you ran with the squirrels in the New Forest.'

'Squirrels? What are you after?' She tried to push me away but I held on and then started to gently rub the spot on her back. She gave a startled little 'Oh', then sighed.

'You know how you tracked them, followed their habits, with those little radios on collars.'

'Mmmmm. That's my job. Mmmm. Don't stop.'

'How effective are those transmitters? What range do they have?'

'A . . . mmmm . . . mile and a half. Why?'

'Got any kicking around? Any that could conveniently go missing?'

This time she did lever me away.

'It'll cost you,' she said, looking me in the eye.

'How much?'

She took off her glasses, laid them on the tray of slides and shook her hair out, then put her arms around my neck.

'Did I mention money?'

I took Domestos with me because he was better than a warrant card. Norman Reeves, the manager of the Shadwell Arms, the farthest-flung pub in the McCandy empire, was also the longest-serving employee of Big Mac. Without Domestos there he would have had me out on my ear for asking questions, let alone demanding to go into the pub's cellar.

The Shadwell was a backstreet boozer within a stone's throw of the Tower of London, but few tourists were encouraged to find it. The cellar floor was cleaner than any flat surface in the bar.

'How many kegs do you get through in a week?' I asked Reeves.

'Usually two or three kils or 22s and, say, six firkins or 11s or tubs, whatever we've been selling most of,' he answered carefully.

I knew enough from my own days as a barman to decode what he'd said. Strictly speaking, beer came in casks and a pressurized keg was a type of container—not a type of beer, as many think. They were known by the size of their contents: a 'kil' was a kilderkin (18 gallons) and a firkin was half that, all the imperial measures being in multiples of nine up to a barrel (36 gallons). Metric containers were measured in hectolitres, but just to confuse the foreigners, publicans referred to them by their imperial equivalents: 22 or 11 gallons. A 'tub' was slang for anything which wasn't a regular imperial or metric size, say ten gallons, and you'd get low-volume beers or cider in those.

'Are they all collected when the draymen deliver?'

'Yeah, we leave them out back. I don't have room to store empties down here.'

'And when do you get deliveries?'

Reeves looked at Domestos, who nodded, before he answered. 'Mondays, Tuesdays, Wednesdays, when-ever . . .'

I frowned at him.

'Whenever the wholesalers deliver.' He shrugged.

'You don't buy direct from the breweries?'

'No, we shop around.'

'And do the wholesalers charge deposits on the kegs?'

'Nah,' he chuckled. 'We'd get a new wholesaler if they did.'

'How many do you deal with?'

'Four or five. What's this all about?'

'Mr McCandy's called me in as a sort of efficiency ex-pert. But we don't talk about it, OK?'

'Sure, sure. Never seen you.'

'Good,' I beamed, enjoying my newfound sense of power. 'Do you have a rota for barmen for Mr McCandy's pubs?'

'Yes. Mr Nigel sends one round every week so we can swap staff if there are any gaps.'

'Just what I need. Get it, will you?'

He got the nod from Domestos and disappeared up-stairs.

'I need two of those in the back of the van,' I said to Domestos and pointed at a row of kegs. Then I picked my way carefully through puddles of spilt beer to have a look at the damp-rotted noticeboard tacked to the cellar wall near the hatch doors which lead on to the street.

There were regulation safety notices about carbon dioxide, no heavy lifting and electrical circuits in cellars and one other which I stole and folded into the back pocket of my jeans.

Domestos was grunting up the stairs to the bar. He had to move sideways as he had an 11-gallon keg under each arm. I could see that they still had green plastic caps on the syphon unit where you plugged in the beer pipe.

'No, Domestos,' I said gently. 'Empty ones.'

A day and most of a night later I was sitting in the Transit again, watching the back door of the Centre Pocket club. This time I had Big Mac McCandy sitting next to me and in the back Domestos snored gently.

'You sure this thing'll work?' He prodded the radio receiving unit on the dashboard.

'Up to a mile,' I said, hoping Zoë had been straight with me. 'Watch.'

I flicked the On switch and the centre one of the three orange lights began to flash. I'd had Duncan the Drunken solder the tiny squirrel collars to the underside lip of the two kegs I'd borrowed, and right now they were about fifty yards away on the pavement, in a stack of about a dozen, outside the Centre Pocket. It was nearly five in the morning and we'd been there since three.

They came round the corner at about half five, in a box-backed truck with no markings. It stopped outside the Centre Pocket and two guys in jeans and zipper jackets with the name of a well-known London brewery stencilled on the back got out.

'Cheeky buggers,' breathed McCandy as we watched them roll up the back of the truck and start loading the kegs.

The snooker club had obviously been the last hit on

their run, as they were lucky to get the Centre Pocket's kegs on board.

'How many do you think they've got there?' McCandy asked me, thinking along the same lines.

'Dunno. Forty? Fifty? They reckon you need about sixty to smelt down a ton of aluminium. Scrap value, twelve hundred notes a ton.'

'You know a lot,' he said suspiciously.

'I asked around.' Then I saw the look in his eyes. 'Discreetly,' I added.

'They've left a couple,' he said suddenly and loudly, but we were well away and they couldn't have heard. 'They know you've bugged those two.'

'Relax. The two they've left are stainless steel kegs, not aluminium. There's no smelt value in them but if you stick them in the back of an old car and put it through the wrecker, they add to the dead weight scrap content.'

I wondered if I'd gone too far, showing off like that, but McCandy let it go.

The truck pulled away and turned the corner. I started the Transit and flicked on the receiver. The flashing light alternated between the centre bulb and the one on the left.

'It's crude, but effective,' I said. 'And we keep out of sight. With so little traffic this time in the morning, I figured that was important.'

McCandy weighed the receiver in one hand.

'If we lose them,' he said, looking straight ahead, 'you'll need surgery to remove this.'

I put the pedal to the metal.

The smelter turned out to be in no-man's-land between Barking and Little Ilford, though there are people who live in Ilford who don't know there's a Little one.

It was tucked away in the corner of an old factory site which the developers called a prospective industrial park and the local residents called waste ground. We found it when the receiver started blinking right but there was no obvious right turn. Doubling back, it was McCandy who noticed something wrong with the shabby picket fence, but he told me not to stop but see if we could get round behind.

They'd been very clever, you had to give them that.

A whole section of ten-foot-high fence had been fixed so it could be slid aside to provide access to the site. The box truck had literally driven off the road, replaced the fence, and nobody would have been any the wiser if we hadn't had the transmitter bugs. The smelter itself was a good three hundred yards from the fake fence. The give-away was its chimney—it usually is—though these guys had given the problem some thought and had kept it to no more than ten or twelve feet high and had fitted a fan on top to disperse the smoke. There were enough other old buildings, piles of scrap iron and even broken-down cara-vans to screen the place from casual passers-by, not that there would have been many of them.

Right next to the smelter—a one-storey brick building with double iron doors—was a black fuel tank, perhaps the remains of some heating plant.

'That's where your diesel went,' I said to McCandy.

I had parked the Transit at the south end of the site, around the corner from the hole in the fence. Big Mac and I were standing on the bonnet looking over the fence and I had given him a pair of binoculars which were no bigger than opera glasses but twenty times more powerful. I'd got them from a passing acquaintance who didn't use them for bird-spotting. Well, not in the conventional sense.

'They nicked your tankers when their tank was running low. Drive it in there, transfer the fuel and dump the rig the next day.'

McCandy grunted and handed the glasses back.

The two guys we'd followed were unloading the truck, adding their haul to a rack of kegs already there. It wasn't only McCandy's pubs getting ripped; this was a well-orga-nized operation, probably buying kegs from freelance chancers at a couple of quid a go. To the side of the smelter, there were two cars, one a Porsche, and a motorbike parked.

'Let's get closer,' said Big Mac and he put his hands on the top of the rickety fence and side-jumped over.

I hesitated just long enough for Domestos to feel the need to cough discreetly, and then I followed.

We picked our way through the mud and over the junk until we were within a hundred feet of the smelter; so close I imagined I could feel the heat. We could certainly hear voices and the clanging of empty kegs and they were so confident they even had a radio on, tuned to the World Service.

Big Mac led the way around a burnt-out caravan and then stopped short. I almost bumped into his shoulder, but halted myself. Physical contact was not advisable, I reckoned.

Then I saw why he'd stopped dead: a big, sleek, brown Doberman bitch was coming at us at Mach 2, ears back in attack mode.

I looked around frantically for a weapon, and despite the junk all around, couldn't decide on anything likely to stop the dog. McCandy still hadn't moved, except to go into a fighting crouch. I did the sensible thing and moved back to give him room to get on with it.

'Hello, Louise,' he said, holding out a hand. 'There's a good girl.'

The dog skidded to a halt and rolled over, exposing her stomach and extending her tongue to wrap around Big Mac's hand.

'How long have you had this strange power over dogs?' I asked.

'Ever since she was a puppy and we gave her to my son Nigel,' he answered without looking up. Then he said: 'Louise—stay.'

The dog stayed. We moved nearer the smelt.

From behind a pile of building rubble we could see at least five men working. One had what looked like a home-made wrench which undid the pressurized seal on the top of the keg. That way the steel spear which fed carbon dioxide into the beer could be removed. It had to be unsealed in that way or it would have blown up as they put it in the furnace. One of the others had the job of collecting the seals and lopping off their tubular spears with a power saw. I'd heard that most smelting operations were given away when people found hundreds of discarded steel spears. They hadn't found a way of making money out of them. Yet.

McCandy and I could see right into the crude smelting oven they had constructed. Not that you need anything fancy. If you have enough diesel to burn, once you hit the right temperature, the aluminium kegs just collapse in front of your eyes. It was almost as if a giant invisible hand crushed them. One minute they were there, shaped and intact against the flames; the next minute they'd folded and turned to liquid which the smelters ran off to cool in moulds made out of kegs cut lengthwise. That was a bit of a giveaway if you ask me, as it was a none too subtle hint as to where the aluminium had come from.

One of the smelters pulled off a pair of asbestos gloves and sauntered out of the smelt and over to the Porsche. He opened the boot and took out an insulated cold box, the sort you take on picnics. He opened it and handed out small bottles of Perrier. It was thirsty work.

'Is that Nigel?' I asked McCandy softly and he nodded.

The two guys who'd brought the truck began to load it with the half-keg-shaped ingots.

'Do you want to follow them, Mr McCandy? Find out where they're selling the stuff?'

Big Mac shook his head. He was still staring across the site at the back of his son's head.

'Griffin Scrap Dealers in Plumstead, south of the river,' he said without turning round.

'Oh. Er . . . one of your . . . er . . . businesses?' I stood back a bit, just in case.

'Yep,' he said grimly. 'Got it in one.'

* * *

'You want me to *what*!'

'I want you to grass my son Nigel.'

'You want me to turn him over to the Old Bill? Your son?'

'And his mates. The whole shooting match,' said Big Mac, reasonably. 'Well, I can't can I? I'm not a grass.'

'Neither am I,' I protested.

'But everybody knows I'm not. I have my position to think of.'

We were sitting back in the front of the Transit, back in the City. Domestos had been sent to pick up McCandy's Jaguar from the car park of a well-known firm of solicitors.

'They send people down for smelting nowadays, Mr McCandy. The breweries have got together and they press for prosecution. It's not just a slap on the back of the legs with a ruler any more.'

'I know that,' Big Mac said philosophically. 'Prison was an education for me. It taught me how to manage people, how to plan ahead, watch your stock control, expand your options and diversify in a static market. I think of it like other people think of school: maybe the best days of your life. Doesn't mean you want to go back, though.'

He lit a small cigar and I regretted that I'd given up smoking again.

'When I think of all the dosh I've spent on private education for Nigel, and he's still daft enough to think he can cross me . . . a spot of stir will be the making of the lad.'

I had a nasty feeling he was right.

'He'll thank me for it one day, but he mustn't know it was me. That's why you've got to do it. I don't care how. I need twenty-four hours to clean out the Plumstead yard. Make sure we don't have any of his—mine, I should say— metal there.'

'But . . .'

'I'm sure you'll think of something, Roy. You seem a

resourceful lad to me. And that old taxi you run about in. Send me the bills for having it repaired. In fact, I'll open an account for you at one of the garages and put some credit behind the counter for you. Have a year's free diesel on me. How's that?'

'Very fair, Mr McCandy. But are you sure about this?'

'Absolutely.'

'I'll need a few expenses.' It was worth a shot.

He produced a wallet and dealt me ten ten-pound notes on to the dashboard.

'What about Mrs McCandy, Nigel's mum?' I tried. 'Won't she be upset if he goes down?'

A slow smile lit up his face.

'Mortified. Absobloodylutely gobsmacked. She'll have to resign from about five hundred committees and stop putting on airs and graces.' He opened the door of the Transit and made to climb out. 'Get it done,' he added.

Then, when he was standing in the road holding the door, he said: 'Or you will be. Done, that is.'

Later that morning, when I'd worked things out, I visited one of the few genuine ships' chandlers left in London and spent some of McCandy's money. Then, just short of opening time, I called at the Shadwell Arms and, using the McCandy name, got the landlord, Norman Reeves, to take me into his cellars again.

'I need a couple more kegs, Norman,' I told him. 'And I want them in the back of my van now without anyone seeing us.'

'What's going on?' he asked irritably.

'Why don't you ask Big Mac himself?'

'Will these two do?' He dragged two 11-gallon lager kegs towards the hatch which led to the street.

'Fine. One more thing. What do you use to unscrew the spears?'

Reeves pretended to look stupid. He was a gifted impressionist. 'Don't know what you mean. Them's sealed containers. You can't tamper with 'em.'

'Not even when you want to recycle some old beer, or maybe water down some good beer? I know. Now where is it?'

To my surprise he gave in before I could invoke Big Mac's name again. He reached behind a stack of boxes containing crisps and cleaning materials in equal proportions and produced a long-handled tool adapted from an adjustable wrench.

'Just lock on to the pressure seal and turn anti-clockwise,' he said.

'Thanks, Norm. Shall I get Domestos to return it when I've finished?'

'Don't bother. I've got a spare.'

The balloon went up, so to speak, at ten past seven the next morning.

It wasn't a balloon, of course. It was a large cloud of noxious orange smoke which even the fan they'd fitted to the smelter chimney couldn't cope with. It blew back and out of the oven itself, the smelters on duty running blindly out on to the waste ground, one of them, blinded, even tripping over the back bumper of the Porsche. I hoped it wasn't Nigel. He had enough to worry about.

Short of a big arrow coming down from heaven and pointing 'Here They Are', there wasn't a better way of spotting the smelter. And the assembled hordes of policemen and brewery security men took the hint, smashing through the fake fence and surrounding the choking, crying smelters.

I was watching from the far end of the site through my binoculars, standing on the Transit as Big Mac and I had done the day before. It had all gone according to plan. McCandy had made some excuse to keep Louise the Doberman at home and the naval distress flares I'd packed into the empty kegs had worked a treat once they'd been pushed into the oven.

It had taken me a couple of dry runs in packing them with sheets of plastic so they didn't rattle or fall out when the smelters took the spear out. And they were so light, the extra weight wouldn't have been noticed. When I was satisfied, I'd called the hotline number on the notice I'd stolen from the cellar of the Shadwell Arms on my first visit. The notice had explained that keg theft was illegal and gave a phone number for anyone spotting anything suspicious.

I'd done it that way, and let the brewery guys call in the cops, so I could stay out of the action.

After all, I had my reputation to think of.

Watching people getting arrested must give you an appetite. That, and the fact that I owed her for a couple of squirrel collars and had to return her radio receiver, led me to drag Zoë out of her lab for an early lunch.

Over a bottle of Othello, a fine headbanging red wine, in a Greek restaurant off the Tottenham Court Road, I told her some of what I'd been up to. (Rule of Life No. 5: Always tell the truth, but not necessarily all of it or all at once.)

She seemed most concerned about the damage to Armstrong, but I told her not to worry, he was being well looked after. That reminded me I owed her for the transmitter collars and I reached into the back pocket of my jeans for the remains of Big Mac's folding money.

As I pulled out my depleted wad of tenners, something else came with it and fluttered to the floor under the table.

Zoë bent over and picked it up. It was the notice about keg thefts I'd pinched from the pub and it was folded so that the pay-off line, printed in red, was clearly visible. It said: KEG THEFT HOTLINE—TO CLAIM YOUR REWARD, and there was a number.

'What's this?' she asked, handing it over.

'Think of it as extra car insurance,' I said. 'You can never have too much.'

Martin Russell

DIAMOND AND PEARL

MARTIN RUSSELL became a crime writer by accident (he originally intended to write humorously) but he holds definite views on what a suspense thriller should be: first and foremost, it should grip as firmly as does this skilfully told tale.

Martin Russell has written more than thirty crime novels, and a volume of short stories. He is unmarried, and lives in Kent.

'ARE SIX BOTTLES going to be enough?'

'I should *hope* so.' Miss Kerridge's tone was severe. In her estimation, half a dozen bottles of champagne between a staff of twenty-four was roughly the equivalent of a Roman orgy in the reign of Caligula: old Mr Smithers, who had founded the firm, would have spluttered into his beard at the mere sight of the goblets laid out on the reception desk. 'There's sparkling wine, too,' she pointed out, 'for those who prefer it. What more do we need?'

'Nothing, Kerry. If you say so.' Reg Barcroft, junior partner in the practice, murmured the emollient in a way that produced from Miss Kerridge one of her suspicious glances, eyes slanted behind her spectacles, silvered head listing slightly to the left. She was never quite certain whether young Mr Reginald was being deferential, as befitted her thirty-six years' devoted service to the firm, or slyly satirical, as suited his character. While not wholly disapproving of him, she was keeping her final opinion on hold, pending a performance rating over a five-year span.

'In any case,' she went on, granting him the benefit of the doubt for the moment, 'there isn't room for more bottles, unless we stack all the in-trays . . . and you know what happened before.'

Reg nodded solemnly. 'The wrong letters in four wrong envelopes. One quartet of highly mystified clients.'

'So we'd best not repeat that mistake. Personally,'

averred Miss Kerridge, giving an extra polish to the presentation cut-glass fruit bowl arrayed on a square of cloth at the centre of the desk, 'I'm not in favour of office parties in any shape or form. They just create disorder.'

'You'd sooner decamp to a pub or somewhere?'

'A restaurant,' she corrected him. 'A civilized meal, with speeches afterwards. Far more acceptable, in my view.'

'I think, Kerry, you're in a minority of one.'

Miss Kerridge winced for the second time. She tolerated Mr Reginald's mode of address only because the alternative was worse: for some months after his arrival he had referred to her uproariously as Miss Kerridge of Justice, which he seemed to regard as a joke of such penetration as to warrant unending repetition, even when her initial wintry smile had long since evaporated. People these days were insensitive, she found. Free and easy nominal relationships were now taken for granted among the younger generation. She sighed. Old Mr Smithers would have kept it to surnames and salutations, and quite right too.

The telephone buzzed. Reg picked it up. 'I'm afraid we're closed,' he informed it. 'Try in the morning, would you? Nine-thirty. Many thanks.' Dropping the receiver, he leaned across to deactivate the switchboard. 'Safe at last,' he announced. 'How about asking the girls to fetch in the food, Kerry? Malcolm should be showing his face soon.'

And that was another thing. The only proper title for the senior partner was Mr Corfield. Here again, Miss Kerridge remained the only one in step. Everyone else referred to the nephew of old Mr Smithers as Malcolm or, worse still, Malc: and, what was worst of all, he seemed to like it. Miss Kerridge heaved another sigh. Either the world had drifted out of touch, or she had. No doubt it was something of each.

An hour later, she felt calmer. The ice had crazed and was starting to fall apart, helped along by the cocktails which had been Mr Reginald's personal contribution to the occasion. Strange, how people who had been working

shoulder to shoulder all day should have to readjust themselves, begin again from scratch when they reassembled in the same place for a different purpose. Before long, it would be time for the presentation and the speeches. Miss Kerridge hoped nobody would look to her for a few words. However, she had scribbled a paragraph or two on a slip of office paper folded into her sleeve, just in case.

'Sausage roll, Janet?'

She accepted one from the conveyancing clerk, Liz Embury, an engaging young woman of whom she unreservedly approved. They swapped smiles. 'It seems to have warmed up nicely,' Miss Kerridge remarked, not alluding to the sausage and pastry. 'The presentation in about ten minutes, would you say?'

'Twenty,' Liz suggested. 'By that time, everyone will be past caring whether Malcolm makes a speech or not.' She gazed pensively at the shock-haired figure of the senior partner, who was discussing golf with a circle of litigation staff members by the window. 'You wouldn't think, would you, he was getting on for fifty? He still looks thirty-five. When you think, all the work and responsibility . . . How long is it since his uncle died?'

'Fourteen years.' If asked, Miss Kerridge could have quoted the precise date. 'Mind you, my dear, he'd been in poor shape for quite some while before he . . .'

'Passed the reins to Malcolm,' Liz finished tactfully. 'Who certainly seems to have risen to the challenge. Although he's looked a little thoughtful just lately. Have you noticed that?'

Miss Kerridge nodded. 'He has a lot on his mind.'

'Show me a lawyer who hasn't. Do I detect signs of movement?' Liz demanded, dumping her sherry glass on an adjacent tray. 'Reg is twitching a bit. I believe we're going to have the presentation now, whether we like it or not.'

Moments later, Reg Barcroft called the gathering to order and took up station alongside the reception desk. 'I'm not going to make a speech,' he proclaimed, to general deri-

sion, 'but I'd like your attention for just a moment so that
the business part of this event can occur, prior to our getting back to enjoying ourselves—sorry, Malc. Seriously,
we're looking forward to hearing from you. But first, it's my
very pleasant duty . . .'

Lifting the cut-glass bowl reverently from its cloth, he
implanted it into the receptive palms of his partner, who
examined its design with appreciative intensity. 'It comes
from all of us,' Reg continued, 'with our best wishes for the
firm's increasing success and prosperity—naturally, since
we're all in it together—plus our personal thanks to yourself
for all you do to make our tasks . . . well, you know what
I'm driving at, so now I'll shut up and invite you to address
the horde.' He stepped aside, leading the applause lustily.
Malcolm Corfield faced his audience.

'An extremely affable horde,' he declared. 'Don't panic,
I'm not about to make a speech either. But there are one or
two things. As you know, Reg and I felt we could hardly let
an occasion like this slide by without some sort of ceremo-
nial rite, though I wasn't anticipating a personal gift: that's
a bonus, and I do thank you all, at the same time voicing
my gratitude for the way you've pulled together, the lot of
you, to bring the firm of Smithers, Corfield and Barcroft to
its present enviable status in the legal profession. I'm not
going to embarrass anyone by singling them out, with one
notable exception . . .'

He turned to regard Miss Kerridge, who went bright
pink. 'If diamond is the value of our jubilee,' he said gravely,
'then Janet here can only be described as the pearl at the
heart of our existence.' Mirth and applause rippled across
the room. 'The debt we owe her can scarcely be put into
words, but when I tell you . . .'

Malcolm paused to frown at the floor. Presently, as
though with something of an effort, he looked up again.
'Out of the sixty years this firm has served the community,
no fewer than thirty-six of them have been favoured by Janet's expert and tireless contribution to the smooth running

of the office machine, first in the later years of my uncle and subsequently . . .'

Once more his voice faded. Reg gave him a quizzical glance. 'Emotion getting the better of you, Malc? Let us know if you want a hankie.'

'I'll be fine . . .' His partner was clutching the rim of the desk. Concern manifested itself among the staff. Moving forward, Reg gripped his arm.

'What's Tracy been putting in the sandwiches?'

'Nothing,' protested the office junior.

'Just as I suspected. You should open your own takeaway, love. You'll make a fortune.' Reg spoke gaspingly. By now he was unequivocally holding his partner up, trying to impel him towards a chair which someone had dragged forward. Malcolm's knees were splaying; his head lolled. He seemed to have no control over his limbs. Miss Kerridge hurried to his side.

'Give me his other arm,' she instructed. 'Careful, now . . . Valerie, my dear, do you think you can slide the chair a little this way? That's much better. Now if two of you can hold it steady while we . . .'

Between them, she and Reg manoeuvred the racked frame of the senior partner into the desired position, where he sprawled untidily, arms hanging loose, legs contorted, chin resting on neck. Reg stood back to eye him in puzzlement. 'Never seen him like this before. Should we fetch a doctor?'

'At once,' Miss Kerridge said forthrightly.

Reactivating the switchboard, Liz put a call through. While she was talking, the figure in the chair began to slide floorwards. Despite all efforts to arrest his descent, he arrived in twisted fashion at carpet level where he lay motionless, face down. Kneeling, Miss Kerridge felt his pulse. After a few moments she looked around at a circle of appalled expressions.

'I don't think it's any use,' she told them. 'I'm afraid he's gone.'

* * *

It was approaching eight o'clock before the police concluded their preliminary inquiries. Statements had been taken; the misshapen form of Malcolm had been removed after an examination by the police surgeon, who had had a murmured exchange with the investigating officer, Detective-Inspector Lazard, before departing to return to his supper. Most of the staff had been allowed to go, leaving Reg, Liz and Miss Kerridge to answer the residual questions. At a signal from the Inspector, Miss Kerridge joined him at the window. Lazard referred to his notes.

'Office administrator,' he read aloud. 'Which means, Miss Kerridge, I take it, that you more or less run the place?'

'That's putting it a little strongly, Inspector. My job is to keep things ticking over at ground level, so to speak. Staff supervision, office stationery . . . all that.'

'So you're well acquainted with the people here. Any internal problems—hidden tension, personality clashes—you'd be likely to know of them?'

Miss Kerridge agreed cautiously that this was probable.

Lazard further lowered his voice. 'What I'm wondering is whether you can put your finger on any particular animosity between Mr Corfield and a member of staff in recent months. Anything outstanding.'

'That might have placed a strain on his heart, you mean?'

'It wasn't a heart attack.'

'Not his heart?'

'No. He was poisoned.'

Miss Kerridge gave the Inspector a straight look. 'Is that what you think?'

'It's not what I think. It's what all the symptoms indicate, unmistakably. Exactly what it was, we shan't know until tests have been carried out.'

Miss Kerridge sat heavily on the window-sill. 'I see,' she said faintly.

'This is why I'm asking. Can you point me at someone who might have had reason to want Mr Corfield . . . out of the way? To put it bluntly.'

'Quite inconceivable, Inspector. I can't imagine Mr Corfield making enemies.'

'Single, was he?'

'Yes. Like his partner, Mr Barcroft.'

Lazard glanced across at Reg, who was talking in an undertone to Liz. 'Did they see eye to eye?'

'The partners? They seemed on the best of terms.'

'You see,' the Inspector resumed after a pause, 'there are only two practical alternatives. One is that the dose was administered by accident—which seems unlikely. Is any sort of toxin kept on the premises?'

'We do have mice,' Miss Kerridge admitted. 'This building is so old, vermin are inclined to come in through the cracks from time to time, and our Man Friday, Mr Ridgeway, who does the stamping and completions for us, is also responsible for dealing with the pests. He keeps mouse bait somewhere. I'm not quite sure what he uses.'

Lazard made a note. 'I'll be having another word with Mr Ridgeway.'

'But I'm sure he'd keep any stuff like that well tucked away. What's the second alternative, Inspector?'

'That Mr Corfield gave himself the dose, on purpose.'

'Suicide? Oh, that's nonsense. He'd no reason.'

'Can you be sure of that? He might have had concealed worries. Health. Business problems.'

'As far as I know, he was a very fit man. Played golf twice a week. As for business . . . well, I can only say the firm has been exceptionally active just lately.'

The Inspector looked at her. 'Anything about this strike you as somewhat odd, Miss Kerridge?'

'In what way, Inspector?'

'Didn't Mr Corfield's uncle, the firm's founder, die in a similar way?'

Miss Kerridge blinked. 'Now that you mention it, it's

true that he did collapse in the office from poisoning, fourteen years ago. In his case it was certainly suicide. That was the verdict recorded at the inquest.'

Lazard gazed past her at the street lamps outside. 'I can recall vaguely . . . Some kind of an overdose, wasn't it?'

Miss Kerridge signified assent. 'Mr Smithers was on tablets for a chest condition which caused him a lot of distress. One day we found him slumped over his desk with an empty cup next to his face. He'd put fifteen tablets, or thereabouts, into his coffee and drunk the lot.'

'How many was he meant to take?'

'According to my brother, who knew about such things, it would have been two a day.'

The Inspector's abstraction deepened. Presently his attention returned to the room. 'Doesn't get us very far, does it? Not as regards Mr Corfield, that is. We may know more tomorrow, after the various wineglasses have been examined —although, there again, we're up against problems.'

'Why is that?'

'Even if we find traces of a poison in one of 'em,' he explained, 'we've no means of establishing who put it there.'

'No. No, I see.'

'To some extent we may have to rely on bluff.'

'Interrogating everyone,' Miss Kerridge hazarded astutely, 'in the hope that the guilty party will assume you know more than you do?'

'Something of the sort.' Lazard looked mournful. 'Always tricky, an event of this nature during a social occasion when everyone has a drink in their hands and no one's taking much notice of the physical interchange of glassware. How do you narrow it down?'

Miss Kerridge pondered. 'Suppose the mouse bait is normally kept by Mr Ridgeway in a wineglass? It could have accidentally found its way on to the drinks tray. One of the girls might have taken it from his room to make up the numbers.'

'Wouldn't she have noticed it already contained crystals, or whatever?'

'She could have taken it for crushed ice,' Miss Kerridge said feebly.

The Inspector sniffed. 'Maybe it's time we stopped surmising. Mr Ridgeway himself can no doubt—'

'Do you want to see his room first, Inspector?'

'It's an idea.'

Up in the Man Friday's second-floor lair, Lazard carried out a rapid search of the fitments and furniture, sneezing from the dust which billowed from shelves and cupboard-tops. Miss Kerridge said apologetically, 'The cleaners do come in regularly, but with so much lying around . . . Have you found something?'

Turning, he showed her a glass tumbler he had removed from a high shelf. 'What's this stuff?'

She peered. 'Sugar crystals, perhaps, for coffee?'

'We'll ask Mr Ridgeway.' Returning downstairs, Lazard had a muttered word with his sergeant before informing Miss Kerridge and the others that they could depart. Under the Inspector's supervision Miss Kerridge locked up the premises, the keys to which were then passed into his custody. 'We'll be here,' he pledged, 'first thing in the morning, to open up, so that you can push on with your own work while we're nosing around and getting in your way. I take it, Mr Barcroft, you're now in sole charge of the business?'

Reg looked a little startled. 'I suppose I am. Sorry, Inspector, if I sound obtuse. I'm a little devastated at the moment.'

'Sleep it off,' Lazard advised, 'and we'll talk in the morning.'

With his sergeant he took off in a police car, leaving the three of them irresolute on the pavement. Reg said blankly, 'Not quite the ending to the party we'd envisaged. Can I give anyone a lift home?'

'I've my car round the corner,' said Liz. She looked pale, and sounded taut.

'Kerry? Can I drop you off?'

'If you're sure, Mr Reginald. I don't want to cause any inconvenience.'

He gave a hollow laugh. 'I think we can withstand a little extra. 'Night, Liz. Try to get some sleep.'

Packed into the front seat of Reg's Vauxhall Carlton, Miss Kerridge permitted herself to sag as he backed into the street and drove off. The first half-mile went by in silence. First to speak again was the surviving partner.

'Where was the Inspector off to in such a rush, Kerry, do you know?'

'To see Mr Ridgeway. He wanted to ask him about something he found in his room.'

'Don't tell me Mike's under suspicion?'

'I don't know that anybody is. I have the feeling—and I believe the Inspector does—that what happened this evening was accidental.'

Reg's gaze left the road briefly. 'How come?'

Miss Kerridge considered before replying. 'If Mr Corfield was poisoned,' she said precisely, 'as they suspect, then it's quite on the cards that mouse bait is to blame. It's also feasible that it found its way into Mr Corfield's wine-glass by chance. Mr Ridgeway, you see—'

'Keeps the stuff in a tumbler in his room.' Reg nodded. 'I've seen him put it back there.'

'So have I. I knew what it was when the Inspector showed me, though I pretended not to be sure. They'll have it analysed anyhow, won't they?'

'You bet. Apart from which, Mike will tell them all they want to know. Question is,' Reg added after a pause in which he throttled back to a statelier pace along a residential street, 'how would any of the bait have got accidentally into Malcolm's drink? And why didn't he notice the taste?' Bringing the car to a halt beneath a street lamp, he sat tapping the wheel with his fingers. 'Kerry, I'm flummoxed. Unless Mike had more bait in another container which he'd brought downstairs, and somehow or other—'

'If he did, the Inspector will hear about it from him,' Miss Kerridge observed. 'The immediate priority, Mr Reginald, if I might suggest, is to keep things ticking over until you can find a new partner to help run the business. Have you anyone in mind?'

Reg looked hunted. 'It's rather soon to be thinking about it. I've not got down to making any plans . . .'

'But you do intend to carry on?'

'Oh, sure. Give us a spot of time, Kerry, to get myself together. We shan't replace someone like Malcolm in a hurry.'

'Why not?'

He looked at her as though she had struck him across the face. 'Well . . . you surely know that as well as I do. Malcolm had everything at his fingertips. He knew everybody. He's virtually irreplaceable.'

'I question that,' Miss Kerridge said briskly.

'How do you mean?'

'I mean, Mr Reginald, that you may find yourself with more of a task on your hands than you imagine, when you take over. There's some salvage work to be done.'

'*Salvage*? Kerry, what the blazes are you on about?'

'I'm referring to the deficit on the clients' account.'

Reg choked over the wheel. Recovering partially, he said in a strangled voice, 'You're not serious?'

'It's hardly an occasion for jokes,' she said on a note of rebuke. 'The clients' account is in deficit to the tune of thirty-eight thousand pounds.'

'How do you know?'

'Mr Corfield told me so himself.'

'*Told* you?'

'Two weeks ago. He called me in one evening, after the rest of you had gone, and unburdened himself. Said he'd met this young woman who had infatuated him, and he'd been drawing on the clients' account to spend large sums of money on her. Now he was in a complete financial mess and didn't know how to get out of it. He wanted my advice.'

Reg gaped at her. 'Did you give him any?'

'What could I say? I know nothing of cash-juggling on that scale. I did suggest he might remortgage his house to pay the money back.'

'Did he think that was an idea?'

'He'd already taken out a second mortgage, to spend on the woman. He'd come to the end of his resources.'

Reg bowed his head to rest it on the wheel. 'I don't believe I'm hearing this,' he groaned. 'I can't take it in . . . Have you told this to the Inspector?'

'Goodness, no!' Miss Kerridge was appalled. 'First I wanted to acquaint you with the situation, in case there was something you could do.'

He sat breathing heavily against the dashboard. Finally he raised his head. 'I'm beginning to see,' he said slowly, 'why you're so anxious to convince Lazard it was an accident. You think Malcolm committed suicide—is that it?'

Miss Kerridge gestured. 'It would have been a way out,' she said simply.

Reg sat up straight. 'There is something I can do. I can raise a loan on my own property, square the account before the deficit comes to light. It's the only solution, if we want the firm to survive.'

She clasped her hands. 'Do you think it's possible?'

'I'll see about it tomorrow. With luck, I can get the cash through in a day or so—my credit's good—and have the account restored to normal in time to avert disaster. My God, Kerry, what a blinder. Old Malcolm. I never dreamt . . . Why didn't he confide in me? We could have thrashed it out together.'

'I expect,' Miss Kerridge said tactfully, 'he didn't want to worry you.'

'Like I'm not worried now?' Restarting the car, Reg accelerated away in the manner of a man who has reached a decision. 'Help me stall the Inspector, Kerry, in the morning. Keep at him with the accident theory. If it does come

out eventually that it was suicide, it won't matter—I'll have the firm's finances straight again by then. Is it a deal?'

Miss Kerridge relaxed into her seat harness. 'It's a deal.'

The atmosphere at Smithers, Corfield and Barcroft the following morning was dreamlike, verging on nightmare. After an early interview with Inspector Lazard, Reg went out, giving Miss Kerridge a significant glance as he left. With the aid of Valerie at the switchboard, she did her best to fend off clamorous clients until she was called in by the inspector, who had taken over Malcolm's office to conduct his inquiries. He asked her to close the door.

'We've established,' he said abruptly, 'that it was a rodenticide that killed Mr Corfield. I've also verified with Mr Ridgeway that it's mouse bait he keeps in that tumbler in his room, *and* that there's less of it remaining than there should be. All of which starts to add up. The point is—'

'I have a confession to make, Inspector,' Miss Kerridge interposed, her voice tremulous.

He paused to study her. 'Fire away,' he invited.

'I did know that it was mouse bait. And after you left last night, I remembered something. A month or so ago, Mr Corfield asked me to arrange for some bait to be put down in his room here, because he'd found mouse-droppings on the carpet. So, without troubling to mention it to Mr Ridgeway, who was very busy at the time, I brought some down in an old teacup and placed it myself. There, along the skirting-board.' She pointed.

Lazard's eyes flickered aside, then returned to her. 'Was it taken?'

'It went.'

'And the teacup . . . ?'

'There were some crystals left in it,' Miss Kerridge said bravely, 'so I put it away in the bookcase over there. I thought it might come in handy if the mice came back.'

The Inspector sprang up. 'Which side of the bookcase?'

'On the right.'

He opened the relevant door. 'It's not there now.'

'That's what I was afraid of.'

Lazard returned to Malcolm's desk. 'Mr Corfield could have come across it and cleared it out.'

'Yes; or the cleaners. They might have discovered it yesterday and taken it through to the kitchen—we have one at the back, where Tracy makes tea and coffee for everyone —and left it on the worktop with the crystals still inside. Then—'

'You're suggesting that Tracy might have made coffee in it for Mr Corfield, without emptying it first?'

'Nothing of the kind. Tracy would never do such a thing. But Mr Corfield himself might have. He was careless in that way. He could well have thought the cup held sugar crystals. They do look rather like them.'

Leaning back in Malcolm's chair, the Inspector hugged his chest with his arms, frowned downwards for a space. 'So, we have a scenario in which Mr Corfield wanders out to the kitchen to make himself coffee—was he in the habit of doing that?'

'Occasionally. And he might well have done so last evening, when Tracy and some of the others were occupied with getting the food ready for the party. Things were a little chaotic at the time. What if Mr Corfield just grabbed up the first teacup he could find . . . ?'

'It's plausible,' the Inspector allowed grudgingly. 'Certainly it squares with the fact that we've so far discovered no trace of poison in any of the wineglasses. That had me stumped, I'll admit. Well now, Miss Kerridge, let me see this kitchen of yours. That teacup may still be around.'

'If so, Inspector, I'm afraid it's probably been rinsed out like the rest. All the crockery was thoroughly washed, ready for use, before the party.'

Lazard placed his face in his cupped palms. Surfacing presently, he remarked, 'One way and another, this is turning out to be an exercise in frustration. Show us the kitchen, anyway.'

Tracy was there, buttering bread rolls. She looked up wide-eyed as they entered. Miss Kerridge said reassuringly, 'We shan't disturb you, dear, for long. Whom are you doing those for?'

'Peter Follick in Litigation. He hasn't time to go out for lunch. Liz Embury wants some too.'

'Keep you busy, don't they?' Lazard's gaze roamed the kitchen. 'We're looking for a teacup.'

'Here's one.' The girl held it out.

'No—a particular one. It might have been brought in here yesterday evening for rinsing out, before the party got under way.'

'What does it look like?'

'It's chimney-pot shaped,' said Miss Kerridge, 'with a curved rim. Pale blue exterior, white on the inside.'

Tracy's brow puckered. 'Don't remember seeing it.'

'It must be here. It's gone from where I left it in Mr Corfield's room, and it hasn't found its way back to Mr Ridgeway's den, so . . .' Reaching past the girl, Miss Kerridge tugged open the drawer of one of the kitchen units. Instead of closing it at once, she felt about inside it with her right hand, a little urgently. After a moment she glanced up. Tracy and the Inspector were watching her. She said, 'It's not here.'

Lazard twitched an eyebrow. 'Did you expect it to be?'

'I thought perhaps it might have been stowed away there.'

'Inside a drawer? Rum place for a teacup. Although as a matter of fact, Miss Kerridge,' the Inspector went on, selecting his words with apparent care, 'it so happens that you're absolutely right. The cup *was* inside there.'

'How do you know?'

'We found it, last evening. Unwashed, with coffee traces at the bottom. Oh, and two sets of fingerprints.'

Miss Kerridge took in breath. 'Fingerprints . . .'

'One lot, on the handle, match up with those of Mr Corfield which we found on a ballpen and several other

objects from his desk. So he was obviously the last to use it. Correction: the second last. The final handler left prints on the base and the rim. Consistent with the way it would have been held as it was deposited in that drawer.' Lazard demonstrated in mid-air with finger and thumb.

Miss Kerridge regarded him steadily. 'Whose prints are those?'

'Ah. That should tell us quite a lot, shouldn't it? Would you be agreeable, Miss Kerridge, to giving us a sample of yours, along with everyone else?'

'You're not implying—'

'No: I'm asking. And here's another question for you. What made you go straight to that drawer to look for the teacup—and why were you so thrown when it wasn't inside?'

The tight look on Miss Kerridge's face disintegrated slowly into a kind of a smile. 'That was rather smart of you, Inspector. You set a little trap, didn't you? I should have tumbled to it. What put you on the scent?'

Positioning a stool, Lazard sat her gently upon it. 'The fact that young Tracy here has sharp eyes. She spotted you last evening, coming out of Mr Corfield's room at about five-fifteen with that blue teacup, and saw you take it into the kitchen. When I learned from Mr Ridgeway that the cup had recently gone missing from his shelf, I started putting two and two together . . . but it still only made three. So, having unearthed the cup last night, I waited to see whether someone might volunteer any information about it.'

'Surely it must have been obvious—'

'Which you, Miss Kerridge, duly did. You concocted that fable about Mr Corfield making coffee for himself and grabbing the first cup he came across. When, in fact, it was you who made the coffee for him . . . on top of those lethal granules which the cup already contained. You took it in to him, and later on it was you who carried the empty cup out, choosing a moment when the kitchen was unoccu-

pied so that you could slip it into the drawer.' The Inspector studied her curiously. 'Why did you do that? You must have guessed it would be found.'

Miss Kerridge sighed, and thought for a moment. 'What I hoped originally,' she explained, 'was that it would be assumed that the poison was in one of the wineglasses, which had been rinsed out before Mr Corfield—' she paused delicately—'succumbed to the effects. You see, I knew there would be a time-lag of an hour or so between ingestion and expiry. My brother trained as a pharmacist, and I've often picked his brains on matters relating to drugs and toxins. So I tried to work it that the mouse bait took effect well after the party had got under way.'

'Your accuracy,' the Inspector said heavily, 'is to be commended.'

'Of course, I did mean to rinse the cup out. Only as I reached the kitchen I heard somebody coming along behind me and I rather lost my head, so I hid the cup quickly inside that drawer, meaning to come back later and see to it. Then it occurred to me . . .' Again she paused to glance up at the girl, who was gazing at her in horrified fascination. 'Would you like to run along, my dear? This can't be pleasant for you.'

Lazard gave Tracy a nod. She went out. 'It occurred to me,' Miss Kerridge resumed, 'that by leaving it there, unwashed, I might be able to sow a little confusion if it became necessary . . . lead the police to think that Mr Corfield had given the poison to himself, either by accident or design. I was forgetting about fingerprints, and I was reckoning without Tracy's observation.'

The Inspector leaned against the sink. 'What I don't understand is . . . why?'

'He was about to ruin the firm, Inspector. I couldn't allow that, could I, now?'

'Ruin the firm? How?'

'Never you mind,' Miss Kerridge said crisply. 'All being

well, the danger should be averted quite shortly. That's all that counts.'

'The life of the senior partner, by comparison, doesn't matter a fig?'

'All things are relative, Inspector, are they not? My responsibility throughout has been to the staff in general. When I was first appointed there were just five of us, but the same principle applied. The firm was their livelihood. Mine too. One simply can't permit human excess or negligence to interfere with that.'

Lazard's mouth hung open as he surveyed her. 'If that's the way you feel about it . . .'

She rose from the stool. 'You know, Inspector, you're conning me a little, aren't you? You've really no conclusive evidence. But don't worry, I shan't go back on my admission. I've felt for some while that it was time to put the record straight. Last time, it was just too absurdly easy. I suppose it's been nibbling at my conscience ever since.'

'Last time,' he repeated. 'We wouldn't be talking about an occasion fourteen years ago, by any chance?'

'Dear old Mr Smithers,' she said reflectively. 'He was completely past it, you know, Inspector. Health breaking down, neglecting his clients' affairs . . . but he would *not* admit it, utterly *refused* to lift his hand from the helm. He had to go. It was the only possible way to protect the continuity of the firm. You do see that, don't you? If you don't, you're not the man I've been taking you for.' She gave a sudden, piercing shriek of laughter as he shepherded her from the kitchen.

Eric Wright

TWINS

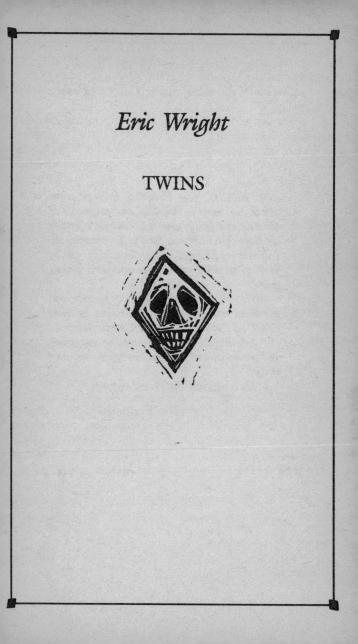

ERIC WRIGHT, now Canada's foremost crime writer, was born in England but emigrated to Canada as a young man. He lived for a year in the North, on Hudson's Bay, before entering the University of Manitoba, where he paid his way by working on construction sites and as a fishing guide.

He now lives and lectures in Toronto, but has found time to write seven outstanding crime novels, all featuring Inspector Charlie Salter.

Eric Wright has also written for magazines and television, and is an accomplished short-story writer.

He is married with two daughters.

'I WANT TO GET IT RIGHT,' he said. 'After making the mistake in the last book about how long it takes to get from Toronto to Detroit, I want this one to be watertight. So just go along with me until I'm sure that it'll work.'

They were standing on the edge of an old mineshaft about ten miles north of Sudbury. The shaft had been sunk in the 'thirties and to reach it they had had to claw their way through dense scrub pine and pick the locks on two chain-link fences that guarded the hole. At least it was too late in the year for mosquitoes. She wondered how he had found this place.

He seemed to hear what was in her mind. 'I found it two years ago,' he said. 'I came up here hunting with Art. Someone told us we might find a bear along at the garbage dump but we missed the road and came to this place.'

He was a writer of detective stories. As far as he could, he liked to 'walk the course' of his plots until he was sure they would work. She always went along as a primary test that the story was possible. The stories often took them to some pleasant places, so it was like getting a second holiday, but this time she had come because she needed to know what was in his mind. Sudbury in October is not a popular vacation spot. 'Tell me again,' she said. 'How does he get her to come this far? I wouldn't.'

'You just did,' he pointed out.

'That was research. Unless you make your villain a

writer, you're going to have trouble. What is he, by the way?'

'I haven't decided yet. It's not important. I want to make sure this works, then I can flesh it out.'

'Yes, but it doesn't work if the reader can't believe she would stumble through a quarter-mile of bush in this godforsaken landscape. You've got to find a good reason.'

'I'll find one. Let's get the plot straight, shall we?'

'This isn't the way you usually work. Usually you get the characters first, then let the plot grow out of them. So you say, anyway.'

'Yeah, but this plot is ingenious. I mean, the villain thinks it is, so I want to test it before I spend my time creating his world. OK?'

'OK, so now he kills her. Right? And drops the body down there.' She kicked a small rock over the edge of the hole and listened hard, but there was no 'ploomp' or rattle of the sound of the rock reaching bottom. It must go down hundreds of metres.

'That's right. He throws the gun in after her; he's made sure it's untraceable. Then he drives south to the motel in Parry Sound where they have a reservation. When he gets there, it's dark.' He looked at the sky turning pink in the west. 'He registers as her.'

'Where did you get this idea?'

'From us. People are always saying we look alike, as if we're a couple of gerbils.'

'Where does he change his clothes?'

'In the car, on a side road, probably the Pickerel River road, somewhere quiet. He doesn't actually have to change much: just put on a blonde wig, lipstick, glasses.' He looked down at himself to show what he meant. Both of them were dressed in sneakers, blue jeans and heavy bush jackets that came well below the waist. 'Then he checks in at the motel as her, saying "her" husband is turning the car around or picking up beer or something. The point is the motel people have seen "her" and believe that he is there, too. An

hour later, he goes to the motel office, as himself, to ask for a wake-up call, so now the motel people have seen "her" and him. Then, around midnight, the fighting starts. The people in the units on either side hear a hell of a row going on, sounds of someone being smacked around, and it goes on so long they complain to the desk, and the night clerk phones over and asks them to pipe down.'

'The row is on tape, right?'

'Right. Then early in the morning the row starts again and there's a lot of door-banging and the neighbours see "her" leaving, walking away. At breakfast-time, he checks out, leaving a message in case his wife returns. He tells the clerk she walked out on him during the night. She's probably gone to another motel. His message is that he's not going to wait around; he's gone home.'

'So he left the motel in the blonde wig, then came back quietly as himself a bit later. Wasn't he taking a chance?'

'Not really. If anyone saw him, he could always say he had tried to follow his wife, but she disappeared. And that's that. He goes home and when his wife doesn't appear that day he reports it to the police. But in circumstances like these it looks likely that the wife has simply gone off somewhere. It's a few weeks before he can get the police seriously interested.'

'And when they do take it seriously, do they find her?' There was not much light left now. In the east the sky was almost black.

'I don't know. It doesn't matter. A few weeks is as good as six months.'

'They'll suspect him. After the row.'

'But they won't be able to prove anything. When he leaves the motel after breakfast, he checks in with the Ontario Provincial Police in Parry Sound in case "she" has checked in with them, and he does the same thing all the way down to Toronto, establishing a solid time trail with no gaps for him to drive back up to Sudbury. Then it's easy to make sure he's covered for the next week in Toronto.'

'It might work,' she said. 'Have you figured out how you are going to solve it? How Porter will, I mean.' Gib Porter was the writer's hero.

'Not yet.'

'You could start with a hunch. You could find out what time he left Sudbury and why it took him five hours to get to Parry Sound. Did anyone see his car parked along the highway, stuff like that?'

'Why would anyone be suspicious?'

She pondered. 'Her father. He never liked the man she married, never trusted him, so he hires Gib Porter.' Now it was close to dark. 'What about the car? Someone might have seen their car parked along the highway.'

'It's rented. Perfectly ordinary rented car. If anyone sees it they won't memorize the licence plate. They'll just assume that it's a couple of hunters. But I haven't seen anyone around, have you?'

'No, I haven't. Who would be wandering around this moonscape?' She had to admit that he seemed to have everything covered. 'In the meantime, old buddy-boy, we'd better be getting back.' She walked away from him, towards the road. She needed to know one more thing.

'It'll work, all right,' he said. 'It's going to work.' He reached inside his jacket and pulled out the little hand-gun he had bought in Detroit. 'Don't turn round, Lucy,' he said. 'I said, *don't turn around.*'

And that was it. It wasn't a game. She said, 'It isn't going to work,' as he pulled the trigger once, twice, three times.

Everything else went smoothly. His wife had often criticized his plots for being too complicated, but this one worked. Two hours later the night clerk at the Sturgeon Motel in Parry Sound signed in Mrs Harry Coates, a blonde lady with sunglasses (though it was quite dark), while her husband unloaded the car. During the night the clerk had to call them twice to ask them to pipe down because they

were fighting and arguing so loudly that the guests on either side had called to complain. The rowing ended in the early morning with a lot of door-crashing, then Mrs Coates came to the desk to check out. She still had sunglasses on, but now the clerk thought they were probably covering up a black eye. Her husband, she said, had left her, taken a train or bus back to Toronto, maybe even hitch-hiked—she didn't know or care. She left a message for him in case he called. He never did, though.

She drove home and waited for two days for him to return, then she called the police. They made some routine inquiries, but they weren't very interested. The story of the night in the motel was clear, and the guy was almost certainly putting a scare into her by taking off for as long as his money held out, but pretty soon he would use a charge card or something like that, then they would be able to reel him in. They did establish that he had a girlfriend tucked away in a condominium on Sherbourne Street and they kept an eye on her place, but she was as mystified as they were, and he certainly never showed up. Nor did he try to call her. A month later the police assumed foul play and sent out a serious inquiry, and she began the process of establishing her legal position if he should have disappeared for good. When the first snow fell she knew they wouldn't find him until the spring at the earliest, and then what would they find? A body, with no money in the wallet, and the gun that had killed him. (She had thrown *his* gun, from which she had removed the ammunition the night before they started their trip, when she realized what he was planning, into the French River on her way to Parry Sound.) And what would they conclude? That he had been picked up hitch-hiking, robbed and killed and dumped into the mineshaft by a local thug. There was still the very slight risk that someone had seen them when they went into the bush that evening, but it was a chance *he* was prepared to take, so it was pretty small. Since the chance of finding the body in the first place was about ten thousand to one, the furthest remote chance

that someone saw them near the mineshaft was an acceptable risk. All she had to do was nurse her grief for the few weeks while the police made their inquiries.

The plan had been perfect, or pretty good. If she had not long known about his lady-friend, tucked away in her condominium, and if she had not come across his fishing tackle box with the loaded gun, the wig, and the make-up kit, packed ready to go, while she was searching for a pair of pliers, she would never have wondered what he was up to. After that it was just a matter of getting hold of a gun herself, and giving him every chance to prove her guess was wrong. The rest went exactly as he had planned.